DISA

HEAVEN'S WAIT

DISASTER AND TRIUMPH

HEAVEN'S WAIT! TALES FROM VOWELLA

Book 4

by

BARBARA MCLAUGHLIN

This book is a work of fiction. All characters in this novel are fictitious.

© 2022 Barbara McLaughlin Publishing
All Rights Reserved

This book or any portion thereof may not be reproduced or used in any manner whatsoever without the express written permission of the author/publisher.

Copyright infringement is against the law. If you believe the copy of this book you are reading infringes on the author's copyright, please notify the author at:

barbarajmcl@heavenswait.com

ISBN: 978-0-9912777-6-6

ACKNOWLEDGEMENTS

Cover illustration and design by Julia Semionova.

To my dear father, Robert J. Marsicano: As this first series comes to a close, you remain my eternal inspiration. To my family: your continued support and love during my ongoing journey keep me on track. To Brad Schreiber: your honest consulting through the years has taught me so much. Thanks for continuing to support me. To Julia Semionova:, your artistic talent is remarkable. Thank you continuing to make Heaven's Wait such a detailed visual wonder. To Akira Ross: I cannot fully express how grateful I am for our collaboration, which has added an amazing layer to this series – music. You have taken my elementary melodies and orchestrated them into beautiful works of art. The music captures the very essence of Heaven's Wait. Who knew we would create a soundtrack for a book series! Though the music can't be heard on the written page, it will be part of everything surrounding this book series. Thank you for believing in the music. *Barbara*

OTHER WORKS BY THIS AUTHOR

RJ AND THE VOWELLANS

HEAVEN'S WAIT! TALES FROM VOWELLA

Book 1

INNOCENTS AND CURIOSITIES

HEAVEN'S WAIT! TALES FROM VOWELLA

Book 2

WONDERS AND TRUTHS

HEAVEN'S WAIT! TALES FROM VOWELLA

Book 3

TABLE OF CONTENTS

Gifts to Share 1
Usual Vowella 3
Idyllic No More 25
First Intruders 31
Emergency Plan 39
Luring Voice 51
The Bugs Attack 72
A Plan for Bait 88
Another Attack 99
Time for Action 110
Leadership 122
Jimmy's Jungle 132
In Town with the Gum 149
Back in the Jungle 154
Another Night Away 169
Stolen Hat 178
The Other Side 190
Limoncinas 206
Ready to Go Home 229
New Jungle Challenges 234

Revisiting the Plan 245

Strategy 258

The Battle 269

For Love of Home 288

From Now On 313

PROLOGUE

Gifts to Share

From: RJ PLOM
To: My Dearest Descendants
Cc: Ma and Pa in Heaven
Subject: Contributions During Challenging Times

As I write to you at this time, I am inspired to share with you my notion that something deep is slowly evolving in our lives here in Vowella Valley. When I first arrived in Heaven's Wait, the Vowellans were naive, innocent, and often shallow in thought. I had much to offer them as a stranger to their land, but I must admit, my way of thinking wasn't that much more complex than theirs. I had plugged along through my earthly life never giving much thought to the deeper meanings that lie beneath all we say and do.

Well, now I am bearing witness to the fact that beings can become richer individuals when they become fully aware of their gifts and are brave enough to share them. In the last story I sent you, young Kip Fig Wig shed her inhibitions and fears in order to sing for me in front of the whole town during the lavish parade the young folks of Vowella put together for me. I saw in her what it truly means to attain your potential.

I'm still not clear if there are negative consequences to surrendering to those gifts, but I do know now that there are positive ones.

Young Mok Fog Bob and I have discussed some interesting questions after thinking hard on that moment. What have the Vowellans learned from Kip Fig Wig's surprising moment during the parade? If all of us were able to shed whatever we hide behind to blossom in our own way, like she did, would our lives be any different? Would we be able to do things we can't even imagine? Could we do something valuable with those things? Could we depend on those things during times of trouble?

I think you'll find some answers in the story I have sent you this time. Enjoy and learn from the Vowellans' experiences.

Till next time and with much love,

Grandpa Rob
Museum of Messages
New Life City, Heaven's Wait

Attachment: Heaven's Wait! Tales from Vowella: Disaster and Triumph

CHAPTER 1

Usual Vowella

*Soft as a pillow, magnetic, warm, comforting...*thought Mok Fog Bob, as he replayed again and again in his mind his sweet first kiss with Kip Fig Wig. He hoped that reliving the moment would forever emboss it onto his brain for future reflection.

Mok lay on his stomach on his sleeping cot with his floppy round feet hanging over the bottom end, his head hanging over the top end, his arms flopped over the sides. He tried to picture the moment of the kiss to fully capture the romantic experience. Yet his vision had been hampered because he had been too close to her face to watch what was happening. He remembered her long lashes brushing his cheek, as well as a flash of disappointment running down his body when his eyeglasses interfered with the ticklish effect of those lashes. But nothing interfered with the warm emotions that now lived within him.

The kiss had come only minutes previously, after the

two teens had congratulated themselves for doing a great job of producing a special parade for the Vowellans' dear mentor, RJ PLOM. It had been a natural conclusion to their joy, as they had sat face to face on their knees on the familiar bench in front of the Fog Bob Box. Mok replayed the kiss again, knowing minutes were ticking on, pushing it farther away from when it had occurred. *What can I do to keep that from happening? What can I do to keep this special feeling inside alive?*

As much as he wanted to stay awake to keep the moment on permanent replay, sleep gradually wrapped him. And quick dreams of various blissful scenarios of his first kiss with Kip tucked themselves into his treasure of memories.

The first morning sun rays beamed through Mok's window, shining on his calm, sleeping face. An out of place tapping sound disturbed his ears, and though he was sleepy, curiosity made him force open his heavy eyelids to investigate the source of the sound. The annoying rhythm of the tapping gradually drove him into full consciousness, and he rolled onto his back, his left arm draped across his forehead. He felt around his nightstand with his right hand for his glasses and awkwardly shoved them onto his face.

Immediate thoughts of Kip and their tender moment flooded his mind. *Please don't ever go away.*

The tapping continued. Though Mok hated to abandon his sweet memory, he couldn't resist investigating the source of the persistent sound. He rose from his cot and took a look in his full-length mirror to make sure his blue and gray pajamas were properly aligned to Fog Bob standards before hopping out of his room and down the bedroom hallway toward the kitchen. The tapping grew louder as he approached the kitchen and its adjoining dining/conference room, as did the faint sound of an accompanying voice.

"What the heck," said Mok aloud. A quick scan of his surroundings told him no one else in the household had yet to rise. Standing between the kitchen and the dining room, he listened harder to determine the location of the source. The sound paused for a moment. Of course, it did, just when he was listening his hardest. *Could it be a critter in the walls,* he thought? *Or maybe in the attic?* The sound seemed foreign to the household.

When the tapping resumed, Mok tapped his floppy left foot three times in response, just to see what would happen. Three taps echoed back. He tapped his foot four times. Four taps responded. He narrowed the source of the sound to the dining area and crouched down by the long narrow dining table.

"What are you? Who are you? What do you want?" he called, hoping he wasn't being too brave while thinking, *please don't be a giant rat or snake or other creepy critter under the floor.*

"Munkee, is that you?" said a muffled voice that seemed to seep up from the floor. "Munkee, are you up there?"

"Punkee? What the heck? Where are you?" Mok was quick to recognize that the muffled voice was that of Kip.

"Under the floor. Open the trap door, will you?"

Mok rushed to push chairs away from the dining table, under which lay the Fog Bob's trap door to Vowella's underground tunnel system. "Punkee, are you under the door in the floor?" he hollered.

"Of course I am, Munkee. Where else would I be?" Kip's light tone made Mok relax his tense muscles, kneel under the table, and rush to open the door.

Finding the recessed handle, he pulled the heavy trap door up and back. Kip climbed up the vertical stairs until she reached the floor's edge. Then, she scooted herself to a safe spot on the dining room's stone floor. She made herself comfortable by taking a cross-legged pose under the long, narrow table, her translucent side fins brushing the floor. Mok sat facing her, but since his legs were attached to each other from his crotch to his ankles, he bent his knees and planted his floppy round feet in front of Kip.

"Punkee, what in Heaven are you doing here, especially this early in the morning? No one else here is even up yet." With his thin, pointy fingers, Mok scratched at his thick brown hair and attempted to flatten the many unruly strands that stuck straight up on the crown of his head. The way he peeked at her from the corners of his eyes suggested his apprehension that something might spoil the memory he was holding so dear.

Kip looked at Mok with tender eyes, memories of their moment together the previous evening also lingering in her mind. Her expression then changed to frustration, her eyebrows wrinkling into a frown, her eyelids narrowing the view of her spectacular turquoise eyes.

"Do you know that when I tried to go out my front door earlier to breathe in the morning air, there were townsfolk sitting in our front yard calling for me to come out and sing? What is that all about? Just because I sang that one song at the parade, they want me to sing for them all the time?"

Mok couldn't help but smile. "Well, come on, Punkee. Do you blame them? What happened to you when you sang was something never seen in Vowella before. They want to experience that moment again. I think you have some fans now."

"Fans? I don't want fans. I'm not that interesting. I lead a very boring life."

Mok chuckled. "Not anymore. You are now the most interesting being in the valley. You're able to transform into some kind of rare state, with side fins that morph into a fan of magnificent colors. None of the rest of us can say that. *I'm* a fan. *I* want to see you sing again too."

"I'm not ungrateful, Munkee, but I'd like to be able to step outside my front door without being stared at or having others want something from me. I've never been one to seek attention from others, like the Net Ken girls. I don't know what to do about it. I needed to talk to you but look. I had to sneak through the tunnels just to get here."

"Well, I think there's good news and bad news," Mok stated. "The good news is that you have touched some lives in incredibly positive ways because you took a leap and exposed your true nature to everyone. The bad news is that you're probably going to have to tolerate avid fans for a while. Folks will eventually get used to your gift, but you might need to give them a little of what they want in the meantime. What might not seem too exciting or fun for you might mean something huge to someone else. G.G. told me he felt 40 years younger after hearing you sing, that a long-lost spirit awoke in him. He wants to feel that again. Do you see what I mean?" Mok took her hand, gently rubbing his slender thumb over hers.

"Yeah, I see," said Kip, her eyes examining his sincere face. "And I love your great grandfather. I just need time to adjust to others seeing me as something different than the frumpy little Fig Wig sitting on the sidelines who still needs her quiet time."

"Tell you what! I need to do a couple of chores at the Ham Bat Pad. When I'm done, let's sneak up to the Cave of Hope and away from your newfound popularity for a little bit. Would that help?" asked Mok with hopeful eyes.

"Of course, Munkee. That sounds nice. When you're ready, why don't you use the tunnels to come over to the Bin, and we'll sneak out the back door of the massage studio."

"Good idea. I'll see you in a while." Mok shot her a shy glance before leaning in and giving Kip a quick peck on the cheek. He appreciated the flush that washed down her cheeks as he helped her once again through the trap door and down the vertical stairs. Once the chairs were rearranged to their original positions around the dining table, he returned to his room to change into proper daytime attire and stuff a few necessary items into his backpack. His desire to see Kip again encouraged him to finish chores at the Ham Bat Pad as quickly as possible.

Dawn peeked into Vowella Valley, bringing clear early morning skies. RJ rocked in his chair on his tiny front porch and cradled his morning cup of RJ's blend coffee. He observed Mok in the distance hurrying up Valley Road toward the Ham Bat Pad. He thought back to the fabulous parade his dear Vowellans had performed in his honor and shook his head at their devotion to him. He felt blessed beyond words to have earned such loyalty from them.

The fact that Kip had given the Vowellans a taste of what it was like to enter a truly authentic state during the parade had been phenomenal. RJ felt such pride that she had grown enough as an individual to allow herself to fully bloom. He already knew that Mok held special gifts that were beginning to show their face. But knowing that Kip also possessed them gave him hope that all of the Vowellans would someday be good on their own when, sometime in the future, it was time for him to leave them.

RJ stood and strolled down his short path to the main road. He turned toward the southern sky in the distance. Thinking back to the strange dark cloud that had appeared in that sky during Kip's performance, he held onto hope that it had been just a coincidental, one-time occurrence. Since the day of the eerie Rufo Fineha, RJ had been trying to push fear of unknown dangers to the Vowellans from his mind. He couldn't help but worry that more concerning surprises might be in store for them.

As RJ lingered on the road, lost in thought, Mok approached him from the rear. "Good morning, Mr. RJ. The sky is sure clear today, isn't it?"

RJ, a bit startled, turned and grinned at him. "To say the least. It's a beautiful thing, isn't it?"

"Sure is. Well, I need to go. I'll see you later, Mr. RJ." Mok started to hop away.

"Hold on there. What's your hurry this morning?"

Mok hopped to a stop, turning toward RJ. "Aw, Kip's a little anxious about the overly exuberant fans that are loitering in her front yard, waiting for her to sing again. She's not used to that kind of attention. I told her I'd sneak her up to the caves after I finish my chores, so she can get away from it all for a while."

"Hmm. Good idea." RJ nodded his head in agreement while pondering the situation. "Maybe we should plan to have her give a couple of informal concerts soon, so the folks will back off a little. You know, satisfy their need to keep the connection going."

"Sounds good, Mr. RJ. I'll talk to her about it and get back to you later. Okay?"

"Sure thing," chuckled RJ. "You go on now. Oh, and by the way, Uncle Nick is flying in with Uncle Jake this afternoon to work on the tennis court. You might want to stop by to check on its progress."

"Thanks. I'll do that." Mok turned and hopped away, hollering behind him. "See you, Mr. RJ."

Mok was so efficient at finishing his hobby jobs that

before he knew it, he and Kip were working their way up Zint Path toward the Cave of Hope.

"Tell me about the lyrics to your song again, Punkee. I really like the part about the moon." Mok exhaled deeply as he and Kip approached the cave.

Kip sucked in deep breaths and exhaled at a pace much faster than Mok. The steep hike up the mountain to the caves was enough to challenge the fittest of Vowellans. She plopped herself onto the large flat rock that sat outside the cave, overlooking Vowella Valley. She welcomed a moment of recovery as well for her Fig Wig weak legs, which always needed massaging after strenuous exercise.

"Thanks, Munkee. Well, you know I wrote the song for my papa during the time he was missing. Though we all missed him terribly, I needed to tell him in my own way how his absence affected me. While Mama cried all the time for him and my sister went mute, I found my own way of dealing with the loss by writing about it. I needed to express how empty I felt when I couldn't touch his face or feel his warmth, how I missed his kisses, his smile, and how he made me feel safe."

Mok, who had been standing to the left of the rock, pulled Kip to her feet, and they made their way through the cave's entrance, past the cleverly engineered floor of old doors that RJ and the Rug Bums had constructed after Mok and Kip's fall into the deep hole beneath it. They moved on to the central cave room, made cozy with dozens of wall candles and colorful pillows on which to lounge. Mok grabbed a round gold and green pillow for

Kip and a long purple body-type pillow for himself. He arranged them side by side by the central fire pit, where embers always glowed, thanks to Kip's mother, Niv, and her aunt, Pip.

He tossed a couple of chunks of koolibarba bark onto the embers to make things cozier for them. They plopped onto their respective pillows.

"Well, I think you expressed your message perfectly. The melody is the perfect accompaniment, and that chorus is the best. Did you really think about those things when you looked at the moon when your papa was gone?"

"Of course, Munkee! I'd think the same things for you if we were ever apart for some reason."

"Well, that won't happen if I have anything to say about it." Mok shot her a momentary frown at the thought. "Will you sing the chorus for me, Punkee?"

Kip lowered her head in shyness before raising it again and looking straight into Mok's deep blue, bespectacled eyes. She opened her mouth, and the angelic voice emerged, first softly, then with confidence.

> *One moon,*
> *Till you come back home that one moon,*
> *Cuz I know that where you are can't be too far,*
> *Under sky, that's where you are,*
> *Till you reach out from afar,*
> *You'll be with me under one moon.*

Her side fins displayed tiny traces of a flutter. Before Kip had a chance to lower her eyelids downward, Mok leaned into her and stole a new soft kiss. He cupped her left cheek with his gentle hand and stole another and then another. Kip looked into his eyes adoringly, as he did into hers. His hand dropped to take hers, and he sincerely said, "Thank you, Punkee. That was beautiful. You're beautiful. Don't ever be afraid to show your beauty."

Kip grinned and lowered her eyes to look at their entwined fingers. Gently rubbing the back of his other hand with the delicate fingers of her other hand, she said shyly, "I never knew kissing felt so good, Munkee. Did you?"

Mok watched the firelight reflection bounce through her bright orange curls. He felt self-consciousness creeping into him. "Of course not, Punkee. I've never kissed anyone like that before you. So you like it then?"

"Yes, I like it," giggled Kip. "But only with you. I mean, it would be yucky to kiss San or Lek like that." She scrunched her nose and stuck her tongue out, causing her puffy yellow lips to shrivel.

Mok chuckled and grinned at her. Their eyes locked as they heard new buzzing in their ears and felt new tickles in their chests. They leaned toward each other and practiced their newfound delight several more times. As they studied each other anew, each of them began to understand that all their years as childhood buddies was fading away.

They sat by the fire pit for most of the morning. After reminiscing and laughing about the awful day they had spent in the cave's deep hole and the rescue that had followed, Mok talked to her about RJ's suggestion that she do a performance or two for the Vowellans. Kip shared her fears about exposing her true nature to so many who had yet to realize theirs. Mok assured her that her singing would do nothing but inspire folks to discover and unfold their true potential. She agreed to give it a try as long as he was willing to be by her side throughout.

Because Mok and Kip were so wrapped up in each other, they forgot the cave's echo phenomenon. Kip's angelic voice had echoed out of the cave and down into the valley. The ears of the Vowellans who were outdoors perked up at the sound, and the memory of her parade performance flashed through their heads. By the time Mok and Kip hiked back down the path to the valley, a crowd of admirers was gathered on Zint Path. Mok wrapped a protective arm around Kip and pushed her through the crowd with his other arm. Several of the Vowellans, seeing how Kip cowered in their midst, realized their fandom was overwhelming and backed away to give them space for the time being. They allowed the couple to move on without being followed.

Mok and Kip caught sight of a plane coming in for a landing at the southern field. Uncle Jake and Uncle Nick were arriving to work on the tennis court. The teens waved at the plane and hurried toward the field until they spotted a strange, thick, dark cloud accumulating over the far southern sky. They stopped, realizing that the cloud was hovering over the dreaded Southern Swamp, which lay far beyond the southern field.

"We'd better go on home, Punky. That cloud does not look happy. Anything coming from the Southern

Swamp can't be good."

"You're right, Munkee. I don't want unhappiness spoiling our special day together."

After one last treasured kiss, they smiled at each other and headed north toward the comfort of their homes.

"Hey, RJ," asked Jake, as he stepped down from the plane's side door and gave his brother a bear hug. "What's that ugly thing hanging out there in the sky? Looks like a pretty mean storm will hit us soon."

RJ frowned and squinted at the cloud to see if he could spot more details in the distant darkness. A creepy feeling flushed down his body, and he warned, "I'm not sure. I think you guys better do what you need to do, then get out of here. I don't want you in the skies if it comes our way."

"Aw, we'll be fine, little brother. That cloud is pretty far south. I don't think it can move that fast," reasoned Jake.

"I'm not going anywhere until I've had my usual dose of Vowellans. They're too much fun to bypass," announced their cousin Nick as he also emerged from the plane. "Where are they anyway?"

"We're right here, you bag of bones," cackled Pun Rug Bum, emerging from the hangar in front of several others from his clan. "Where the heck have you been? We were expecting you last week."

"Oh, I got hung up on a remodeling job at the Café, you lazy lug," replied Nick. "But that's done now, and I'm ready to tackle this tennis court project. We brought a ton of supplies, so we'd better start unloading."

"You get started," teased Pun, pretending to walk away. "I think it's my nap time."

"Pshh," replied Nick. "You want a tennis court; you get to work."

Pun chuckled and turned toward the plane.

The lazy Rug Bum was one of Nick's favorite sparring partners. They couldn't wait to do battle with each other on the new tennis court when it was complete.

Tug and Gun Rug Bum barreled out of the plane hangar on forklifts and pulled them up to Jake's small plane. Pun helped them unload the cargo while Nick and Jake chatted with RJ. They reminisced about the Game of Winnit, the recent event that had resulted in the Vowellans winning the big prize of a real tennis court in Vowella and to this moment, that of building it. RJ told them about the fabulous parade the Vowellans had put on for him and about Kip's song, which had transformed her and entranced everyone else.

Nick and Jake expressed interest in watching the video that Doc Fog Bob had taken of the parade, but RJ quashed that idea after noticing that the cloud to the south was beginning to churn and rumble.

"You know what, guys? I don't like the looks of that sky down there. It might be better for you to save the video for another time. You can come back to see it when things look a little more peaceful." RJ frowned at the southern view.

Nick and Jake agreed. Most days in Vowella were

beautiful. There was no sense in sharing the sky on this day with the gloomy blob. Once the supplies were unloaded, they headed back to New Life City.

As the plane disappeared into the northern sky, RJ and the Rug Bums closed shop and headed toward their homes. RJ alerted the townsfolk about the impending storm before settling into his little cottage, where he would be safe and dry.

Surprisingly, the next few days in Vowella Valley were simply beautiful. No clouds dotted the sky, so Nick and Jake returned for a couple of days of work with the Vowellans on the foundation for the new tennis court. During the off hours, they stayed at the spacious Ham Bat Pad. The Rug Bums and Net Kens worked on the excavation and leveling, while folks from other clans helped to haul pipe, cement, rebar, fine wire mesh, specially processed clay, and all the other necessary supplies.

The court was situated just south of the Rug Bums' maintenance yard at the south end of town and north of the southern field. This meant that the Rug Bums would have to practice restraint whenever other Vowellans passed their porch to play tennis. History had shown that the townsfolk had been mercilessly harassed by the Rug Bums, who, as a result, had been placed under strict surveillance by the town's Council of Elders. The Bums' behavior was slowly improving, but impulsive incidents still occurred now and then. Gun couldn't help but sting a few butts with his side-swiping-from-the-rear move with his scratchy rugs once in a while. And though Dun tried his best, an occasional name-calling phrase slipped from his grouchy lips. Habits of decades past were hard to break, especially for the Rug Bums.

The folks of Vowella went about their Friday business as usual. Mok and RJ had arranged for Kip to give an encore performance at Friday's usual Spaghetti Night. They had made a few changes to the normal agenda, pushing the evening's after dinner dancing back just a bit. Since excited fans were still pestering Kip, Wit Fig Wig and Bek Net Ken guarded the main tunnel that ran north to south under Valley Road so Kip could safely get to the Ham Bat Pad for the event. The Ham Bats' Rec Hall, home to most community events, was put off-limits to all who were not performing dinner setup. Setup was one of Kip's normal clan-learn jobs, so she was thankful she was still able to perform her normal duties. When she was done, Mok escorted her to San's room to hide until it was time to perform. Kip was not a happy Fig Wig.

"This whole thing is stupid," whined Kip as her eyes searched San's room for the first time. Her lids stretched open in wonder as she spied San's round frying pan bed, a hat tree on one side of his bedroom window boasting colorful hats of varying shapes, and another tree dripping with a variety of bags that matched his hats. An open door revealed San's ample closet stuffed with coordinating outfits that were crammed onto sagging clothing rods.

"Who in town ever heard of a Vowellan having to hide out because she was suddenly in demand? I don't want this life, Munkee," she complained.

"I know, Punkee. Don't worry. I'm sure it will all go away. Give it time." Mok was equally fascinated by the colorful contents of San's bedroom. It was not usual for friends to visit each other's private quarters in Vowella.

"Will you stand near me when I sing, Munkee? That will help."

"Of course." Mok pulled her close to him and wrapped his long twiggy arms around her frail frame. He detected a lavender scent rising from her tumble of orange curls and paused to let it wander beyond his nostrils and into his memory.

Kip, much shorter in stature, leaned her head against his waistline and hugged him back. "Thanks."

While Mok and Kip remained unseen, RJ observed how Friday's Spaghetti Night proceeded as usual. The Vowellans passed through the buffet line in animated fashion. The Rug Bums displayed their characteristic boisterous antics at the back end of the hall, while the quiet Fig Wigs huddled near the fireplace. The Ham Bats gobbled their food as always, and the others enjoyed the pleasantries that came with the weekly community gathering.

RJ grinned as he remembered the very first Spaghetti Night in Vowella, back in the day when his Ma was still there, and he was new to Vowella Valley. The animated folks hadn't known what to do with the slippery strings of food. It had been quite a comical scene. These days, Spaghetti Night was still a heartwarming event.

When the meal ended, RJ noticed that excitement about Kip's performance began to fill the air. Some Vowellans chattered amongst themselves while others hurried to rearrange the furniture from a dining hall configuration to a theater setup. He was amazed at how emotionally attached the Vowellans had become to Kip and her amazing new gift. He hoped that for this performance, with all the pageantry of the parade gone, the folks would still appreciate what authenticity was about when it was on full display.

Because of her short stature, Kip took her place atop a platform in front of the fireplace microphone, her Fig Wig clan sitting right in front of her, Mok standing off to her right. The crowd quieted while several of the Vowellans craned their necks to view her lovely appearance. She wore an airy, deep purple dress that her mama had made for the occasion, the second dress now in her wardrobe. This occasion deserved better than the usual shapeless overalls she much preferred.

Kip began her performance by singing a couple of Roz Fog Bob's beautiful original compositions. The first piece, "Songlin in Love", was from Roz's recent musical, which had been performed at the town's outdoor venue at Lake Marie. Songlin had been the lead character in the play, a lonely princess looking for love. The second was Roz's thoughtful piece of work about the danger of missing your kids growing up, "No Longer." The townsfolk sat mesmerized by the sparkling tone of Kip's voice and the honest way she communicated the words.

But when the first few lyrics of "One Moon" flowed

from Kip's voice, the townsfolk practically melted in their seats. Because the melody and lyrics had come from deep in Kip's heart, she was able to once again step into her space of pure truth. Her kaleidoscopic turquoise eyes sparkled to the extreme, and her side fins again blossomed into a spectacular backdrop of color for her. She was a sight to behold, having entered a zone that none of the other Vowellans had yet to achieve.

RJ and Mok studied the phenomenon carefully. RJ, from his position at the Rec Hall's south doors, likened it to earthly athletes who entered a certain zone of concentration and performance when competing at a high level. Mok, still standing off to the side of Kip, tried to determine what would happen to him if he were fortunate enough to someday enter that space.

Once the final "one moon" passed over Kip's lips, the Vowellans closed their dropped jaws and wiped heartfelt tears from their cheeks. They cheered and clapped wildly for their newfound idol. They chanted her name and started rushing toward her.

Mok and San Ham Bat hurried to form a barrier around her until she could be escorted from the room. Kip shriveled within their barrier, reaching under her orange curls to cover her ears with her tiny hands. As they moved toward the north exit doors, the unlikeliest of comments filtered through those covered ears.

"Kip, oh Kip," hollered her snooty schoolmate, Jen Net Ken, who waved her netted right hand high above the excited crowd. "Hey, girlfriend, let's do lunch someday soon and hang out, okay?"

Mok and Kip shot bewildered glances at each other. She shook her head as if to say, *now why would I ever want to do that?*

"Hey, sweet thing, how about you and I go out later," suggested self-absorbed Nak Ham Bat, who suddenly appeared behind them, chuckling at his cleverness while trying to touch Kip's waist. "We could walk out to the lake-ood'ly and look at 'one moon.'"

Kip cowered away from him, displeased at Nak's bold gesture.

Mok frowned and swatted Nak's hand away. "Don't ever touch her without her permission, Nak."

Mok surprised himself with his quick and somewhat aggressive response.

Nak backed away and held his hands up in the air. "Hey, I'm so sorry. Kip, I'm so sorry. I was just being a stupid flirt. It won't happen again."

"Okay then," was all Mok could think of as a response.

Kip shriveled and leaned on Mok as they reached the west doors. San backed against the doors to open them, and they hurried her back to San's room at the Ham Bat Pad.

The Vowellans continued to buzz about the performance while they once more rearranged the Rec Hall's furniture to allow for the evening's dancing. RJ grinned at the scene before stepping through the Rec Hall's south doors to inhale a good dose of the valley's crisp evening air. The sudden grim appearance of the southern sky urged him to make a U-turn and head back inside.

He hurried to the Rec Hall's microphone and announced to the townsfolk in his usual soothing voice, "I'm sorry, everyone, but I'm afraid we need to cut this wonderful evening short. A huge black cloud is heading toward the town at a pace I have yet to witness in Vowella. I would like all of you to gather your families and go back to your homes as quickly as possible. Close your doors and windows and keep everyone indoors until we announce the storm's end on the town's loudspeakers. Hurry now and be safe. Goodnight."

RJ monitored the Vowellans' sudden evacuation while Mok discreetly escorted Kip, camouflaged in one of San's ample jackets, down Valley Road to the Fig Wig Bin. They stopped in the middle of the road between their two homes and spied the blackness that was rapidly heading toward them. Though they knew they needed to retreat to their homes, they weren't yet ready to part ways.

"Thanks for taking care of me, Munkee," said Kip, as she pressed her head against his left arm. "I was kind of scared back there with all that attention I was getting."

"You mean you don't want to sit under 'one moon' with Nak Ham Bat?" Mok chuckled, but his tone reflected something else.

Kip looked up at Mok with curious eyes. "Wait a minute, Mok Fog Bob! Do I detect a little jealousy in your tone? Do you actually think I'd do that with him?"

Mok examined her from top to bottom. With a grin,

he confessed, "No, I don't think you'd do that, but I must admit, I didn't like the way he approached you."

"Well, I didn't either. It was creepy." Kip grinned back at him and changed the subject. "Listen, if the storm hangs on for a while, maybe we can catch up with each other in the tunnels sometime tomorrow."

"Sure thing, Punkee. I'd like that." Mok kissed the top of her head through her wild curls and pushed her off toward the Fig Wig Bin. When she reached her front stoop, he spoke to her once more. "And Punkee! You did good tonight. I'm really proud of you."

Kip spread her puffy yellow lips into a satisfied grin and disappeared into the Fig Wig Bin. Mok turned his attention to the sky. By the looks of it, he had to agree that RJ had done well at hurrying everyone home.

CHAPTER 2

Idyllic No More

San Ham Bat awoke to a deep, blasting hum. His overly sensitive ears, common to all Ham Bats, could barely stand the prickly groan, which also vibrated through his head. Accompanying the hum was a chorus of wails and moans. He soon realized his own moans were part of the chorus composed of the those of his fellow Ham Bats.

Fahbee Flingbee, San's tiny flying creature friend, awoke with a start when a particularly painful groan spilled from San's throat. Fluttering around San's head, he swooped and dove in his attempt to attract San's attention. "Hey, Señor, what's wrong? What are you yelling about? Are you sick or something? Señor! Talk to me."

San pressed the palms of his chubby hands against his fan-shaped ears and pinched his eyes shut as he writhed in pain. Fahbee hovered in front of San's face, flapping his wings madly. He hollered at him again and again. Fahbee failed to grab San's attention despite his extreme acrobatics and shouts.

Seeking relief, San rushed into his closet, flipped on the light switch, and slammed the door. Fahbee managed to swoop through the last crack of airspace before the door hit the frame.

Within the closet, the vibrating hum was muffled significantly. San dropped his hands from his ears. He shook his head and leaned forward in hopes of relieving himself of the wave of nausea that had washed over him.

"Señor San, what's going on? I've never seen you like this," chattered Fahbee nervously. He perched on the shoulder of one of San's hanging jackets and stared. "What can I do? What can I do?"

"Ugh! Just give me a minute, Fahbee." Sweat dripped from San's brow onto the closet's tile floor. He inhaled and exhaled deeply as he patiently waited for the nausea to pass. When it did, he lifted his hefty torso back to a standing pose and wiped his face with his hands. "Good grief, what is that awful sound-ood'ly out there?"

Fahbee cocked his head to the side, his beak appearing more crooked than usual. "I don't know, Señor. All I heard was your yelling. Something bad is bothering your ears, huh?"

San panted with a bit of a chuckle. "Yeah, something really bad."

"Well, put your earmuffs on and open the door for me. I'll see what's going on."

"Yeah, sure," mumbled San as he scrounged through the messy mountain of colorful shoes at the bottom of the closet. "Here they are."

San hurriedly shoved the earmuffs onto his head and worked them to a tight fit over his aching ears. While shaking sweat from his limp yellow hair, he cracked the door open far enough for Fahbee to slip through. Once Fahbee's curly tail cleared the jamb, he slammed it shut again.

Fahbee's first stop was San's bedroom window. "It's still so dark outside. I can't see anything there."

His second stop was the bedroom door, which was open a few inches, enough to allow Fahbee a decent view of the Ham Bats' courtyard. He gasped at what he saw. Chubby Ham Bats of all sizes and ages ran frantically back and forth within the courtyard, their hands pressed against their ears, their moans reaching high volume. Parents chased their children in attempts to install earmuffs over their ears. The children wailed at the idea of removing their hands from their ears long enough for the muffs to be fitted. The Ham Bats were in definite need of help.

"Señor San, Señor San, open the door." Fahbee kicked at the door with his tiny, webbed feet. San could not hear him. Fahbee shouted in his loudest Flingbee voice.

By chance and curiosity, San cracked open the door. Fahbee swooped in before San closed it tight again.

"Your folks are in trouble, Señor San," hollered Fahbee with deep concern as he continued to swoop. "You need to help them. Whatever noise is hurting your ears is making them go crazy too. They need to get their earmuffs on."

"Yes, yes, they do, little buddy. Come on. Let's go." San grabbed Fahbee and shoved him into the front shirt pocket of his print pajamas. Making sure his own earmuffs were tightly in place, he left his room to help his fellow kinsfolk.

San fought his way through the courtyard of panicked Ham Bats on his way to his parents' quarters on the west side. He entered the room to find his mother, Lan, carefully adjusting Baby Kal's earmuffs.

"Oh, good, honey, you're wearing your muff-ood'lies. Promise me you won't take them off." Lan turned to make sure he had his muffs properly in place. "Please go help your dad. He's making the round-ood'lies to make sure everyone is safe. But check on Paz-ee and Jaz-ee first. Your grandparents are our first priority."

"Of course," shouted San. "But where is that noise-ood'ly coming from?"

"Heaven knows," yelled Lan. "It's best if we just focus on protecting everyone's ears at the moment. Now go!"

"Okay. I'll be back-ood'ly." San hurried off, his hand over his pocket to assure himself that Fahbee was all right.

San and his dad, Mat, directed everyone to the Ham Bat Rec Hall, where the Ham Bats could comfort and attend to one another. Puzzled and scared, they huddled together and calmed the children. When Lan entered the hall with Kal, she was relieved to see that Paz-ee and Jaz-ee were safe and comfortable in their earmuffs, as were the rest of the Ham Bats.

The out of place sound of moans and wails in the

near distance drew RJ out of a calm sleep and up onto his feet. He stepped onto his tiny front porch garbed in a brown flannel robe and matching slippers. Detecting that the sound came from the Ham Bat Pad and that it was most unusual for it to be filled with light so exceedingly early in the morning, he cut through the crop fields toward the Pad. He could barely see the narrow path that bridged the two buildings because of the unusual darkness of the sky. He felt grateful it had not yet begun to rain.

RJ banged and banged on the south doors of the Rec Hall yet no one inside noticed his presence. He frowned when he saw that the room was filled with Ham Bats, each wearing a set of earmuffs. San finally noticed RJ's waving arms through the glass and rushed to open the door for him. The Ham Bats, desperate for help, crowded around RJ.

"What is that noise-ood'ly, Mr. RJ?" asked sweet Tam as she wiped tears from her chubby cheeks.

"Yeah, our ears are aching," added San.

"In all my days, I've never heard anything like this-ood'ly, RJ," said Paz-ee. "What do you think is going on?"

"Why, I don't know," answered RJ, as he scanned the room filled with miserable Ham Bats. "All I hear is a strange, low hum. It's certainly not affecting me like it is all of you. Have you checked around to see if a piece of equipment is acting up?"

"Yes," said Mat. "But we couldn't find anything wrong-ood'ly."

"Do the earmuffs help?"

"Quite a bit," said Mat. He briefly lifted his left muff

and winced at the increased volume.

"Okay, you folks stay here. I'll go see if I can find anything around the outside of the building. Hang in there. I'll be back."

RJ stepped through the south doors and searched the sky. It was nothing but black. He performed his analysis aloud. "Strange. It's near dawn, and there's no sign of light in the sky. No stars. The only light is coming from the Ham Bat Pad, from the bedroom lamp in my place, and coming off the streetlights along Valley Road."

He listened hard to the drone in the air. It sounded like a deeply vibrating electronic device. It was certainly louder outside than it had been within the Ham Bat Pad.

The pajama-clad, ear-muffed Ham Bats again crowded around him when he stepped back inside.

"Well, the sound is definitely coming from outside, but it's too dark to see anything at this point. We'll have to wait until daylight to find out what's going on. Just try to hang in there as best you can." RJ examined each Ham Bat face. He saw disappointment in some, worry in others, and hope in still others.

"We'll be okay," assured elder Paz-ee. "We'll cook up some scrambled eggs and toast-ood'ly. Daylight will come-ood'ly before we know it."

"Yes it will," agreed RJ. He helped Mat, San, and Nak set up tables and chairs while other Ham Bats headed to the kitchen to whip up some food.

CHAPTER 3

First Intruders

Within the quiet of the domed, stucco Fig Wig Bin, Kip's mother Niv awoke to the subtle moaning that drifted from grandmother Lil'la's room. Niv stepped into her fluffy green slippers and padded across the floor of the Bin's central room.

"Mama, Mama," she called as she reached Lil'la's room. "Are you all right?"

Lil'la rolled over in the dark to turn on her tiny bed lamp. "Oh, Nivee. My arm is really aching for some reason. I must have been sleeping on it."

Niv sat on the left side of Lil'la's bed and leaned over to examine her left arm. Lil'la held it up for her, groaning in the process. Niv gently touched a growing, inflamed bump on her upper arm and frowned at her discovery.

"Mama, you have a nasty bite here. Your arm's all hot and swollen. I'm going to get you some ice, and then we'll look around. Maybe there's a spider in your bed."

Lil'la grimaced at the thought, but her usual mild manner shined through her discomfort. "Oh dear."

While Niv shuffled back to Lil'la's room from the kitchen, an exceptionally large black insect caught the left corner of her vision. It hurriedly swooped through the dainty sheers that covered the Fig Wig front entryway, sneaking away from the Bin.

"Goodness sake!" Niv ran into Lil'la's room and draped a bag of ice over her arm. "There was a giant bug out there like I've never seen before. It must be what stung you. Keep that bag on there, Mama. I'm going to get Fil up so he can cover the entrance before it comes back. Will you be all right?"

"I'm fine, Nivee. You go on." Lil'la pressed the ice bag against her arm, wincing while Niv wasn't looking.

Fil and Wit Fig Wig were already standing by the central room's fire pit as Niv entered the space. Seeing the troubled look on her face, Fil asked, "What's going on, Nivee? You were speaking pretty loudly for this time of the morning."

Niv explained the situation and described the flying creature. Fil and Wit rushed to Lil'la's room to examine her arm. It had swollen even more during the short time since Niv had left her.

"Good grief. We certainly don't want this to happen to anyone else," worried Wit. "Lil'la, you stay right there and rest. Nivee, just stay here with her. Come on, Fil. We need to block the entrance right away."

Wit and Fil stepped out onto their front stoop to look around.

"The sky is certainly dark for this time of day, and the air has a strange electric feel to it, don't you think?" asked

Fil.

"Yes, something seems way off here," observed Wit.

They hurried back inside, where they pulled from the entryway's closet two heavy metal panels that normally served as storm doors during the short, annual monsoon season. They carefully fitted them into the permanent braces that they had attached to either side of their arched doorway years previously. They hated to block the fresh breeze that usually flowed into the Bin, especially since it counterbalanced the heat that emanated from their central fire pit, which kept their dainty bodies warm no matter what the season. But they felt right in adding this layer of protection to the Bin while things seemed uncertain inside.

Within Lil'la's room, Niv concluded that the ice was failing to stop Lil'la's arm from swelling more and more. Realizing that Lil'la was now burning with fever, she didn't hesitate to reach out for more help. Her first call was to Dr. Jon Fog Bob.

"The Rug Bums." Niv's eyes widened as she realized the Rug Bums' vulnerable status at their Hut. While in the kitchen, waiting for Dr. Jon to arrive, she felt compelled to warn them about the scary bug. The Rug Bum Hut, just down the road and across the gum tree grove from the Fig Wig Bin, had three wide archways that were completely open to the outside. The thickly furred Rug Bums depended on the open air, along with their suds spouts, to help keep their bodies cool.

"Gusee?" Niv wasn't one to ordinarily call the Rug

Bum Hut on the phone.

"Nivee? Is that you?" Gus answered in a grouchy tone. "Why in heck are you calling me this time of the morning?"

"I wanted to warn you that we had to close up our front door because a mean-looking, giant insect stung my mama. She's getting pretty sick now. Your place is wide open over there. I don't want the same thing to happen to one of you."

"Yeah, I think it's here now. He's an ugly, noisy bugger. Dun's running around right now trying to smash him with his hubcaps. He's waking everyone up," Gus explained. "It looks ripe for juicing, but maybe we should test him out before we add him to our bug juice vat. We sure don't want to get sick. Thanks for letting me know, Nivee. We'll keep our guard up. Dark out, ain't it?"

"Is it? I haven't looked outside. I'm going back to Mama now. Take care, Gusee."

Niv had told Dr. Jon to come to the Bin by way of the underground tunnel system, since their front entryway was now blocked off. By the time Dr. Jon banged on the Bin's tunnel trap door in the floor, Lil'la's arm appeared ready to explode. She panted, and a stream of sweat dripped from her limp body. Niv and Fil pulled the trap door open. Dr. Jon hopped up the vertical ladder to ground level and rushed to Lil'la's side.

Mok hopped into the Ham Bat Café just as Lan and Jan came out of the kitchen carrying heavy trays of scrambled eggs and toast. There to perform his usual, early morning hobby job of writing out the day's menu for the Café, he quickly hopped up to Lan and relieved her of her tray. Her pregnancy had made her already hefty belly more swollen by the day, making it difficult for her to manage the heavy tray. Turning toward the Rec Hall with the food, Mok discovered the pajama-clad, ear-muffed Ham Bats huddled around several tables in the middle of the room. He had never before seen them in their bedclothes.

"Mrs. Lan, what's going on? Why is everyone up so early?"

"Didn't you hear that awful noise-ood'ly outside when you came up the road'l? It's been driving our ears crazy."

"Well, now that you say that, it does sound kind of weird out there. All I noticed was the darkness."

Mok placed the tray on a side table and looked around. Several Ham Bat mamas cuddled their kids and adjusted their earmuffs. Ham Bat males huddled in deep conversation. San rested his head on a table while tiny Fahbee perched on his right muff. Mok gasped when he spotted RJ, clad in *his* pajamas, robe, and slippers, sitting at a table with Paz-ee, Jaz-ee, and Pun Rug Bum.

Pun had been walking back from one of his secret, nocturnal tree-tending sessions up in Jimmy's Jungle when he had noticed that the Ham Bat Pad was alive with light. He had peeked through the north doors and noticed that RJ and the Ham Bats were eating, so he had decided to mosey on in and mooch some breakfast.

Mok approached their table. "Mr. RJ. You're here

too. And you're all in your pajamas. How long has everyone been up?"

"Hey there, Mok. Well more than an hour, I'd say," said RJ. "These poor folks have been having quite a time with their ears. I thought I'd keep them company for a while. Is it getting light outside yet?"

"Barely. A narrow rim of daylight is starting to show around the edges of the valley. The rest of the sky is pretty black. I guess we're going to be in for quite a storm today."

"Well, we've been waiting for daylight so we can try to figure out where that noise is coming from," said RJ. He pulled back an empty chair that was next to him. "Here, take a seat and have some breakfast with us. We'll wait a bit, then go out to see what's going on."

Mok joined the small group. He observed RJ's calm attitude and his soothing words to Paz-ee and Jaz-ee. He chuckled at the way Pun continued to shovel free food into his mouth. He watched the jumpy Ham Bats, with their earmuffs tightly pressed to their heads, slowly drift back to their rooms to get dressed for the day. He listened to the low drone that still hung in the air.

RJ, Pun, Paz-ee, and Mok exited the south doors of the Rec Hall to examine the sky. They were finally able to see the dimensions of the huge black cloud that hung over the entire valley, thanks to the narrow ribbon of blue sky that defined its perimeter. It wasn't long before the composition of the cloud registered in their heads. Thousands of particles within its body frantically jumped about like the loud, fuzzy "snow" that appears on a TV screen when there is no reception. They hovered over all the structures within Vowella's boundaries.

The reality of the situation hit RJ like a brick. All he could do was to whisper to himself, "Oh...my...God!"

"It's not a storm cloud, is it RJ?" asked Pun as his beady black eyes bulged and realization struck.

"No, Pun, it's not. You and Mok better get on home as fast as you can. Paz-ee, get inside now," ordered RJ in an unusually demanding tone. "I think we're in serious trouble here. All of you, tell everyone to stay inside and lock down your houses."

"But what is all of this, Mr. RJ?" asked Mok, who had yet to fully realize their dilemma. "If it's not a storm cloud, what is it?"

"It's a giant swarm of BUGS! Now, go home right now!"

Mok and Pun raced down Valley Road while RJ helped Paz-ee into the Rec Hall. Once assured that Paz-ee had securely bolted the north and south doors, RJ ran back to his place. He threw on some clothes and rushed to lock down the few windows in his little place. He grabbed tufts of his graying hair with both hands as his brain tried to prioritize the many new chores that suddenly came to mind. He now realized why the Ham Bats' ears had been so tortured and was glad that protection was already in place for them. He made phone calls to both the Net Ken Den and the Fig Wig Bin. He assumed Pun and Mok would warn their households.

RJ sank into his rocker when he learned of Lil'la's sting and that Dr. Jon was already treating her. His mind spun. As far as he knew, nothing like this had ever threatened his beloved Vowellans. Natural storms were one thing. The one that had destroyed the town before he had arrived in Vowella had not stopped the Vowellans from rebuilding. But this! RJ couldn't imagine what kind of damage a bug cloud could do or what in Heaven they could possibly do about it.

CHAPTER 4

Emergency Plan

Mok had his fellow Fog Bobs lock all the windows and doors of the Fog Bob Box before he explained the situation to them. Roz informed the clan that Lil'la Fig Wig had already been stung and that Dr. Jon was attending to her at the Fig Wig Bin. Old Dr. Jok suggested that Dr. Jon, the current chief executive officer of the Fog Bob Box, would be of most value caring for Lil'la and that he should stay at the Fig Wig Bin. So Jok took the lead, as he had in his younger days as CEO, and called RJ and the remaining Council of Elders members for an emergency meeting. He told them to come via the underground tunnels, which had just recently been extended to RJ's place, the Rug Bum Hut, and down to the tennis court site.

The Elders, excluding Lil'la, were pulled from the trap door in the Fog Bobs' conference room. RJ was the last to make his way through the trap door.

"How's Lil'la?" he asked without hesitation.

"Not good," answered Roz, who had just made a call

to the Fig Wig Bin. "Her arm is enormously swollen, and her fever is dangerously high."

"So what can we do about it? We can't just let her lie and suffer." RJ's brow wrinkled into a worried frown.

"We need to create an antidote," interrupted Dr. Pol, the Fog Bobs' head scientist and inventor, who had been lingering nearby. "We need to get our hands on a couple of those bugs, so I can develop a medicine to counteract the sting."

"Yes, son. And we don't know how many others will be stung as well," added his father, Dr. Jok. "I think we need to prepare for the worst."

"Well, here," offered Jud Rug Bum. "I brought this along. Dun smashed the bugger in our house before we closed it up. Will this work?"

Jud pulled a large, squashed, ugly black bug from his loincloth pouch. It was wrapped in a banana leaf, and it smelled like a mix of tar and vomit. Everyone hurried to shield their noses with their arms.

"Yeah, we thought this guy might be good for bug juicing until Niv told us about Lil'la. What a waste of a giant bug." Jud opened the banana leaf, exposing the foreign creature for all to examine.

Dr. Pol hopped forward and pulled a small magnifying glass from his lab coat pocket. He described his thoughts as he studied the creepy bug. "Hmm. I've never seen one of this species before. Its body is heavily armored with black plates, and its long, sharp stinger looks like a narrow screw. My guess is that it attacks like a drill, stinging by spinning itself into a victim. This is one mean critter. And it seems its venom is even meaner. Let me work on this and see what I can come up with."

Dr. Pol rewrapped the critter in the banana leaf and disappeared into his lab.

"All right, folks," said RJ, now taking the lead as he paced back and forth within the width of the conference room. "We don't know why this 'cloud' is here or how long it's going to hang over the valley. We certainly don't want anyone else to get stung if we can help it. But we need to assume that there is more to come from these mean buggers since the cloud is so huge. We need to implement an emergency plan."

"Agreed," responded Dr. Jok and Paz-ee in unison.

"So let's talk about our most immediate needs," continued RJ. "Keep in mind that we might have to stay inside or underground for an extended amount of time."

"Well," contemplated wise Dr. Jok." If we need to use the underground, I'd say our first order of business is to protect the entrances. We need to somehow keep the bugs out and at the same time keep the tunnels aerated. We certainly don't want to slip into hibernation mode."

RJ and the Elders nodded as they discussed the first time RJ had discovered the Vowellans. The Vowellans had hidden within the town's original tunnels to escape the terrible storm that had delivered RJ to Vowella Valley. He had found them when he uncovered trap doors to the tunnels that had been buried under layers of storm dirt and debris. Because the back ends of the tunnels had also been buried by the storm, the lack of oxygen within the tunnels had thrown their unique bodies into some kind of hibernation or suspended animation. The fresh air that had flowed into the tunnels once the trap doors were reopened had brought the townsfolk back to life.

"Excellent point, Jok." RJ searched the faces of the others. "Any suggestions?"

"How about that fine wire mesh that Uncle Nick brought in yesterday for the tennis court?" asked Jud. "The holes are much smaller than that mean critter. If the rest of them are that big, the mesh should keep them out."

"Good idea, Jud," agreed RJ. "But how are we going to get to it without exposing ourselves to the outside?"

"What if we drive the Bucket down through the main tunnel to the tennis court site and run out long enough to load the mesh into the back seat and trunk?" suggested old Granny Zen, who had been quietly standing by, listening to the conversation.

"Yes, RJ, that vintage '56 Chevy of yours just might be good for that chore," agreed Dr. Jok.

"We have those heavy-duty Teflon overalls and hoods for work in the jungle that we could use to cover ourselves while we're exposed," offered Jud.

"Okay! We're getting somewhere," said RJ, his expression showing a glimmer of relief that there might be some things they could do about the situation. "What about food? How are the reserves?"

"It depends on how long we need to stay inside-ood'ly, RJ," answered Paz-ee, who was aware of the town's food inventory. "We have an ample stash-ood'ly of dry goods in the Ham Bat side tunnels. And the crop fields are full of fresh produce right now. We need-ood'ly protection to get to them too."

"Wait!" interjected Dr. Jok, suddenly fidgeting, betraying his normal calm. "The animals! They're all out there exposed right now."

"You're right, Jok," said RJ, his eyes widening with realization. "Okay, here's the plan. Zen, go back home and tell Wes, Bek, and a few others to dress themselves in the protective overalls and hoods and herd the rets and hens into the tunnel under the school from the back end. That's their closest access point. Then, drive the Bucket down into the main tunnel, pick up Jud and his boys at the Rug Bum junction, and proceed to the tennis court site to fetch the mesh. No time to waste. Jud, tell Pun to go down to the school junction of the main tunnel and construct a makeshift gate for the animals. Roz, call Wit to see if he's done anything with the wistas. Mok, I want you to stay here with me in case I need you to run an errand."

Roz nodded and hurried off. Granny Zen and Jud headed back to their homes through the tunnels. Paz-ee said he would go back home and organize a crew of Ham Bats and Net Kens to sneak out to the crop fields to haul in as much produce as they could. Professor Nox and young Dok Fog Bob followed Granny Zen back to the Net Ken garage to fetch the other vintage vehicle, the powder blue '54 Chevy. The group decided it was necessary to drive up the north underground tunnel to Jimmy's Jungle to fetch clean water from the ample waterfalls there.

While the folks went about implementing the emergency plan, RJ pounded his elbows onto the Fog Bobs' conference table and cradled the sides of his head in his hands. Praying to the Eternal, he whispered, "How much time do we have? Please don't make us need these preparations. I have a bad feeling about this situation."

Mok hung his head, worrying about Kip while trying not to imagine what the future might hold.

Granny Zen retrieved Jud and Tug at the Rug Bum intersection of the main tunnel. The Rug Bums were fully protected by the overalls that they used for heavy excavation work. More Rug Bums volunteered to help, but space needed to be conserved in the Bucket for the wire mesh, which would not be easy to compress. Zen was quite exposed to the stings of the bugs, except for her head, which was covered with her black wide-brimmed hat with the red feather. Her fashion choice was an attempt to keep the mood light.

The wide tunnel ended, and a ramp led up to ground level just past the new tennis court site. Zen kept the headlights on as the sky's dreary darkness continued to hang heavily over the valley. The Bucket crept toward the materials cage, which sat just ahead and to the right of the makeshift road. The cage had been constructed to keep the youngsters away from the materials and from getting hurt during the construction.

The Bucket's occupants spied a few of the ugly black bugs wandering through the headlights' beams. Jud displayed a worried face, but Tug stared them down to prove his lack of intimidation by the foreign critters. Zen stayed quiet as she came to a stop next to the cage's gate.

"Zen," Jud said in little more than a whisper. He handed her his hubcaps. "You need to cover up. Those things out there look pretty nasty. Hide behind my hub caps when I open the door. If one of those buggers gets in, smash him."

"Oh, you know I will," whispered Zen, her feisty expression beaming through her red eyes.

Jud, on the front seat passenger side, and Tug, directly behind him, slowly opened their doors and stepped outside. Carefully, they opened the cage gate and leaned in to grab the rolls of wire mesh. As in slow motion, they quietly pushed as many rolls into the trunk and backseat of the car as they could. The stray bugs' flight pattern began to zigzag as though the demons were annoyed with the Rug Bums' movements, but they didn't swarm around them or advance. One bug attempted to fly into the car, but Zen swiped at it with a hub cap, and it changed course. Jud closed the gate and hurried back to his seat in the car. Tug pushed on the mesh in the back seat to make room for himself, and in the process, caused a substantial rip in the seat's fabric. Zen shot him a serious frown before backing up and turning the car around. The damage was of lesser importance now. She stopped just inside the tunnel at the bottom of the ramp to enable the boys to secure their first opening, the widest in the system.

Gun and Dun were waiting in their overalls when Jud and Tug returned to the Rug Bum Hut after securing the southern leg of the tunnel system.

"What's the plan, Uncle Jud?" asked Dun, anxious to do something to help the situation.

Jud closed his eyes to map out in his mind the plan for securing the other tunnels. Keeping his eyelids pressed together, he said, "Okay, the way I see it, we should start by securing the outer Ham Bat tunnel at the northwest end, to protect the food supply that will be stored there. Then we can move southwest to work on the Fog Bob outlet. After that, we can cut across to work on the tunnels at our place, the Fig Wig Bin, the school, and wrap things up at the Net Ken Den."

"Sounds like a plan." Dun pulled rolls of wire mesh from the Bucket and strapped them across his back. He stuffed various tools into the side pockets of his loincloth.

Jud, Tug, and Gun did the same. The foursome proceeded to make its way around the outer reaches of the system to secure the original tunnel entrances.

Meanwhile, the Bums didn't concern themselves with the wide exposure at the far north end of the main tunnel, which sat a good distance inside Jimmy's Jungle. The threatening bug cloud certainly didn't extend that far.

By the time the Bums finished their loop around the valley, having covered most of the tunnel openings, there was not enough remaining mesh to cover the Net Ken opening.

"Now what do we do?" Dun's thick eyebrows curled into his worried frown. His brows quickly rose again to a high arch when he heard sudden screeches echoing through the main tunnel.

"Help! Help!" screamed little Sil Fig Wig, who suddenly ran up and down the tunnel in a panic. "Mr. Huge Dude! We must rescue Mr. Huge Dude. He's stuck outside all by himself, and he can't get in. Help! Help!"

Dun chased her down, surrounding her tiny waist with his shaggy blue arm. Pulling her up off the ground, he held her tight as he examined the top knot of wild orange curls that now blocked most of his field of vision. Never having been so close to a Fig Wig, he found himself distracted by the tiny being. Her hair was so orange; her head was so large compared to her body; her translucent side fins looked so fragile as they stiffened from the stress Sil was feeling. And those huge puffy yellow lips!

"Did you hear me, Dun?" Sil yelled into his face. She had never been so close to a Rug Bum either. "Mr. Huge Dude. We have to get him inside. We have to."

Dun put her down, and Sil and the Bums hurried down to the south entrance of the main tunnel, the first one they had secured. Mr. Huge Dude was there, grabbing onto the outer side of the mesh, his eyes expressing their own form of panic.

Jud and Tug detached the left side of the mesh barrier and pulled it back far enough to allow Mr. Huge Dude to pass through. He would not have fit through any of the other outlying openings, so his expression morphed into one of relief once he found himself inside. Dun smashed stray giant bugs in his hub caps while the Bums repaired the barrier. He added them to the pouch he had attached to his loincloth so Dr. Pol would have more bugs to use for the creation of an antidote.

Mr. HD sat against the east tunnel wall, sweat dripping from his furry face, short breaths puffing from his mouth. Sil climbed into his lap and rubbed his scruffy chin. Mr. HD's breaths gradually slowed, his anxiety waning in the supposed safety of the tunnel.

The Vowellans managed to carry out the remaining initial stages of their emergency plan without incident. Dressed in their hooded Teflon overalls, conscientious folks filled the Rec Hall and Ham Bat tunnels with the bounty of valley produce that they stripped from the crop fields and orchards. All the while, they monitored the hovering black cloud. The ear-protected Ham Bats and the Net Kens sorted, packaged, and refrigerated the food to give it maximum shelf life.

Dok and his crew returned from Jimmy's Jungle with enough fresh water to last at least four to five days if rationed. They stored it in one of the Ham Bat side tunnels. Dok felt confident that they would be able to return to the jungle in relative safety whenever it was necessary. The black cloud didn't seem interested in the jungle.

The townsfolk seemed to be well protected if they remained indoors. But covering the Net Kens' outlying opening with aerated material was still of major concern. Though it was well hidden far to the east, at the foot of the Blue Zint Mountains, it was still vulnerable. After conducting a thorough inventory of their limited resources for covering the opening, finding nothing that would allow for ventilation, RJ and the Elders made the decision to seal off the tunnel. Though doing so would further limit living space within the tunnel system if things got bad, the risk of folks getting stung was worse.

"Pun," said RJ. "You and your boys take those old steel doors that are being stored in the Net Ken tunnel and seal their far end opening tight. Then board up the inner entrance of their tunnel at the main tunnel junction. We don't want anyone to wander into it and accidentally fall into hibernation. The Net Kens can access the main system through the showroom garage leg when it's necessary."

"Sounds good, RJ." Pun and his boys hurried off to complete that chore.

Wit Fig Wig wasted no time in herding his precious wistas into the main room of the Fig Wig Bin through the massage studio's outer door. Since the wistas were such fragile creatures, he wasn't about to tolerate them being shoved into the school tunnel with the wild hens and the hyperactive rets. Though Mr. Huge Dude was charged with guarding the animals at the school tunnel, Wit felt he needed to keep the wistas under his watch. The Fig Wigs agreed that they could live with the wistas in their midst for a while. Dok delivered a hefty supply of north side moss to the Bin to keep the wistas well fed, since the sky blue creatures were the valley's source of milk. Wit had asked him to fetch the moss while on his water run, and it had been no bother to collect.

To prevent further intrusion by the ugly black bugs, Wit and Fil Fig Wig decided to add more protection to their home by covering the round vented windows that dotted their dome-shaped home with metal panels that they would normally only use during storms. Keeping the trap door to the tunnel system open would allow ample air to circulate through the Bin. They also made the decision to close the sky vent that defined the peak of the dome by sliding its triangular metal plates into storm position. By doing so, the Fig Wigs would have to refrain from using their central fire pit, but that sacrifice was a better option than becoming victims to more stings. They would simply have to double up on clothing if needed.

"I'm so pleased with the efficiency of our townsfolk," RJ told the Elders as they reconvened at the end of the day. "They did just about everything possible to try to protect us all and prepare us for an indefinite stay indoors. Why don't you go on home now and rest?"

From their home windows, except the few that had been covered, the clans watched the black sky until night descended. There was nothing left to do but sit and wait. And wait...and wait...until the ugly black cloud of nasty insects went away.

CHAPTER 5

Luring Voice

The following morning, Kip lifted her head from the left side of Lil'la's bed. She observed her mother hunched over the right side of the bed, soft sleep sounds spilling from her mouth, her head resting next to Lil'la's terribly inflamed arm. A tear trickled down Kip's cheek as she turned her attention to her beloved grandmother, who was struggling with breaths and moaning from pain. Kip had given her grandmother, whose given name was Lil, the nickname of Lil'la when she was a baby just learning to say words. The Fig Wigs, as well as the other clans, had found the name so endearing that they had all referred to Lil as Lil'la from that time on.

Niv opened her eyes, raised her head, and rubbed the left side of her neck with her left hand. Kip whispered to her, "Mama, how is Lil'la doing?"

"Oh, sweetie, I'm afraid your grandmother is very ill," Niv whispered back, with obvious worry in her voice. "I hope it's not too long before Dr. Pol comes up with something that will help her. Her fever is extremely high, and she's delirious with pain."

"Oh, Mama. We must help her. We can't let anything happen to sweet Lil'la. We can't." Kip's whisper transformed into a sob as she spoke. She rushed from the room into the Fig Wig main room, where the wistas were napping. Niv hurried after her.

"Listen, sweet baby, we must keep it together, for Lil'la's sake. We don't want our pain to add to hers, now do we?" Niv held Kip's head in her gentle hands. She smoothed Kip's kinky curls away from her face and kissed her forehead. "Let's keep hope alive that Dr. Pol will find an antidote. Can you do that with me?"

Kip looked into her mother's sad eyes with her own of sparkling turquoise. She pinched her puffy yellow lips together, wiped her tears away, and changed her expression to that of determination. "Yes, Mama, I can. I can. You go back to Lil'la. Don't worry about me. I'll go check on Silee, Papa and the others. Yes, hope is always alive, isn't it?"

"It is." Niv hurried back to Lil'la. Kip watched her for a moment, then went on to check on her household.

Dr. Jon hopped to and fro in the kitchen of the Fig Wig Bin. He was not having an easy time being patient while his father, Dr. Pol, worked on formulating an antidote for Lil'la's bug sting. Beyond that, he had not slept well in Kip's bed, which was much too short for his tall frame. He was stiff and achy and unaccustomed to being in a strange household. Kip had given up her room for him once it was determined that he would spend the night to keep watch over Lil'la. Dr. Jon's grouchiness made him hop all the quicker.

As Kip checked on the bedrooms that encircled the Bin's main room, she heard the slaps of Dr. Jon's floppy round feet on the marble kitchen floor. She tiptoed over to the kitchen's arched doorway and observed his behavior. From her few experiences with him during massage appointments and from things Mok had told her about his father, she knew how difficult it was to communicate with him. Dr. Jon had firm ideas about how things should be, and there was no bending from those ideas.

Despite that knowledge, Kip slipped into the kitchen to speak to him. She had just opened her mouth when she heard a commotion behind her. The wistas crowded around the Bin's open trap door in the floor of the main room. Wit and Fil rushed from their rooms to see what was disturbing the gentle creatures. Kip joined them at the trap door, as did Dr. Jon.

Mok's top-hatted head appeared through the opening. He hopped up the vertical tunnel ladder until he reached the Bin's floor level. Wit and Fil herded the wistas to the back end of the room.

"What are you doing here, son?" asked Dr. Jon. His expression was that of irritation.

"Papa Pol sent me over, Father." Mok pulled a small vial from his inside jacket pocket and handed it to his father. "Papa worked all night, with the help of Uncle Nox and G.G. They think this is the antidote that will help Lil'la get better."

"How could they possibly come up with something so quickly? Were they able to test it on anything?"

"I'm not sure, but Papa is confident that his formula will be an effective anti-venom, based on other such medicines he's made in the past."

Dr. Jon took the vial, carefully examining its milky gray contents. "All right! We'll have to trust his judgment for Lil'la's sake. I will administer it to her at once. What are the specifications for use?"

"He said to add two drops of the antidote to one half cup of wista milk and a beaten hen egg. Whisk them all together. Then, slowly give Lil'la spoonsful until it's gone."

"Yes, that sounds logical," said Dr. Jon with a nod of his long head. "She's quite delirious at the moment, but I'll make sure the antidote is delivered as instructed. Thank you, son."

"You're welcome, Father."

Dr. Jon rushed to Lil'la's room to check on her current state. Niv was applying a new cold cloth to Lil'la's forehead when he entered.

"Jon, I applied herbal packs to Mama's arm throughout the night. They helped with the swelling, but the fever and the pain. Please help her," pleaded Niv.

"That's just what I'm going to do, Niv. My father sent over this antidote. I need your help to get it prepared." Dr. Jon explained the recipe to Niv. She rushed off to make it while Jon stayed with Lil'la.

"All right, Lil'la," said Dr. Jon in a calm tone as he sat to the right of his ill patient. "I have some medicine for you that should make you feel better soon. Do you think you can lift your head so you can swallow a few sips for me?"

With great effort, Lil'la barely opened her eyes and raised her head while Jon slipped his hand under the back of her skull to support it and raise it more. Niv sat to her right with the antidote mixture. At first, Lil'la turned away from the mixture, hardly able to tolerate the smell of it. Niv insisted and carefully gave Lil'la small spoonsful and made sure she swallowed each one. Niv fought back tears and offered an encouraging grin to her mother during the process.

Outside Lil'la's room, Mok comforted Kip by holding her close, stroking her kinky hair, and whispering soothing words to her. Not having seen each other since the bug swarm had moved into the valley, they took a moment to share their feelings as best they could.

"Oh, Munkee, I'm so worried about my Lil'la. I don't know what I would ever do without her." Kip's voice shook as she spoke the words.

"I know, Punkee. I know. But she'll be all right. I have faith in Papa Pol's medicine for her. Just be patient. I know she will get better soon."

"Thanks Munkee. I needed to hear you say that." Kip looked affectionately into Mok's eyes.

"I need to get back to Mr. RJ now, but I'll come check on you and Lil'la as often as I can. Stay strong for me, okay?" Mok returned Kip's affectionate gaze.

Kip nodded in response and pressed her face against his chest.

They separated quickly when Niv and Dr. Jon passed through Lil'la's doorway and entered the main room. Jon shot Mok a shocked glare before turning to talk to Niv.

"My father told Mok that he was quite disturbed when he realized the toxicity level of the insect's venom," Dr. Jon quietly shared with Niv. "It is quite fortunate that Lil'la was only stung once. At her age, it would be impossible for her to tolerate more stings."

Niv nodded, understanding how serious Lil'la's condition truly was.

"Keep up the herbal compresses, Niv, and give her lots of fluids. Perhaps by the end of the day, we'll start to see some improvement in her condition," he continued. "I'm going to go home now for a bit to freshen up and check on the other Fog Bobs. It seems you folks are well locked down in here. I'll come back a little later to see how she's doing."

"Thanks, Jon. I don't know what we would have done without you." Niv shook his hand before returning to Lil'la's room.

Dr. Jon turned toward Mok with a stone gaze before turning to exit the trap door. "Come with me, son. We have things to do."

Mok shot Kip an alarmed expression before he hopped after his father.

Kip returned to Lil'la's room where she offered Niv relief. "Let me sit with her for a while, Mama. You should get some real sleep. Lil'la's more likely to need your help later when she's more alert."

"You're right, Sweetie," said Niv, sighing at the chance to take a break. "I'll go to bed for a while. Call on Auntee Pip or Auntee Jil if you need help."

"Okay, Mama." Kip looked down at her fragile grandmother and expelled a huge sigh.

Once the two Fog Bobs reached the tunnel floor, words Kip would long remember floated up to her ears, "What do you think you're doing, son? DO NOT get too close to that girl."

"What do you mean, Father?" Mok frowned at Dr. Jon, irritated he would have to defend his actions. "Punkee needed comfort. She's been my best friend my whole life. What's wrong with that?"

"Friendship is one thing. Getting close is another. Clan boundaries must be respected. Remember that, son." Dr. Jon turned and hopped toward the Fog Bob tunnel without a further word.

Mok's eyes burned into his father's back as he hopped away. A knot twisted in Mok's chest while confusion swirled through his head. He whispered, "What boundaries?"

A few hours later, Lil'la began to show signs of consciousness. She cracked her eyes open and slowly rocked her head from side to side. She grimaced at the stiffness in her neck. She spied the room from side to side, trying to remember where she was and what had happened to her. Peeking down to her right, she spotted Kip's tousled orange hair randomly draped over her right arm, as her granddaughter slept with her head on the bed.

"Kipee!" Barely a sound emerged from Lil'la's throat. She tried again. "Kipee!"

Kip awoke with a start. She stood and leaned over Lil'la's face. She touched her forehead, then lifted the herbal pack from her arm. She grinned at the discovery that Lil'la's fever had lessened, and the swelling had decreased.

"I'm here, Lil'la. You're doing just fine. We're all here to take care of you." Kip gently pushed the damp white curls away from Lil'la's sticky forehead. "Do you know where you are?"

Lil'la licked her puffy yellow lips, which had become dry and cracked during the peak of her illness. "Yes, in my room," she whispered. "It was that ugly bug, wasn't it?"

"Yes, Lil'la, but you're getting better now. Doctor Pol developed an antidote for you. Wasn't that good of him?"

Lil'la nodded and smacked her dry lips. "He's a smart one all right."

"Would you like some tea?"

At Lil'la's nod, Kip hurried off to the kitchen and returned with a piping hot mug of ginger apple tea.

With Kip's help in supporting her head, Lil'la leaned forward a bit and took a sip. "Ah, that tastes good," she said in a voice that was a little louder than a whisper.

"What else can I get for you? Do you need a blanket? Would you like a cold towel for your neck or forehead?"

Lil'la peeked at her with loving eyes. "Will you sing

to me, Kipee? I would really like that."

"Of course I will." Kip's lips spread into a wide grin. She began to hum a new little tune that she had composed.

Lil'la closed her eyes, relishing the soothing sound of Kip's voice. Others of her clan slowly gathered outside her room to witness her improvement and to enjoy the heartwarming sight. They sighed with relief, at the same time marveling at the talent that spilled from Kip's voice. They hadn't previously realized that her voice was so pure and mesmerizing.

The pleasant sound of Kip's humming traveled through the open trap door of the Fig Wig Bin and down into the town's underground tunnel system. It drifted into the Fog Bob Box across the street and the Rug Bum Hut down the road by way of their trap doors, which were open as well. RJ had suggested opening trap doors for all the dwellings for the sake of air circulation and ease of communication.

RJ had chosen to stay at the Fog Bob Box while the town was in lockdown. Sitting with Elders Jud, Dr. Jok, and Paz-ee at the Fog Bobs' conference table, he raised his head to listen to Kip's tune. Mok, in the process of raiding the refrigerator in the adjacent kitchen, also perked up at the sound.

"I hope Kip's humming means that Lil'la is getting better," said RJ with a shake of his concerned head.

"I do too, Mr. RJ." Mok responded while the Elders remained quiet.

RJ rose from his chair and sauntered down the Fog Bob's main hallway toward the front doors. Mok followed him. The tall glass panes within the doors allowed a view of the domed Fig Wig Bin across and down the road a bit. RJ and Mok observed that the Bin was locked up so tightly, they couldn't tell what was going on inside.

The huge black cloud that hung over the valley started to show signs of activity. Its dense black center, resembling a target bulls' eye on a dart board, slowly repositioned itself directly over the Fig Wig Bin.

RJ pressed his palms against the glass door on the right. He felt his stomach churn as he watched the shift take place. "Jud, Jok, Paz-ee! Come look at this."

The Elders hurried toward the front doors, followed by others of the curious Fog Bobs - Professor Nox, Rok, Dok, and Dr. Jon, who had rejoined the Fog Bobs after refreshing showers. Through the glass, they watched the cloud thicken directly over the Fig Wig Bin.

RJ fought to maintain a calm voice as he asked to anyone who was listening, "What do you think those nasty critters are up to?"

"Beats me," Jud hurried to reply, a look of disgust washing down his blue furry face. "What a waste! We can't even juice the ugly varmints."

"Mr. RJ, you don't think they're going to attack the Fig Wig Bin, do you?" Mok's eyes widened when it dawned on him that, besides the fact that Kip was inside the Bin, the Fig Wigs had no idea what was stirring above them.

"I wouldn't worry about that, Mok," said RJ, sounding as though he was trying to convince himself of that fact rather than Mok. "It looks like Wit and Fil did a good job of locking the place down. That structure is solid stucco and metal."

As it turned out, there was something to worry about. The heavy cloud began to churn and slowly turn clockwise. It did so quietly, not as the nerve-wracking bug chorus that had tortured the Ham Bats' ears earlier on. The mass took on the shape of a giant, inverted chocolate kiss, its graduated tip targeting the highest point of the Fig Wig dome. Like chocolate suspended over an open fire, it slithered over the exterior of the Fig Wig Bin, totally encasing it in blackness. It thickly hugged the round frame, making the Bin look like a sickly bonbon.

The onlookers within the Fog Bob Box observed in horror. RJ snapped his eyes shut and threw his head back trying to think. He mumbled to himself, "Why would these creatures pick on the Fig Wig Bin?"

Mok gasped and hurriedly hopped back toward the conference room and the Fog Bob's trap door.

"Mok! Where are you going?" hollered RJ in response to Mok's quick retreat. "You need to stay here for now."

"No! I need to go to the Fig Wig Bin to help them. Kip's in there. Lil'la's in there," Mok hollered back as he hopped. "We need to get them out."

RJ rushed toward him. Dr. Jon wasn't far behind.

"No, Mok, wait," explained RJ as he grabbed Mok's

thin arm. "Listen for a minute. Kip is still humming. Do you hear her?"

Mok listened hard. RJ was right. Kip's tune was still drifting through the tunnels.

"The Fig Wigs don't realize anything is going on outside their house," said RJ. "There are no outward signs. Let's not panic them if we can help it. Maybe the bugs will tire of being there and retreat at some point."

"But how can they not know their house is covered? Do you think those ugly critters are being that quiet?"

"That seems obvious, son," interjected Dr. Jon, his cold stare making Mok's insides feel like they were twisting. "Your place is here with your clan at a time like this, not with your trivial friends."

Mok's eyes widened, and he turned away from his father without answering him. He hopped back toward the front door, mumbling to himself. "Punkee is *not* a trivial friend."

What is Kip to me, Mok asked himself as he gazed beyond his front door? She's not just one of my friends anymore. And none of them are trivial, Father. What an insensitive thing to say to me. What is it that I feel for Punkee? Why are my feelings for her so different now? Is this what love is? If it is, why would it be wrong for me to love her?

While Mok and the others within the Box monitored the Fig Wig Bin, RJ, speaking in almost a whisper, pulled Jud Rug Bum aside in the hallway. "Jud, I want you to go back to the Hut and get your boys suited up. Grab all the hub caps you have and meet me in the main tunnel in ten minutes. I think it's time for us to figure out how we will defend ourselves if need be."

Jud shot RJ a serious stare before his thick black eyebrows curled into a determined frown. "You got it, RJ." He quietly retreated through the Fog Bob trap door to complete his task.

Within the usual quiet of the Fig Wig Bin, Lil'la began to perk up. She even asked Niv for a cracker after she drank down a follow-up dose of the antidote. The second dose tasted as bad as the first. She was surrounded by several of the Fig Wig females, each watchful and grateful that she seemed to be improving. Kip had pulled small chairs in for Pip, Jil, Sis, and little Sil, who all felt comforted by staying close to their beloved Lil'la.

Kip kept the atmosphere calm and relaxed with her soothing hums. Every now and then, Sil would join her in their usual harmony. Kip noted the smiles on the female faces. She grinned at Lil'la's peaceful expression, which had only recently appeared on her worn face.

"How about singing us your song from the parade, sweetie, while we go get dinner together?" Niv, tired but in a better mood, asked Kip. "Your songs always make everyone feel so good."

"Sure, Mama. I'm happy to do that." She scooted her chair closer to Lil'la and gently took her hand. Sil scurried to stand next to her while Niv, Jil, and Pip stood and moved on to the kitchen to do food prep. Kip's voice would certainly carry into the kitchen. When Wit and

Zin learned that Kip was going to sing, they crowded into Lil'la's room with their uniquely Fig Wig instruments.

> *Didn't know that you were leaving,*
> *Didn't know how life would change,*
> *Couldn't touch your face with my hands,*
> *Couldn't feel your warmth, how strange.*

Kip's clear, angelic voice filled the air. The pure sweetness of it made the puffy yellow lips of all the Fig Wigs, especially Lil'la, spread into instant smiles. The Fig Wigs closed their eyes and, for that moment, allowed the music to take them to magical places in their imaginations.

RJ, Mok, and the other Fog Bobs watched the bug-encrusted Fig Wig Bin with anxious eyes. They listened to Kip's sweet song drifting through the Fog Bob Box by way of their trap door. The contrast was undeniable. RJ had just returned from the main tunnel where he had instructed the armed Rug Bums to split into pairs and stand guard at each of the intersections that branched off to the Vowellans' homes. Mr. Huge Dude still stood guard at the school tunnel intersection where the town animals were being kept. He was armed with a borrowed set of giant, shiny hubcaps. The plan was to have the guards use their hubcaps to smash any bugs that dared to enter the tunnel system.

A low whine started to compete against Kip's voice for attention. Shivers ran down the spines of those eying the Fig Wig Bin as they watched the unmoving bug mass suddenly show signs of activity. Before the observers' eyes, the solid black mass broke into frantically twitching dots that seemed itching to explode. A sound like chalk scraping against a chalkboard filled the air, only muted by the walls and windows of the Fog Bob Box. Paz-ee Ham Bat pressed his earmuffs closer to his ears.

Mok, whose mind was already going crazy wondering how safe Kip was within the Bin, watched the activity of the bug swarm increase by the second. From across the road, it appeared the bugs were pounding and scratching at the sealed Bin, making it abundantly clear that the Fig Wig Bin was now under full attack. The trigger for the attack finally dawned on Mok, as well as RJ and Dr. Jok.

"Aargh!" Mok turned and hurried back down the hallway to the trap door. "It's her singing," he yelled in a panicky tone. "They're after her singing."

"He's right," shouted RJ, who chased after him. Past moments clicked into place in his mind: the distant gray cloud that first showed itself during his parade; the heavy black sky that took over the valley after Kip sang at Spaghetti Night; the chocolaty crust that hugged the Fig Wig Bin when Kip hummed to her grandmother. The vicious bugs had been patiently waiting for her to sing again, and now their time had come. They were doing everything they could to find their way into the Bin.

Mok tore past the Rug Bum guards and up the vertical ladder to the Bin's interior. The bugs made a deafening sound as they tried to pick at the stucco walls and metal plates with their screw-like front stingers. Kip had already stopped singing because the Fig Wigs had just realized there was something terribly wrong going on outside. They were huddled in the main room with the wistas when Mok emerged from the open trap door. Mok observed the frightened expressions on the Fig Wigs' faces and spoke to them as calmly as he could.

"The bugs have begun their attack," he called to them above the racket. "They are trying to get into your house right now. We need to move all of you out of here."

The Fig Wigs obediently stood, scurried to round up clan members as well as the wistas, and crowded toward the trap door.

"But Munkee, where will we go? Isn't everyone's house under attack?" Kip hollered above the continuing racket.

"No, just yours. Now let's go. I'll explain later." Mok directed the Fig Wigs and their wistas down the steep ladder.

"But Lil'la!" called Fil. "She is still much too weak to move."

"We have to try," said Mok, who heard RJ's voice at the bottom of the ladder. He turned toward the opening. "Mr. RJ, what about Lil'la?"

"Here, Mok." RJ climbed partway up the ladder to hand something to him. "This is the harness we used to get you and Kip out of the hole in the cave, remember? Jud just brought it to me. Use it, or do whatever you have to, to get her down here. She's so light weight, it shouldn't be too hard."

"Okay, Mr. RJ. We'll see what we can do."

While Mok and Fil hurried to deal with Lil'la, RJ and the Rug Bums helped to escort the tiny Fig Wigs down the ladder to safe ground in the main tunnel. They then lifted the wistas down and herded them into the Fig Wig tunnel. Mok and Fil placed Lil'la on a plush wistamere comforter and dragged the comforter across the stone floor to the trap door, where they gently slipped the harness over her fragile legs and sat her up.

"Lil'la, dear." Fil stroked his mother-in-law's damp head and patted her hand. "We're going to put you in this harness so we can lower you into the tunnel. Try to hold on to the straps as tightly as you can. We'll have you down there in no time. Then, you can rest again."

"All right, Fil. Don't worry. I'll be fine," reassured Lil'la as she returned a pat to his hand. She managed a tired grin and then looked toward the task at hand.

Mok planted his floppy round feet firmly into the floor before he raised Lil'la in her harness, while Fil guided her over the trap door. Mok's long Fog Bob arms almost resembled a crane. Fil loosened the harness straps enough to lower Lil'la into the waiting arms of the Rug Bums below. Her body was so light, the process was completed in no time. Roz led them to a Fog Bob cot she had moved to the floor of the main tunnel that would serve as Lil'la's temporary place to recuperate, completing the job.

On his knees, Mok monitored the activity in the tunnel below him through the trap door of the Bin. He watched Wit use gentle taps with his whip to herd the wistas into the Fig Wig tunnel. He watched the Rug Bums follow him with gate materials so they could confine the wistas to that space. While the bugs continued to pounce on the structure, Mok stood to look around the interior of the Bin. He didn't want anyone to be left behind. He jumped when he spied a surprise blob of bedding approaching him.

"What the heck?"

"It's me, Munkee. Can you carry some of this stuff?"

"Punkee, what are you doing? Why are you still in here?" Mok addressed her in a frustrated tone.

"Lil'la's going to need these," hollered Kip above the scratching, drilling sounds. "Here are sheets and her pillows and comforter."

"Okay, okay, I get it. Now get down that ladder, and keep your voice down," commanded Mok.

"Why, when it's so noisy up there?" Kip shot right back at him.

"Just go, go, go!"

Kip hurried down the ladder. Mok quickly followed. Before closing off the Bin for the uncertain future, he scanned the dome's interior one more time. The usual warmth and airiness of the Bin was gone. Its inhabitants were gone. *What a creepy feeling*, he thought. Mok closed the trap door and moved on.

From their view across the schoolyard from their second story living room window, the Net Kens watched in horror as the vile bugs pounded on the Fig Wig Bin.

"What will we do if a swarm decides to attack our

house?" asked Lek, whose obsessive-compulsive tendencies kicked into high gear. "Their jittery behavior will drive me insane."

"Not if you don't let it," responded his mother, Jes, who hurried to wrap her left purple arm around Lek's slender waist. "Going insane won't solve the problem, now will it?"

"I guess not," replied Lek, whose body shuddered.

"We'll figure a way out of this, Lekee," assured Granny Zen. "Don't you worry. RJ has our backs. The Council has our backs. I think even the Rug Bums have our backs on this one."

"Well, I'm staying inside. Don't even ask me to go out." Lek slithered out of his mother's caress and crept toward his room, where he wouldn't have to watch the bug show.

Within the Ham Bat's Rec Hall, the Ham Bats remained huddled together, tightly pressing their earmuffs against their tortured ears. San helped his grandfather, Paz-ee, roam within the Rec Hall to make sure their clan mates' fan shaped ears were properly guarded.

"We'll be okay, Paz-ee. See, everyone has their ears covered, just as you'dl told them."

"Well, San-boy. Let's hope so. I've seen for myself how those bug-ood'lies operate. They are na-a-asty." Paz-ee and the Ham Bats were only able to hear the turmoil. They were unable to view the Fig Wig Bin from the Ham Bat Pad.

Along the side walls of the main tunnel beneath Valley Road, the Fig Wigs scurried and fussed to make themselves comfortable. Roz and Dok Fog Bob moved Lil'la's cot to a quiet spot against the wall on the Fog Bob side of the tunnel, out of the way of increasing traffic. Niv and Pip arranged Lil'la's bedding on the cot and made her as comfortable as they could, considering the circumstances. The Rug Bums paced, waiting to hear what they should do next.

Mok led Kip to RJ, who was standing in front of the Fog Bob tunnel extension, observing the tunnel scene while trying to determine their next steps. Mok opened his mouth to speak when the prickly pounding noise of the bug mass came to a sudden halt. RJ and the Vowellans within the tunnel paused where they stood and listened hard to the sudden silence. They waited in their own silence while they looked toward the tunnel ceiling for the racket to resume. It did not. The bugs had ceased their attack.

Mok turned toward Kip, gently taking hold of her tiny hand while speaking cautiously, trying not to scare her. "Punkee, listen to me, okay? For some reason, the bugs don't like to hear you sing. Thinking back, we realized that the first time they appeared was at the parade. Remember?"

"No, I don't remember," spoke Kip in a voice louder than necessary. She broke loose of his hold and walked away, then back again. "You're saying that all of this is because of ME?"

The vicious bugs again became agitated as she spoke and resumed their pounding. RJ, Mok, and the Rug Bums shot each other worried glances. Kip's turquoise eyes bugged, and her mouth dropped.

She stood silent, and the bugs became silent.

RJ hurried to Kip and placed a reassuring arm around her tiny shoulder. "Kipee, you didn't do anything wrong."

"But look at Lil'la. She's sick because of me," cried Kip in a soft voice. She lowered her head and pulled on her vibrant orange locks. "Why is this happening?"

The bugs again responded to the sound of her voice and resumed their pounding. When she stopped talking, they stopped pounding. RJ and Mok looked at each other in amazement.

"It's not her singing, Mr. RJ. It's the sound of her voice," said Mok with fascinated concern. "Say a word, Punkee. Any word."

"Munkee," pleaded Kip. The bug racket resumed, then stopped.

RJ listened hard before he took hold of Kip's shoulders and made her look at him. "We don't know why this is happening, Kipee. All we can do is try to fix it, which means I think you need to be silent for a while. Can you do this for us, Kipee? We will fix this."

Kip glanced at Mok and then back at RJ. She nodded as a tear fell from each of her kaleidoscope-patterned eyes.

CHAPTER 6

The Bugs Attack

Seeing from their front door windows that the bug mass was quiet yet still attached to the Fig Wig Bin, most of the Fog Bobs and remaining Elders made their way down to the main tunnel. They supposed it felt safer there, where more and more Vowellans were congregating. Dr. Jon tended to Lil'la while Roz, Tov, and Lol hauled down pillows and blankets to help make others more comfortable.

Dr. Pol remained burrowed in his ground floor lab with Dr. Jok, Professor Don, and Professor Nox. They continued to produce more doses of the antidote. There was no way of knowing whether others would be stung as time progressed. Though Lil'la was their only test case thus far, they suspected that two doses of the antidote would need to be administered to anyone who might be stung in the future.

Dok, Rok, and a few others lowered chairs and small library tables to the large rotunda area between the Fog

Bob Box and the Fig Wig Bin. They went about setting up an underground emergency operation base for use by the Elders and others who would be handling the crisis. Dok outfitted the station with lamps, telephones, and electronics equipment that might be useful. He ran long extension cords through the trap door and to the base from plugs in the Fog Bob kitchen and conference room. RJ and the Elders praised his foresight in setting up.

Back up in the Fog Bob electronics lab, Dok contacted Jake with his two-way radio. RJ's brother, back in his office at the airport in New Life City, had recently brought several radio sets to Vowella to make communication regarding the new tennis court, as well as other matters, easier. The telephone system used within Vowella only worked for local calls between the structures, and it wasn't connected to New Life City. Through heavy static and long pauses, Dok and Jake were able to conduct a short conversation.

"Uncle Jake, we're in trouble here. That storm cloud you saw the other day is not what we thought it was," explained Dok.

"Yes, I know. Nick and I tried to fly into the valley earlier on, but we couldn't penetrate the ugly thing. When bugs started congesting my plane's engines, we had to turn around and come back. I feel helpless. How is everyone? Is there anything I can do from here? I'm worried about you guys."

Dok started to tell Jake about Lil'la and the new emergency operations station, but the static increased, forcing Dok to desert the conversation.

Kip and Mok sat silently against the rough, rocky west wall of the main tunnel just south of the operations station. Kip stared straight ahead, as though in a trance. Mok covered her tiny hand with his and gave it a comforting pat every so often. Other Vowellans quietly conversed with each other at a minimal level.

After an hour of silence from above, RJ and the Rug Bums ventured back into the Fig Wig Bin to inspect it for structural damage. Protected by heavy coveralls and hoods, they climbed the Fig Wig ladder into the domed main room and looked around. Everything was in order. The Bin was dimly lit. The fire pit was barely glowing. The air was scented with traces of lavender and rosemary. And the walls seemed secure, except for a few minor cracks here and there. The stucco structure had endured the bug attack very well.

"It looks like those storm panels did their job," observed Jud as he stretched his neck back to inspect the covered round windows within the Bin. "I'm glad we put them up at our place too." There were no windows at the Rug Bum Hut, only large arched doorways. It had been a significant effort for the Rug Bums to cover them with their metal plates, which they had retrieved from the shed at the rear of the Hut.

"Who's over at your place right now?" asked RJ, as he studied the concern on Jud's face.

"Just Gusee, Hun, and Pun, as far as I know. They're cooking up as many gum recipes as they can, so we can store them below. Everyone else is in the tunnels."

"Good, good," said RJ with a nod. But good did not last very long. RJ and the Bums returned to the main tunnel to discover a disturbing new racket. The vigorous pounding by the bug mass resumed, this time sounding more distant and infused with a crackling element.

"What the heck is that?" hollered Jud, already heading down the main tunnel toward the Hut.

"What the devil is that?" shouted Gusee at the same moment, but from within the Rug Bum Hut. A fierce, crunching noise enveloped the dwelling. She, Pun, and Hun were unaware that the Fig Wig Bin had been under attack.

"Sounds like those drill critters are all over the Hut, Gusee," yelled Pun over the racket. "Quick, grab as much of the gum as you can. Then, get down the hatch."

Gusee and Hun, Elder Jud's wife, stuffed as many gum items as they could into their apron pockets and hurried through their trap door. The crunching noise made Pun look toward the roof. Random sprinkles of sawdust fell all around him and into his eyes.

"Hurry," he shouted. "They're working their way through the roof."

Unlike the Fig Wig Bin, the Rug Bum Hut was constructed of wood, its roof layered with shake shingles. The structure was much easier to get through than the Bin, considering not only the softer composition of the wood but also the screw-stingers at the front of the bugs' black armored bodies.

Covered with sawdust, Pun rushed down the ladder. But before he had a chance to close the trap door completely, a small army of bugs broke through the roof and swooped through the crack of the passageway. It swarmed around the bodies of Hun and Pun, then headed northward through the main tunnel toward other Vowellans.

Gusee managed to evade the bugs' attention, but Hun was stung three times, and Pun was stung twice, once on his furry back and once on the top of his head, near his suds spout. Sadly, he had shed his overalls once he had finished his emergency chores.

Mok's keen hearing picked up on the familiar hum of the bugs' flapping wings. Without hesitation, he pushed himself upright on his floppy round feet and pulled Kip to her feet. He scooped her tiny body into his arms and hopped as fast as possible across the tunnel floor and into the Fig Wig tunnel, where RJ, Roz, Lol and a few others were huddled in a quiet conversation.

"Look out," shouted Mok, pushing through the huddle. "The bugs are inside. We need to protect Punkee. Let me through."

He plopped Kip down behind RJ and Roz and hurried up the Fig Wig ladder to open the trap door. Once inside the Fig Wig Bin, he knelt at the entrance and reached down with his long thin arm.

"Hurry, Punkee, hurry. Climb up and grab my arm."

RJ quickly scooped Kip up and lifted her as high on the ladder as he could. Kip hurried up the steps until she reached Mok's waiting arm. As though suddenly empowered with super strength, he grabbed her by one wrist and lifted her up into the Bin.

Below, a few coverall protected Rug Bums guarded the Fig Wig tunnel entrance while RJ helped Roz, Lol, and the few others up the ladder to join Mok and Kip within the Bin. Once RJ reached floor level, he slammed the trap door shut. Mok hugged Kip tight to his body while RJ inspected each Vowellan to make sure no bugs had gotten to them.

"I think we're all okay," assured RJ. He looked at each of the rattled Vowellans with calming eyes. "Quick thinking, Mok. I think we'll be safe here."

"But what about Mama and Papa and Lil'la?" Kip whispered in Mok's ear once they had come to a sit. "Silee's down there. The rest of our clans are down there."

"Shh, Punkee." Mok whispered back as he looked at Kip with tense eyes. "Don't say anything. Do you hear me? Not a word. Let's hope the Rug Bums can protect them."

As the group fell into worried silence, RJ called the other households from the Fig Wigs' phone, telling them to make haste in closing their trap doors.

Down in the tunnel system, the bugs went on a frantic hunt for potential victims along the tunnel paths. Tug, Gun, and Dun, furious at the knowledge that the bugs were invading their Hut, their safe place, led the pack of suited Rug Bums in a charge against the bugs. They smashed a large number of them between their hubcaps as they chased after the dwindling swarm that moved northward within the main tunnel.

A few bugs came to a halt and hovered when they found themselves face to face with Mr. Huge Dude, who was obediently guarding the animals that were being kept in the "school" tunnel. Mr. HD stood at full attention, glaring at the bugs with no fear in his eyes. Tug and Dun, the tallest of the Bums, sneaked up behind the bugs, reached as high as they could, and managed to smash the invaders at Mr. HD's waistline. HD slowly raised his large, borrowed hubcaps and swiftly clanged them together, destroying the bugs that hovered within one inch of his mouth. Mr. HD exhaled a huge breath he didn't know he had been holding.

Though RJ had warned the clans to shut their trap doors, a few bugs managed to find their way into the Ham Bat Pad, the Net Ken Den, and the Fog Bob Box. The Vowellans used what they could find to smash the persistent invaders. Pots, pans, books, and various other household gadgets served as their weapons. They covered themselves with blankets, bedspreads, and towels when they had the chance. But, unfortunately, several folks were stung anyway. Time would tell who and how many.

The Rug Bums, the only Vowellans still in protective gear, finally managed to kill off the rest of the stragglers. They borrowed harvesting buckets from Mat Ham Bat and proceeded to collect the dead insects, knowing that Dr. Pol and his crew would need to produce more of the antidote now that it was clear that several Vowellans had been stung.

Tug was finally able to announce that all the bugs were dead. The tunnels were free and clear. Gun banged on the trap doors while Dun dismissed the Rug Bums guarding the Fig Wig tunnel. Dun climbed the ladder to the Fig Wig trap door and banged.

"Open up now, Mr. RJ. Everything is under control," he hollered.

"Dun! Are you sure?" RJ examined Mok's and Kip's eyes. They seemed calm enough. He reached for the handle and opened the door.

RJ hurried down the Fig Wig ladder, through the curious wistas who were roaming within the Fig Wig tunnel, then northward within the main tunnel.

"Mok, I'll be back in a minute," he yelled. "Keep an eye on everyone for me. I'll assess the situation when I return." RJ veered left at the junction of the main tunnel and the narrow one heading to his place.

RJ pulled himself up into his little cottage. Finding his lightweight gray jacket hanging over the top of Ma's rocking chair, he slipped it on and zipped up the front. He grabbed his framed picture of his dear wife Linda and another vintage picture of his kids when they were young. Those he stuffed down the front of his jacket. He retrieved from his top dresser drawer the small box containing the precious Angelicous pin that Lady Wisteena had given to him on his first trip to New Life City. It signified his discovery that he was in Heaven's

Wait to serve as the Vowellans' Angelicous. He carefully tucked the box into his zippered left jacket pocket. He gave the rocking chair a sad look, as though he was perhaps saying goodbye to it. Since his little cottage was also constructed of wood, he was unsure if it would survive the horrible bug storm. After one more sentimental glance at his cozy surroundings, RJ climbed down his ladder, closing his trap door behind him.

RJ's next stop was the Fog Bob Box. He was anxious to see, through the tall windows of the Fog Bob library, what kind of damage the bugs were inflicting on the Rug Bum Hut. He climbed up the Fog Bob ladder and made his way to the front of the structure, which was now deserted, except for the research lab. By the time he reached those library windows, the bugs had finished their attack on the Hut and had returned to the sky, resuming their black cloud formation.

Tug, Gun, Dun, and a few other Rug Bums, hearing that the horrible crackling, buzzing noise of the bug attack had come to a halt, also entered the Fog Bob Box and hurried to join RJ at the windows. They were not conscious of the interior surroundings of the Box, which they had never before seen. Their focus zeroed in on their Hut, their home, their one concern.

It was fair to say that the Rug Bum Hut had been flattened. What had once been the casual, bungalow-type residence of the Rug Bums stood no more. The bugs had drilled enough holes in the shake shingles to make the roof collapse. They had done the same with the walls, reducing them to large wood chunks that had cascaded onto the floor, in turn causing the metal door panels to slam to the floor in various directions. And the Rug Bums' signature "harassing" porch, the Bums' favorite hangout, had been whittled to a pile of firewood. The only items that stood above ground were two toilets and Gusee's metal refrigerator and stove. Fortunately, the trap door had been upgraded to metal in recent years and set in concrete, so its integrity had been preserved.

The Bums within the Fog Bob Library stood with jaws dropped and bodies stiff. There wasn't a face among them, normally scowling and full of attitude, that wasn't on the verge of tears.

"There's nothing left, Bums," lamented Tug. "We have the little clothes we're wearing, the gum we hoarded, and our sturdy hubcaps. Looks like those buggers even ripped up our harassing rugs."

"Boy, Auntee Gus is going to have a fit when she sees what those nasty critters did to her sparkling kitchen. She's gonna have to let go of her obsession for things being clean," added Gun.

Dun looked up to RJ for relief. Anger worked its way into his words as he spoke. "What do we do now, Mr. RJ? Those buggers have destroyed everything we have. What right do they have to do this to us?"

RJ stared at the flattened Hut in disbelief. Images of helping the Bums build that Hut many years previously flashed through his brain. His focus then turned to the bug cloud. "They don't have the right, Dun. They are definitely trying to get to something inside, and they thought tearing down your place was a way to do that. I'll tell you this. You hang out with the rest of us and help us figure out how we're going to end this nightmare. Eventually, we will build you a new place. I promise."

"Just look at them up there," growled Tug with new determination in his voice. He stomped both feet on the library floor. The bugs hovered in the sky, waiting for another opportune moment to attack. "Those 'drill bugs' think they've got us beat. Well, I say they'll never have us beat."

"Drill bugs," repeated RJ with a nod of his head. "Appropriate name for them. Come on now, boys. We'd better get below and gather reports on the injured."

Aside from Rug Bums Pun and Hun, Elder Jud, his daughter Luk, and her son Tuk were also victims of the drill bug attacks. Casualties amongst the Fog Bobs included Professor Don and Roz's hysterical sister Tov. Among the Net Kens, Wes, Tes, and Vel were stung. And Ham Bats affected were Jak, Jaz-ee, and Elder Paz-ee. Pun and Hun were the only Vowellans who incurred more than one sting. They, of course, fell most seriously ill with high fever, swelling, and delirium much worse than Lil'la had suffered.

Dr. Jon Fog Bob hurried from patient to patient as the victims were gradually brought to the central station within the main tunnel. He found it difficult to care for the folks under such dark, crowded conditions. Before long, he became overwhelmed by the amount of work that lay ahead of him. He hopped back and forth, frantic about which task he should tackle first.

Dr. Jok, having relocated to the tunnel from the research lab, observed Jon's inability to handle the flood of responsibility and stepped up to his grandson with an offer of help. "This is a lot, Jon. Let me help you get organized here. RJ says the Fig Wig Bin is safe inside. It survived the test of a major bug attack with no more than a few cracks. Let's set the Bin up as a temporary hospital. I will assess each case as it arrives at the command base and assign it a priority level. I will send you the highest priority patients first. And I'll find you helpers to nurse the patients."

Jon stared at Jok. The words took a few seconds to sink into his brain. Shaking the confusion from his overly analytical mind, he replied, "Yes, Grandfather. It would be most helpful to have the sick confined to one space. Find as much help as you can. I'll go up into the Bin now."

Dr. Jon recruited Niv and Jil along the way to help with the setup. Dr. Jok, with RJ's assistance, coordinated the assessment and transfer of the sick to the Bin. Several Rug Bums served as the transport team while other Rug Bums kept watch at the tunnel junctions. Niv directed patients to different areas of the Bin, based on their care needs. She, Jil, Min, Zin, and a few other Fig Wigs volunteered to serve as nurses.

In the meantime, the Net Kens cleaned up the tunnels, collected nursing supplies, and delivered them to the Fig Wig Bin. The Ham Bats worked on preparing meals for the townsfolk. Lan took it upon herself to gather up the children and younger teens to keep them safe and occupied while the adults worked on their assignments. She assembled them in the Ham Bats' Rec Hall, where she, Pip Fig Wig, and Mat's sister, Pat, cared for them and kept them busy with fun activities.

Mok and a most guilt-ridden Kip, who couldn't help but feel responsible for all that was happening to the Vowellans, even though the Hut attack hadn't been directly associated with her, served as couriers for Dr. Pol. When new doses of antidote became available, they brought them to Dr. Jon at the Bin. After researching the venom of the vile drill bugs and using Lil'la as his first case study, Dr. Pol concluded that more than one dose of the antidote was definitely appropriate in order for one to recover. Lil'la was slowly recuperating after a second dose, though she was still extremely weak. He also determined that an average adult Vowellan would be able to withstand three or, at most, four stings before the venom became lethal. This meant that Hun Rug Bum, having been stung three times, was in serious trouble.

On Mok and Kip's fifth return to the research lab, Dr. Pol asked Mok to urge RJ to work on an immediate plan to eliminate the massive cloud of drill bugs before anyone else fell victim to their stings. Mok nodded, grabbed Kip's hand, and quickly returned to the emergency operations station.

RJ, Dr. Jok, and Granny Zen convened at their makeshift operations base in the rotunda of the main tunnel to examine their options. Three Elders...Lil'la Fig

Wig, Jud Rug Bum, and Paz-ee Ham Bat, were now ill.. Other potential decision-making adults were either ill or busy with emergency assignments. The disabled Council decided to add Jes Net Ken, Professor Nox, Fil Fig Wig, Mat Ham Bat and Roz Fog Bob to the Council, not only to represent the clans, but to also serve as an official "disaster committee." Dr. Jok thought that with more minds at work, they would be able to concoct a plan for saving their town.

In the meantime, RJ sent Tug, Gun, and Dun, in full protective gear, up to the remains of their Hut to search for clues among the rubble. He hoped they would come across some tidbit of information that would either give them ideas for fighting the drill bugs or tell them about the bugs' vulnerabilities, if there were any.

The Rug Bum trap door was heavily weighted with wood chunks and sawdust. Tug, balancing on the upper steps of their vertical ladder, pushed and pushed on it, trying to open it just a crack for viewing. After a fair amount of sawdust slid through the door and down the ladder, he was able to push the door up far enough to peek at the ground beyond the opening.

"Hey, dudes, it looks pretty quiet out there. The bugs are back up in their cloud. The sun is shining on the cloud way out there in the distance. And our Hut is demolished. What a mess on the floor."

"Well, get out of the way, you hogger, so we can go out there," grouched Dun. "Does it look safe?"

"Uh, I think so, as long as the bugs don't come after

us." Tug gave the trap door a forceful push, flipping it back, allowing space for the Bums to climb to ground level. He was then quick to slam it shut again.

Dun's instinct was to stand guard with hub caps held firmly in front of his torso, eyes fixed on the ugly bug cloud. Gun moved around the floor with angry stomps, an occasional grumble rumbling from his throat. Tug kicked wood chunks from his path while his squinty eyes searched the rubble for clues or salvageable belongings.

"Hey," Tug grunted with a hint of sadness. "Here's Daddy's megaphone. We'll take it back. He'll want this when he wakes up."

"Yeah, if he wakes up," said Gun, his tone echoing a fear not usually heard in Rug Bums. "He didn't look too good when we left. Two stings ain't good."

"Better than three," replied Tug. "I think Pa will pull out of it."

"Hey, look at this, dudes," said Gun as he picked up a mangled mass that had once been a porch rug. "Those buggers sure know how to destroy our fun. How are we going to harass folks without our rugs?"

Dun turned his attention away from the cloud, shaking his head at Gun. "We don't even have a harassing porch anymore, you bozo. It'll be a long time before we're harassing folks again. Maybe this is a sign that we're supposed to stop doing that."

Gun threw Dun a confused glare before continuing to rummage through the rubble. "Hey, here's something else." He picked up a sawdust covered cookie sheet onto which Auntee Gus had rolled a pizza dough thick layer of gum. Several dead bugs were attached to it. "They even tried to ruin our lunch."

"No, look," said Dun as he scurried over to Gun to take a closer look. He pointed at the corner of the sheet that was closest to him. "Look at how the screw-stingers on these bugs here are stuck in the gum."

"You're right," agreed Tug, blowing sawdust away from the sheet. At least two dozen dead bugs were revealed. "They're all stuck that way."

"This has to mean something," said Dun. "Let's take it back." He shot an angry glance at the quiet bug cloud before turning toward the trap door and shouting to the sky. "We're going to get you critters. Somehow, we're going to get you."

The three furry brutes grabbed a few stray bug juice jugs that were scattered here and there before hurrying back down to the safety of the tunnels.

CHAPTER 7

A Plan for Bait

"What do you make of it, Pol?" asked RJ, as the disaster committee and Dr. Pol examined the cookie sheet of gum. RJ had summoned Pol from his lab when Dun and the others had returned from their clue-finding mission. The committee was confident that Pol, so experienced at research on the valley's gum, would find significance in the Rug Bums' discovery.

"Hmm. It's obvious that once the drill bugs' stingers enter the gum, they are stuck. In all these cases, there is at least fifty percent penetration of the stingers into the gum. My initial guess is that, once the stingers get stuck in the gum, their screw shaped nature keeps the bugs from pulling them back out."

Roz, her body bent from the waist, her face as close to the tray of gum and bugs as Dr. Pol's, asked curiously, "Do you think they're attracted to the gum?"

"It's hard to say, Rozee." Doctor Pol picked at the plated armor of a dead bug with one of his fancy instruments. The stench of the black fluid oozing from the body forced their heads to jerk back.

"So how can we use this information to our advantage?" asked RJ, who was standing behind them, his arms folded, his head cocked to the side.

"Perhaps if we find something that attracts them to the gum, we'll be able to trap them by laying out trays with gum that is of this approximate thickness," Dr. Pol offered with a shrug. Research had yet to be done. He could make no further predictions.

"But there are so many of them," added Dr. Jok with a disbelieving shake of his head.

"Well, why don't we experiment and see what happens first," suggested RJ. "Then we can worry about numbers."

RJ and Roz left the meeting to search for Gusee. She was the one who generally had a handle on the gum supply. RJ and Roz quizzed the Vowellans they passed in the main tunnel as to her whereabouts. They quickly learned she was in the Fig Wig Bin, tending to her brother Pun.

When they entered the Bin, they were taken aback by the scene. Sick, moaning folks were in cots or beds scattered throughout. Dr. Jon and the Fig Wigs bustled about, checking fevers, bringing cold compresses, making sure the ill were properly hydrated. The job was indeed overwhelming. Mok and Kip had been given a new assignment by Dr. Jon, that of scheduling and administering timed doses of the antidote to the sick.

Despite the care from everyone, the mean venom of the drill bugs took its sweet time to dissipate within a body. RJ's heart broke to see his precious Vowellans in such a state.

He spotted Mok leaving one of the side bedrooms and called to him. "Mok, do you know where Auntee Gus is?"

"She's over there in Kip's room with Uncle Pun and Mrs. Hun," said Mok, pointing him in the right direction. "Do you need her to do something for you?"

"We need to get some gum from her, babe," said Roz in a quiet voice. "We need to experiment with it to see if it will help us catch the bugs."

"Interesting. Well, let me know if you need a runner. I'd be happy to help. Auntee Gus is not going to leave Uncle Pun anytime soon. He is much too sick. Those two wouldn't know what to do without each other, you know."

Roz looked into her son's eyes and smiled. Her admiration for his sensitivity and awareness of others shone. She placed a gentle hand on his cheek. "I'm so glad you're my son. You know people well, don't you?"

"Yeah, I guess I do," he said sheepishly. They followed RJ into Kip's room.

Pun was barely conscious, his breaths infrequent and shallow. The top of his head, home of the worst of his two stings, was terribly swollen, preventing his suds spout from producing cooling suds for his body. Gusee sat at his side, cursing at him for "being so stupid and getting stung." She dealt with her frustration and worry the only way she knew.

In the bed next to Pun, Hun Rug Bum, surrounded by young Sun, Hun's son Lum, and Niv Fig Wig, hung on for dear life. Three stings were almost more than her aged body could bear. RJ spent a moment sitting at her side, holding her hand, and whispering soothing words.

He then crouched down next to Gusee at Pun's bedside. "How's he doing, Gusee?"

She simply shook her head from side to side.

"I hate to disturb you right now, but I need to ask you something." RJ gently rubbed her furry blue back and explained to her the experiment they wanted to try. "The gum on the cookie sheet. What can you tell me about it?"

"Not much. Pun brought me this new experimental resin earlier in the week. It was different from the normal stuff," said Gusee, never allowing her eyes to stray from Pun's sweaty face.

"Where did it come from, one of the grafted trees in the gum tree grove?"

"I don't think so. Heck, I don't know where it came from." Gusee's voice reflected a rising shortness and annoyance.

Pun moaned from where he lay and slowly turned his head toward them as drool fell from the side of his mouth. "Jhuh," he whispered between thin breaths. "Jhuh, jhuh."

"What's he trying to say, Auntee Gus?" asked Mok, who had been quietly standing in the background.

"I don't know." Gusee leaned closer to Pun's face. "What are you trying to say, you bundle of bones?"

"Jhi...Jhuh," whispered Pun. "Jhi...Jhuh."

"What the heck is "Jhi...Jhuh?" snapped Gusee.

"Jhi...Jhuh," he whispered again. This time, Mok was also leaning in.

"Are you trying to say Jimmy's Jungle, Uncle Pun?" Mok asked gently. "Are there gum trees up in Jimmy's Jungle?"

With every ounce of strength he had, Pun nodded.

Gusee pulled her head back and turned to look at Mok. "How'd you know that, boy?"

"I don't know. Maybe because I've seen Uncle Pun coming from the direction of the jungle in the early morning hours. It just clicked."

"Well, good for you, Mok," said RJ as he perked up. He leaned in to speak to Pun. "Hey, buddy. Is that where this new resin came from?"

Again, Pun slowly nodded.

RJ patted Pun's arm. "Good job, Pun. We'll take it from here. You just take it easy now."

Roz, who had been witnessing the conversation, turned toward Gusee. "It looks like the gum can trap the bugs' stingers, Gusee. We suspect that if they can't escape it, they die. Is there any gum from that batch left that we could experiment with?"

Gusee gave her a vigorous nod. "Yeah, there is, actually. I shoved it in our tunnel behind the bug juice barrels right after Pun and Hun got stung. Ain't nobody gonna mess with our gum."

"Okay! Thanks so much, Gusee," chuckled RJ kindly, patting her arm as well. "You stay right here with your brother. We'll let you know how things go."

RJ and Roz, with Mok tagging along behind, left the Fig Wig Bin to begin the next phase of their emergency operation.

San Ham Bat sat in another room of the Fig Wig Bin with his stricken grandparents, Paz-ee and Jaz-ee. They were showing signs of improvement after receiving a dose of the antidote. Though they were very weak from the sting each of them had endured, they felt some relief from the pain and swelling. Paz-ee's inflammation was on the back of his hand, and Jaz-ee's was on her left leg. They lay on the floor atop bedding brought from their frying pan beds at the Ham Bat Pad. The Rug Bums had tried to fit them onto the long, narrow Fog Bob cots that had been brought to the Bin, but their ample bodies simply wouldn't fit onto the cots or any of the other beds within the Fig Wig Bin.

San sat on the floor between them, holding hands with both. He told them silly stories about his funny little buddy, Fahbee Flingbee, who lazed in his pocket most of the time. With his eyes closed, Paz-ee smiled at the story of how this crooked-beaked, lazy-eyed, Spanish-speaking Casanova of the flingbee had come into San's life at Lake Marie. Jaz-ee like the story about San's fishing experience that day, when he found a squishy yellow ball that contained a liquid tasting like "a piece of heaven in your mouth."

"I sure wish I had a drop-ood'ly on my tongue right now," whispered Jaz-ee, still so tired. "The 'sweet cream taste' sounds so good-ood'ly."

San's upper body straightened from its casual slouch. He looked from one grandparent to another. "Well, then, I'll go get you some," he proclaimed. He jumped to his feet and left them without a further word. Fahbee, who had been hidden and silent within San's shirt pocket the entire time, poked his head out to see what would come next.

Paz-ee and Jaz-ee glanced at each other with puzzled expressions. "It was only a story, right?" whispered Jaz-ee. Paz-ee yawned and shrugged his hefty shoulders.

San ran northward through the main tunnel, passing various Vowellans, as well as Mr. Huge Dude, along the way. He waved to Mr. HD, who dutifully continued his watch over the hens and hyper rets that were penned in the school tunnel.

Upon arrival at the Ham Bat Pad, San hurried to his cluttered bedroom closet. Despite his well-dressed outward appearance, his closet revealed his lack of organization. He kicked mounds of clothing and boxes of shoes out of his way. He pushed hangers full of colorful coordinated outfits to the right side. His wide body demanded room from which to operate. Once San was able to reach the left side of his top shelf, he retrieved the hidden ceramic mug that housed the floppy, hairy yellow ball that he had found at the shore of Lake Marie. Though it had been a while since he had looked at the squishy orb, it seemed to be intact, secured by a bag clip from the Ham Bat work room.

"Do you think the limoncina is still good-ood'ly,

Fahbee?" he asked his little buddy, who now balanced his tiny, winged body on the top edge of San's pocket.

"Oh, of course, Señor," assured Fahbee. Limoncinas, desired for their delicious drops of liquid, had been commonplace in his home country. He therefore thought he was the all-knowing limoncina expert. "It becomes even better with age."

"Good! This might be just the thing-ood'ly to perk up my grandparents. Let's go."

San and Fahbee hadn't traveled far down the main tunnel, when Lek Net Ken joined them. The red eyes surrounding his head searched the tunnel floor for possible cracks as they walked along. His compulsive tendencies ran on overdrive during the current stress. But so did his sensitivities. "San, I'm so sorry to hear about Jaz-ee and Paz-ee. Are you going down to the Fig Wig Bin to see them?"

"Yeah, I've been keeping them company while everyone else-ood'ly is busy with assignments."

"I'll go with you then. I want to check on Auntee Tes and Uncle Vel. Granny says they're feeling pretty crummy." Lek's two right-facing eyes suddenly focused on the yellow scraggly hairs that protruded from the mug San carried. "Hey! What's in there?"

"Oh, remember that yellow squishy thing-ood'ly I found out at Lake Marie a while back? Remember you wanted to take it from me?" San loved digging at Lek about his peskiness.

All Lek's eyebrows bent into a circular frown at the

fact that he also had a couple of the odd objects hidden away in a dresser drawer at home. He had never figured out what to do with them. "Yeah, I remember. Did you find out what it is?"

"Yes! It is common where Fahbee comes from." San opened the top of his pocket, and Fahbee's curlicue tail emerged. San looked at Lek, almost hesitant to reveal the orb's good quality. "It's called a limoncina. One drop of the nectar inside the ball-ood'ly makes you feel like you've eaten the best thing ever. I'm going to give some to Jaz-ee and Paz-ee. So don't try to talk me into giving it to you-ood'ly, Lek."

"I won't. That does sound pretty cool though." Lek's mind calculated when he might be back home to pull his limoncinas out of his drawer and experiment with them.

They reached the operations base in the tunnel's rotunda, where several folks huddled. Curious about current news of the bug situation, they worked their way toward the central tables where RJ, Granny Zen, Dr. Jok, Jes, Fil and Professor Nox discussed current matters of concern. At a side table, Roz, Mat, and Mok worked on spreading Gusee's small batch of experimental resin onto a few cookie sheets and regular everyday resin onto others. All seemed quiet on the outside. San and Lek approached Mat.

"What are you do'd'ling, Daddy?" asked San. "That doesn't look very appetizing."

"It's not for eating, son," chuckled Mat. He pointed toward the bug-infested sheet the Rug Bums had recovered. "See that there? We're experimenting to find the best way-ood'ly to catch more of those nasty buggers."

"Ah! I hope it works. I hate what they did-ood'ly to Jaz-ee and Paz-ee." San pulled the limoncina from the mug. "So, Daddy, do you think it's okay if I give them a drop-ood'ly of this yummy liquid I found at Lake Marie? I thought it might cheer them up."

Mat frowned at the hairy, alien-looking orb. But old Dr. Jok, who had been half-listening to the conversation, gave a quick gasp, his face lighting up. He rose from his chair and moved close to San.

"OH! Is that a *limoncina*?" Jok's jaw dropped in amazement. "Why, I haven't seen one of those since I was a youngster. We used to pull them out of the lake and treat ourselves to drops on special occasions. I can't believe you found one."

"Yeah, it was buried under clob-ood'lies in my fishing bucket. The drops taste amazing. And the nectar seems to last'l a really long time."

"Oh, it will last forever," confirmed Jok. "It's so rare to find one these days. This would be a fine thing to give the sick folks. It's completely harmless. It won't improve their condition, but it might soothe them for a while. When you get to the Bin, tell Dr. Jon that I approve of administering drops to the patients. May I open the limoncina to remind myself of the delightful aroma?"

"Of course, Dr. Jok." San removed the bag clip from the straw that had been inserted into the flesh of the limoncina and passed the mug to him.

Jok closed his eyes while inhaling a whiff. "Aah, just as I remember."

"Well, that's wonderful. It would be so nice to help-ood'ly the sick folks," said Mat, waving his hands in his excitement. In his usual clumsy manner, he accidentally bumped Dr. Jok's arm with a careless hand. A fair amount of limoncina nectar spilled onto one of the cookie sheets of Gusee's resin.

"MAAAATTT!" hollered everyone within range.

Mat shrunk into the nearest chair and shook his head in embarrassment. "I'm so, so, so sorry. Is there enough left-ood'ly to take care of the sick folks?"

Matt's remorse saddened San. "I'll make it work, Daddy. You didn't mean to do-d'l it. I'll go over to the Bin now and see how far-ood'ly it goes."

Lek, curious to see for himself what the limoncina's nectar would do, encouraged, "Yes, let's go."

With that, they headed across the main tunnel.

Meanwhile, Mat looked sadly at his worktable. "Well, I guess I ruined this sheet of gum-ood'ly. I'm sorry, everyone. I hope this doesn't ruin your experiment."

"I say we go ahead and put the sheet out along with the others and see what happens," suggested Dr. Jok. "We have nothing to lose at this point."

"So true," said RJ. "Good idea, Jok. So, let's get these gum sheets outside. We can monitor their status from upstairs in the Fog Bob Box. Agreed?"

"Agreed!" echoed the committee. The members nodded in typical Vowellan animated fashion before making their way up through the Fog Bob trap door and to the front library windows.

CHAPTER 8

Another Attack

Tug Rug Bum, fully suited in protective gear, proceeded through the Rug Bum tunnel and up the ladder to the trap door of the Rug Bums' destroyed Hut. He carried a stack of cookie sheets, each lined with gum and separated by banana leaves. RJ and Jok had instructed him to set the bait for the drill bugs as safely and efficiently as he could. Working fast, he lifted the trap door with the top of his head, just far enough to slide the trays out onto the cluttered Hut floor. He fanned them out, placing them within easy reach of the door, with the tray that had been compromised by the limoncina nectar to his far right. After pulling the banana leaves from the tops of the trays, he looked up at the black bug cloud. It appeared to turn angry, churning within itself.

Tug slammed the trap door shut just in time to evade the bugs' new, rapid invasion. A narrow ribbon of villains swooped down from its cloud to the Rug Bum property. The drill bugs swarmed the trays in massive numbers in a frantic blur of activity. Tug listened to the commotion above him, hoping with eyes scrunched closed that the metal door would keep him safe.

While San and Lek visited patient after patient within the Fig Wig Bin, distributing rationed drops of the limoncina nectar to the sick folks, RJ and most of the committee members stood in the Fog Bob Library to watch the bugs' behavior. Roz and Jes remained at the emergency station to handle new issues that arose.

RJ, Dr. Jok, and the others watched from the tall library windows as the drill bugs attacked the gum in crazed fashion. Dr. Jok shook his head at the sight. "Well, they are certainly attracted to something out there. It's hard to tell whether it is the gum or the limoncina."

"Hopefully, it's not the limoncina," replied RJ. "If it is as rare as you say it is, it won't be of much help. Let's hope that Pun's gum is doing its job."

"Me and my clumsiness," added remorseful Mat Ham Bat with a sad shake of his head. "If only I hadn't spilled the nectar-ood'ly."

He hung his head and slapped his chubby left hand again and again against the glass window in a display of frustration. The vibration of the glass rattling in its frame caught the attention of the drill bugs. The somewhat diminished swarm of bugs suddenly turned its attention away from the gum sheets and instead toward the tall, square-edged building up the road that was the Fog Bob Box. Perhaps taking the rattling as a cue that the structure had the potential to give them access to the underground and Kip's voice, the drill bugs resumed a ribbon shape and positioned itself facing the Box. They were clearly more agitated as they observed the movements of the committee members behind the glass of the Fog Bob library.

"OH NO!" yelled RJ, realizing what was about to happen. "Let's go. They're going to come straight at us."

He and the Vowellans hurried down the long Fog Bob hallway toward the trap door. Behind them, one of the tall library windows shattered as the powerful armored bugs blasted through the glass and began their rapid swoop through the building.

"Hurry Jok! Hurry Zen! Get down the ladder quickly," commanded RJ above the horrible clatter of the bugs' armored wings. The two precious elders were his primary concern. Mat, Professor Nox, Fil, and finally RJ raced down the ladder as quickly as their assortment of odd body shapes would allow. RJ slammed shut the metal trap door, but not before each of the committee members had been inflicted with a sting. The bugs didn't sense other vulnerable targets, so they swooped out of the broken library window and returned to the trays of gum.

Back at the operations station, Mok, Roz, and Jes came to the aid of the victims. Mok and Jes hurried Dr. Jok and Zen to the Fig Wig Bin. Roz called for Dok and Wit to help deliver Mat, Nox, and Fil there as well. She also called on Dun, Tug, and Gun to hunt down any stray bugs that might have infiltrated the Fog Bob tunnel. And she issued an alert to close all trap doors until further notice. During the activity, RJ sat down at the meeting table and examined his forearm where he had been stung. With her urgent assignments complete, Roz sat beside him, also taking a hard look at the damage.

"It doesn't look anything like the others' stings, RJ. You may have lucked out." Roz grabbed a cold compress from the ice chest that sat behind them. Settling back beside him, she pressed it against the sting for a few moments, then removed it. "Look, it's no more than a little prick in your skin. The others' stings are already so swollen and discolored."

RJ shrugged. "Maybe it's because I'm not a Vowellan. I'm of a different species than the rest of you, you know."

"Yes," Roz said with a nod and a grin. She leaned over and wrapped him in a sweet hug. "You've been with us as long as I can remember, so I do forget about that little fact. What did we ever do before you came here?"

"You lived a much less complicated life, for sure," he chuckled. He looked into her deep blue eyes, and the memory of the first time he saw her, as a mere 7-year-old, flashed through his mind. After the storm that had brought RJ's plane down into Vowella Valley, RJ and his Ma had found her cowering behind a pier under the original porch, the only structure that had survived the unusual weather event. She had been frightened and delirious and separated from her clan. She had been the first Vowellan RJ had ever seen. "You were my first friend in Vowella, Rozee. We've had a special relationship all these years, haven't we?"

"Why yes, RJ. You've been my hero since the first

time I saw you." Roz shot him an adoring look. "I don't know what we would have ever done without you all these years."

"You know what? You would have been simply fine. Your lives just would have been different without exposure to the human way of life. Let me say this, Rozee. If anything does happen to me with this sting and all, I trust you and Mok to take charge here. Jon is tied up with the sick. Pol is busy with the antidote. With all the Elders now out of commission, we're going to need good leadership to get through this disaster. You two are the best and most sensible I know. I trust you to make whatever decisions are necessary to end this nightmare. Will you do that for me, Rozee?"

"Of course, RJ." Roz shook her head and hugged his shoulder. "But let's not get ahead of ourselves here. Let's get you a dose of the antidote. Maybe you'll be just fine."

"Maybe."

Roz walked RJ to the Fig Wig Bin, where Dr. Jon administered his antidote. Since RJ was still feeling all right, he and Roz returned to the operations base. They instructed Dok, Nak, and a few others to go to the Net Ken Den and the Ham Bat Pad to cover all the windows with their storm panels. They now knew that windows were vulnerable targets. The body of the Den was composed of granite, and the Pad was constructed of stucco with a tile roof. Adding the storm panels would theoretically make the structures safe from bug attacks.

The town's living space had shrunk. More and more folks had been forced to the tunnels. RJ and Roz closed the Fog Bob Box, except for Dr. Pol's lab, which was windowless in the center of the building. The Rug Bums, garbed in full protective gear, searched for stray bugs when it seemed safe and covered the Box window spaces with storm panels as well.

Tug Rug Bum once again lifted the Bums' trap door with the top of his head. Through the goggles of his protective gear, he peeked at the outside view. Six hours after the attack on the Fog Bob Box, the black bug cloud hung immobile in the sky. Night was taking over the valley. Tug quietly pulled the cookie sheets, one at a time, through the hole and into burlap bags. He worked quickly, not stopping to examine them. He hurried them to the operations base, where RJ, Roz, Mok, San, and Lek were discussing the status of the sick over at the Fig Wig Bin.

San and Lek had distributed drops of limoncina nectar to the patients until they ran out. Mok had held his G.G.'s hand until he had settled into a deep sleep.

"Old Dr. Jok is very ill-ood'ly, as is Granny Zen," reported San. "Judging by sweet Lil'la's slow progress, it seems the older folk-ood'lies are experiencing much more serious reactions to the venom than the younger folks."

"Yes," added Lek. "Auntee Tes is already showing sign of recovery, as is Mrs. Tov. But Mrs. Tov is still hysterical over her stinging incident, so Mrs. Niv sedated her with that local sage-like plant the Fig Wigs like, lavexlava."

"And Uncle Pun is now fully alert, Mr. RJ," said Mok. "But Father told me to tell you that poor Mrs. Hun is still in grave condition with her three stings."

The conversation changed focus when Dun and Gun appeared with Dr. Pol. The Rug Bum boys had gone to fetch Pol when they heard word that Tug had retrieved the gum sheets. They had dressed Pol in a protective suit. He had carried his top hat in his hand, since the head cover was too small to accommodate it.

Tug laid the sheets out on the left side table while everyone crowded around. Removing his head cover and replacing it with his top hat, Dr. Pol took a hard look at the gum sheets. He pulled a magnifying glass from the front of his protective suit and examined the trays closely.

"It appears the drill bugs went after all of the trays with Gusee's gum, doesn't it," he commented. "The trays with the regular gum...not so much. The new gum definitely trapped the bugs by their screw-stingers. They can't back themselves out of the gum once they're screwed in, so they stay and die a slow death."

"Good! They deserve it," proclaimed Dun, tired and distraught from stress of the situation.

"But look at this tray," observed Dr. Pol as he moved his magnifying glass over to the last tray on the right. "You can barely see the layer of gum because there are so many of these ugly creatures stuck in the gum."

"That's the sheet that the limoncina spilled onto, isn't it," stated RJ, frowning while still sitting in his chair at the main operations table. He didn't need to look to know the answer.

"Yes, I'm afraid so, RJ," answered Pol. He looked at each weary face that was within his range of sight. "It looks like these varmints love the nectar. Where do you think we can get our hands on more?"

It became clear to the disaster committee that their best solution at this point for ridding themselves of the drill bugs was to infuse massive quantities of the gum from Pun's gum trees with the bug-attracting limoncina.

"San, honey, have you seen any more of the limoncinas at Lake Marie recently?" asked Roz.

"No, that's the only one I've ever seen-ood'ly. I've been hoarding it because I didn't know if I'd ever find another one. I'm glad it did some good-ood'ly for the sick folks, but it's too bad it's gone now."

Lek squirmed and fidgeted as he listened to the conversation. He had been hoarding two limoncinas since he had stowed away and gone to New Life City on RJ's plane several months previously, while RJ had been on a buying trip. He had been unaware of their unique properties. Now he had a moral battle going on inside of him. If he said nothing, he could keep the two precious squishy balls for himself. If he forfeited his personal wants and turned them over to the committee, he could help his town rid itself of the dreaded bugs. Since he was a Net Ken, putting anything ahead of inborn greed was exceedingly difficult to do. But at the same time, Lek the individual was such a nice guy, how could he even think twice?

Jes was quick to pick up on Lek's unease when she returned from the Fig Wig Bin. "What's wrong, son? You look like you're about to crawl out of your skin. Is there something you need to talk about?"

Lek's ten eyes spun in their sockets. He turned so his front facing eyes focused on RJ and Roz. "Uh, yeah, Mother. Mr. RJ, I have a confession to make. A couple of months ago, when you took a trip to New Life City, I stowed away on your plane."

RJ stared at Lek for a long moment. He cracked a sideways grin and chuckled. "Ah, so you're the one. I knew someday the truth would come out."

"Oh, Lekee, you know better than to do that," said Jes in a slight reprimanding tone. "So why is that making you jittery right now?"

Lek continued to look at RJ rather sheepishly. "Because, Mr. RJ, while you were in the city, I sneaked into the forest behind Uncle Jake's office to look around. I found some ponds in the forest where limoncinas were breeding, or whatever they do. I netted a couple of them and brought them home. They're in my room right now. I never knew what to do with them."

RJ knew how difficult it was for Lek to part with things. Collecting was his life. "Lek, will you let us have them?"

Lek's plentiful eyes examined the many hopeful faces surrounding him, those of RJ, Mok, Roz, Dr. Pol, Jes, and San. He turned and headed north in the main tunnel, hollering behind him, "I'll be right back."

San, in the meantime, ran up to the workroom behind Valley Store to fetch a couple of mugs and straws for the limoncinas. He and Lek reconnected in the main tunnel and headed back to the base. San gave Roz and Jes a detailed lesson on opening the limoncina to access the liquid.

Roz watched curiously as San carefully twisted the straw through the pliable surface. "How did you learn how to do that, honey? It appears you were well-taught."

"Oh, it was my little buddy, Fahbee. He knew all about these limoncinas."

"Well, it looks like Fahbee's method is quite useful for preserving every drop of the nectar," observed Jes.

While Lek and San ran their errands, Mok hopped over to the Fig Wig Bin to check on his great grandfather. Dr. Jok was in the moaning, feverish stage of the sting reaction, not realizing Mok was even there. Mok also peeked in on Pun, who was fortunately becoming more alert by the hour. Pun's strong and able body had helped him withstand the terrible effects of his stings. The top of his head remained quite swollen, but a few cooling bubbles now made their way from his suds spout.

Mok thought it might be useful to dig for more details about the gum trees in Jimmy's Jungle. He sat at Pun's bedside, careful not to disturb Gusee, who was sound asleep, her head resting on the opposite side of the bed. Pun turned his head to look at Mok.

"Uncle Pun, can you tell me exactly where your experimental gum trees are in Jimmy's Jungle? It looks like their resin is excellent for catching drill bugs. You should be so proud," whispered Mok. "Are there several trees or just a few?"

"There are a whole bunch of them past a clearing off to the left of the central coffee farm. There's a skinny trail that leads there. Old bug juice jugs are hanging from the trees to mark the way. Must be ten years since I planted those gum trees. They're just busting with good resin right about now. You should be able to collect a hefty amount up there." Pun sighed after saying all those words. "Sure wish I was strong enough to go get it for you."

Mok patted his damp, furry arm. He couldn't remember if he had ever before touched a Rug Bum's shaggy fur, much softer than he would have thought. "Don't you worry about that, Uncle Pun. You did a great job taking care of all those trees you planted way back then. We'll take care of getting the resin down here."

"Take Dun with you. He's the best tapper we have, the little bugger. He'll know how to be smart about the extractions."

Mok patted his arm one more time before rising. "Will do, Uncle Pun. You take care of yourself now."

CHAPTER 9

Time for Action

Before heading back to the command station, Mok searched the Bin for Kip. She had been serving as nurse around the clock, along with the other Fig Wigs. Hours had passed since they had seen each other. He found her slumped next to the Massage Studio's interior door, her head leaning against the wall, sweat dripping from her orange curls and the bandanna that covered her forehead. She looked wilted and extremely sad.

Mok slid down the wall next to her, knees up, floppy feet planted on the floor. "Punkee, you're working much too hard. You need to take care of yourself, so you don't get sick too."

"Can't you see that's what I'm trying to do?" she snapped in a voice she had not intended to use. She placed her tiny hands over her closed eyelids and sighed. In a whisper, she continued. "I'm sorry, Munkee. This is all too much for me."

"Listen, Punkee. You need to quit beating yourself up over this whole thing. You didn't bring the drill bugs to the valley. You're not responsible for everyone being sick. The drill bugs are. You brought nothing but joy to everyone here with your fabulous voice. Don't forget that. Someday, all of this will go away, and you'll be able to sing for us again. I know it."

"Why would I want to sing again? What good has it done?" she again whispered.

"It has made folks happier than I've seen them in a long time, that's why..." Mok paused.

A ticking noise commenced, at first unidentifiable. Mok's first thought was that someone was throwing rocks at the stucco exterior of the Fig Wig Bin. The noise began at a slow pace, but that pace increased rapidly. The disturbing sound soon became the frantic racket they had heard earlier on, as the drill bugs once again descended on the Bin. It was impossible to confirm that that was the case, now that all the town's windows had been covered with storm panels, which eliminated all views of the Bin from the outside. But previous experience left the Vowellans who were inside with no doubt.

Mok watched Kip cover her ears and roll her body into a tight ball. He watched the sick and weary surrounding him cry with fear and frustration. He watched Dr. Jon helplessly hop from patient to patient. He watched the Rug Bums stomp and curse the black cloud that hovered just outside the Bin's domed ceiling. He closed his eyes and breathed deeply in an attempt to control his resentment that the Vowellans were being held captive in their own town, having to live a disaster like none they had ever known, one they had no experience in handling. *There must be a way to end this nightmare*, his thoughts told him again and again.

"Ssh, now, Punkee," he whispered to Kip. He wrapped his long, skinny arms around her trembling, curled up body and pulled her next to him. "The bugs must sense you're here. Mouth closed from here on out, okay? I'll take care of you."

Kip nodded, raised her head, and lifted her heavy eyelids, exposing her spectacular kaleidoscopic eyes to him. Mok's heart melted at the sight of them, so bright and rich with multiple shades of turquoise. Still holding her close, he pushed her bandanna back into her curls. He pressed his cheek against her damp forehead, then gently kissed it twice. Her tense yellow lips spread into a sweet grin, and she raised her face to his. That familiar tickle rose in his chest, and he couldn't help but lean into her lips and gift them with more kisses.

The tickle rose in her chest too. Kip looked deeper into his eyes, placed a tender hand on his cheek, and kissed him back. No words were needed to communicate their feelings for each other.

"MOK!" Dr. Jon's voice broke into their private moment with a jolt. He towered over them like mean schoolmaster.

Mok and Kip jumped to attention while continuing to sit on the floor. Kip lowered her head, but Mok looked straight into his father's eyes.

"I want to speak to you this instant." Dr. Jon opened the Massage Studio door, stooped his tall body to fit through the short, curved opening, and hopped inside.

Mok pushed himself upright and patted Kip's head before following his father into the room. The door slammed behind him.

"What is the meaning of this, son? Your behavior is entirely unacceptable on many levels."

"Father, I was just comforting--"

"You were making a spectacle of yourself. Such behavior is inappropriate under these circumstances. It is inappropriate under any circumstances. I told you to stay away from that girl," barked Dr. Jon.

"Father, Punkee's my best friend. I'm not going to stay away from her," Mok stated clearly.

"She is obviously more than that, and I will not allow it. You are heading into forbidden territory, son. Fog Bobs don't do that." Dr. Jon took a serious and stubborn stance, glaring at Mok coldly.

"Don't do what?" Mok frowned, feeling hairs rise on the back of his neck and the familiar twisting of his insides. It took all he had to refrain from exploding at his father. "You're going to forbid me from having feelings for someone else? You may control much of my life, but you can't control that. I won't let you."

"Clans do not cross that line. A Fog Bob will never cross that line. Our reputation is at stake."

"You mean your reputation, father? You may be the only one who cares about that. And you know what? The only thing that is inappropriate is this conversation we're having. There are so many important things to do right now. You need to get back to your patients." Mok flung the door open and exited the Massage Studio in a huff.

When he reentered the Bin's main room, Mok realized that the drill bugs had once again retreated to the sky. The Bin was calm and quiet. The folks had resumed either resting, nursing, or guarding. He hopped around the Bin in search of Niv. It was so very crowded with cots, makeshift beds, patients, and scurrying helpers. He eventually found her in a side room dabbing Hun Rug Bum's face with a cool cloth.

"Mama Niv," whispered Mok as he observed the grave condition of Hun Rug Bum. Her damp, shaggy blue fur had faded almost to the gray color of Mr. Huge Dude's feet. Her left cheek was massively swollen, her left eye buried under the bulbous sting site. "Sorry, Mama Niv. Do you have a minute?"

Niv placed the cloth in a nearby bowl and rose, guiding him to a quiet spot outside the room. "Of course, honey. What is it? You look terribly worried."

"I am, Mama Niv. Kip is a worn-out mess, and I fear the bugs know she's here in the Bin. They are after her for whatever reason. Can you afford to let her leave for a while? May I take her to the operations station so the committee can see what this stress is doing to her? Maybe they can help us decide what to do about the situation."

Niv flinched at the thought of her daughter being in danger. "Of course, honey. I don't understand why she is the target of this miserable attack, but I trust you, and I trust that she'll be safe in RJ's and the committee's hands. Do me a favor, though. Find Wit down in the tunnel with the wistas. Tell him what's going on, okay?"

"I will, Mama Niv. Thank you." Mok left her and

returned to Kip, who remained cowering next to the Massage Studio door.

"Punkee, come on," he said softly as he reached down and pulled her up by her armpits. "I'm taking you to Mr. RJ. Your mama says it's okay. Let's get you out of here for a little while."

Emotionally drained and exhausted, she complied. Without words, she took his hand and allowed him to lead her to the trap door and down the Fig Wig ladder.

Roz took one look at Kip and hurried to embrace her. She glanced at Mok for answers. RJ rose from his chair and did the same.

"I think the drill bugs are attacking others in an attempt to get to Punkee," theorized Mok aloud. "Her voice seems to set them off. Look at her. She's a wreck. We need to do something, Mr. RJ. How can we protect her? How can we keep the bugs from trying to find new ways of getting into the tunnel system?"

RJ's eyelids showed initial signs of drooping. "I'm not quite sure. We've done all we can to secure all potential entrances. We could keep Kipee in the research lab, but that is so isolating."

Kip grabbed a piece of paper and a pen and scribbled with a trembling hand. *I don't want to be isolated. I want to be able to help with nursing or food or whatever else needs to be done.*

"I know, Punkee, but we need to protect you," reminded Mok.

They were then interrupted by a phone call from the

Ham Bat Pad. Roz answered and reported, "Oh no. Something is scratching at the storm doors at the Rec Hall. We must do something. All the children are there."

"Dun!" Mok hollered down the main tunnel in quick response. "Grab your boys. Trouble at the Ham Bat Pad. Let's go."

The Rug Bums, still suited in protective gear, assembled themselves with hub caps in hand and took off north through the tunnel. Mok left Kip in Roz's hands while he, Dok, San, Lek, Bek, and Nak hurried behind them to the Rec Hall to evacuate Lan, Pip, Pat, and all the children to the Ham Bat tunnels. Considering the massive quantities of food that had been stockpiled in those tunnels to feed the townsfolk during the disaster, only nooks and crannies of space remained.

Each adult took responsibility for three to four children, and Mok called Roz for more adults to come care for the remaining kids. The children cried and called for their parents. The tunnels seemed the safest place for them for the time being.

The Bums temporarily slid the storm panels away from the south glass doors, which were still intact, so they could look outside. Once the Rug Bums finished their inspection of the Pad and the grounds surrounding it, they concluded that what had sounded like drill bugs pounding on the storm doors had been a few stray hens pecking frantically trying to get indoors. The Bums quickly retrieved them. The Pad, protected by its tile roof, stucco walls, and storm panels, was otherwise in solid condition.

Mok and the other teens returned to base. He looked from Kip to Roz to RJ. "Mr. RJ, we need to go after the gum and limoncinas. We can't go on like this anymore. The children are miserable. Everyone at the Bin is in a bad way. We're helpless without a weapon. If gum and limoncinas are all we have at this point to fight the drill bugs, then we need to get them in our hands. Are you okay with that?"

"Absolutely," RJ was quick to respond, though through a huge yawn. "I have one hundred percent trust in you getting the job done."

"But son, how do you know you'll be safe? And how will you know where to go?" asked Roz, worry hanging from her face. Her attention quickly diverted to RJ, whose head started to drop. She grabbed his shoulders and investigated his face. "RJ, what's wrong? Is your sting bothering you?"

"No. It's okay. I'm just suddenly so sleepy."

"Mr. RJ," Mok interrupted, trying to finish his conversation with him. "I have another idea. What do you think about putting the children and many of the others into hibernation? You know, just as you found all the Vowellans in the tunnels when you first got to Vowella. Do you think that would work? Folks have suffered enough trauma. And if we do that, there will be less folks to take care of while we try to fight the drill bugs."

"That's actually a good idea, Mok," RJ said through yet another yawn. "I don't know why I didn't think of it myself. Start with the children and the Elders once they recover. Now, before I fall asleep on you, tell me how you're going to find what you need."

"Uncle Pun has already told me where his gum trees are in Jimmy's Jungle. Lek and the younger Bums have worked at the nearby coffee farm, so we should have no trouble locating the trees. But I don't know about the limoncinas. Uncle Jake's place is on the other side of Jimmy's Jungle, right?"

"Yes, but none of you have ever been outside of the valley," RJ pointed out.

Mok grabbed Kip's notepad and pen from her. "Can you draw us a quick map, Mr. RJ, since you know your way there?"

RJ sketched out a quick lay of the land beyond the jungle. "Once you get through the jungle, you'll see flat space that extends almost as far north as you can see. On the far east and west sides, forests line the flat space. Way out in the middle of the horizon, what looks like stacks of boxes is the skyline of New Life City. On the far right of the horizon, you'll find the airport, the Materiality Zone, and Uncle Jake's airplane hangar. Call Uncle Jake once you clear the jungle. He'll guide you there."

RJ's voice started to fade, but his brain was still working. "How will you find your way through the jungle? Darn, I wish I were strong enough to fly us there."

"You wouldn't be able to anyway," reminded Roz. "The bug cloud is in the way."

"Yes, how *will* we get through the jungle?" That little obstacle hadn't occurred to Mok.

"I know the way," said a barely audible voice coming

from San's shirt. Fahbee Flingbee poked his curly tail out of the front pocket.

"What was that noise?" All Mok heard was a tiny vibrating sound.

"What, Fahbee? Do you really know the way-ood'ly?" asked San, who had been standing back listening to the conversation.

"Hey, I heard him say that too," said Nak. He turned toward San's shirt. "Fahbee, are you sure about that-ood'ly?"

"I traveled that route when I first came here. And I've roamed the jungle many times with the other flingbees since I've been here," added Fahbee while turning his tiny body around, exposing his head for all to see.

San translated, since only the Ham Bats could hear him speak.

RJ's speech began to slur. He sounded like a Fog Bob whose scalp had been attacked by fog. "That's incredible. And Lek, do you think you can find the limoncina ponds again?"

"I think so," Lek said nervously, remembering the fright he had felt when he had last been in the forest. "I saw the ponds from the plane and...and...I didn't walk too far before I saw the limoncinas and...and...then I netted them...and...then I saw the blue monster...and..."

"What blue monster?" said a slow, low voice that suddenly came from the school tunnel entrance just a few yards away. "What did it look like?"

Everyone made a startled turn toward the voice. RJ's

head finally hit the table.

"Mr. Huge Dude?" asked Mok in wonderment. "Was that you speaking?"

"Yes," Mr. H.D. said shyly, his head hanging, his eyes focused on the tunnel floor. He walked closer to the conversation. "Did the 'monster' look like me, Lek?"

Lek, on the verge of freaking out not only over the rapid sequence of events but at the fact that Mr. HD was speaking to him, stared at him while his side eyes spun in their sockets. Trying to remember his 'monster', he looked him up and down. "Yes, he looked just like you. Was that you at the ponds?"

"No, but I know the ponds you're talking about. I was there with my brother when I was suddenly taken away and delivered here. My brother must have been who you saw."

"That's amazing," said Mok with a shake of his head. "Mr. HD, thank you so much for speaking up." He turned toward RJ. "Mr. RJ, can you hear me? I think we have it covered."

"RJ, RJ." Roz hollered at him and pulled him back to a sit in his chair. "Can you hear me? Does all of this sound like a good plan to you?"

"Yes, a good plan." RJ's head flopped back, his eyelids closed, his speech slowing like a dying tape player. He continued to say all that needed saying. "Thanks, Rozee. Thanks Mok. You'll do a fine job with all of this. Just protect the Elders. Very important."

RJ's head hung back as he forced his eyes open to say

one more thing. "Rozee, remember back when my Pa was stung in the jungle? It made him sleep for months. But one day, the sun shone on him, he woke up, and he came back home. I promise I'll be back when the sun shines in the valley again."

Roz took his face in her gentle hands and spoke to him reassuringly. "Yes, I remember that, RJ. Don't worry. We'll take care of the Vowellans, and we'll take care of you. We'll carry out our plan, and before you know it, the sun will shine in Vowella again. You go to sleep now, sweet man."

"I will." RJ slipped into a deep slumber.

Dok and Nak carried him to the Fig Wig Bin and placed him in a room with Dr. Jok. Dr. Jon looked him over and determined that needing to sleep was the only after effect of RJ's drill bug sting. Niv made him cozy with soft pillows and a fluffy quilt. RJ was now down for his own period of hibernation.

And the Vowellans were now on their own.

CHAPTER 10

Leadership

"Papa Pol," said Mok to his grandfather, Dr. Pol. "What can you do with the two limoncinas that Lek gave us? Do you know the ratio of gum to limoncina you need to make effective bait for the drill bugs?"

"Not yet, Mok-Mok. My guess is that maybe a third of the limoncina's nectar spilled onto the gum. I'll start working on that right now. By the time you get back from the jungle with the resin, I should have an answer for you."

"Thanks, Papa." Mok huddled with the new disaster team to plan the next steps. "Moms, who can we spare right now to go up to the jungle with us?"

"Well, I'd like to keep as many Rug Bum guards here as I can. The Fig Wigs definitely need to stay at the Bin. And we need Jan and Kan Ham Bat at the least to work the Ham Bat kitchen to provide food for all of us here. So, I'd say take a couple of Rug Bums and some able-bodied Ham Bats and Net Kens with you. I'll keep Jes and Dok here to help me out. If the two-way radios will work for us, Dok will keep the communication going between us."

"Sounds good, Moms. Now, how about putting folks into hibernation?" Mok's brain was multitasking at a furious rate. "Will you be able to handle that on your own?"

"Sure, babe. Don't worry about that. Jes can help, and I'll get Wit and the Rug Bums to assist too. We can use the Net Ken tunnel, since the back end is already sealed. We'll simply seal off the front end, which will eliminate the oxygen supply. The folks will go into a kind of suspended animation, like their bodies are on pause. Then, they'll quickly recover once they have access to oxygen again. I was with RJ and his Ma, you know, when he first found and uncovered the trap doors in the ground. Once oxygen entered the clans' tunnels, the folks popped right back to life. It was an easy process. I don't think the folks will resist. They'll probably be glad to sleep until this nightmare is over."

"All right, then. Let's see. I could use you, Nak, and you, Bek. Dun needs to come as our expert resin extractor. San, you and Fahbee need to come so you can guide us through the jungle. Lek, you and Mr. Huge Dude need to come so you can lead us to the limoncinas. Bek, who from your clan would also be good at cutting through the jungle with their clippers?"

"Well, believe it or not, probably Jen and Nel. They're really efficient, especially with all the extra practice they get by cutting folks' hair. Most of the best foliage cutters we used when we were building the tunnel up to the jungle were stung. The girls probably won't like it much though."

"Well, I don't think any of us like what we're having to do right now," Mok stated bluntly. "With the new tunnel extension, we'll use the Bucket and the '54 Chevy to drive north into the jungle. Nak and Bek, gather up as many containers as you can find for the resin. Once we're in the jungle, you two can shuttle the cars back and forth with the gum. Dok, please go find Dun and tell him to report here with one more Rug Bum. Lek, please gather enough of the Teflon protective suits, hoods, and goggles for all of us. Hopefully, there are enough to go around. San, please have your Auntee Jan pack up some food and drink for us. Punkee, I want you to stay here with me to take care of last-minute details. You're coming with us too."

Kip's eyes widened. She stared at Mok without speaking.

Mok turned to her and whispered, "We need to get you out of town for a while. And besides, I need you to help me stay strong."

Kip searched his eyes and gave him an understanding grin.

"And one more thing, everyone." Mok looked at each young face. "Make sure to go to your families to say goodbye. We don't know how long it's going to take us to get through the jungle. It might be a while before you see them again."

The newly formed rescue team, composed of mere teens who months before had no more worries than playing stick ball in the rain, took a serious look at each other, realizing the importance of their mission. Bringing back the goods that would hopefully save their people and their town was in their hands. They would venture to places unknown, stepping out of their idyllic comfort zone for the greater good. They had no choice. They exchanged nods, telling each other they were ready for the challenge. They then went their separate ways to carry out their assignments.

As predicted, Jen and Nel were not pleased that they were assigned to the mission.
"You want us to what?" screamed Jen, pacing back and forth in the Net Ken's stainless-steel kitchen. "Are you out of your mind?"
"You want us to leave the perfectly safe granite walls of this Den? Why should we have to sacrifice our comfort for the good of others who don't care about us? That makes no sense," Nel hollered as she leaned her fashionably clad body against the stove, twisting her spiky hair in her purple fingers like she had no plans of going anywhere.
"And why do you suppose others don't care about you? You girls never think beyond yourselves. Don't you see the bigger picture here?" explained Bek, who knew his task of convincing them to go would be a frustrating one. "The bigger picture is that none of that matters. If we don't work together as a community, we may never get back to our normal life. We'll eventually run out of food. We may even lose friends or family if the bugs are able to

really penetrate our safe zone. That's not the future any of us wants."

"Aw, quit being so dramatic, Bek," moaned Jen, annoyed. Not having had exposure to the sick, she had no idea what the townsfolk were dealing with.

"He has to be dramatic. This is serious stuff," said Lek as he walked in on the conversation. He tried another angle. "You girls should be proud that you're the ones who were selected for the job. It's only because you're such awesome cutters. Just think, you'll be the heroes who cut through the jungle, and everyone will love you in the end."

"Well, Nel, you have to admit, that does sound pretty fantastic." Jen's red eyes glistened at the thought. "Let's do it."

"Whatever you say, Jen." Nel grinned at her, and the two clueless girls sauntered off to their rooms to sharpen their clippers.

Dun and the other Rug Bums held a meeting in their tunnel. The Bums decided that Sun was the best choice to accompany him and assist him with the gum extraction. She was sturdy and conscientious when it came time to work. The other Bums would remain in town under the leadership of Tug and Gun, who would prepare the "army" for their war with the drill bugs.

Dun and Sun swung by the Fig Wig Bin to see Uncle Pun and Auntee Gus, Jud and Hun, and a few others on their way out.

"Try to get the most you can out of those trees, you

two. I know you'll do a great job," said Pun, who was sitting up and alert. "I sure hope there's enough there to do the job for us."

"Don't worry, we'll make the most of whatever we find," assured Dun, now fully aware of the responsibility he was accepting.

"Be careful out there, young'uns. I want to be able to slap those furry backsides of yours again," added Gusee.

"Ha, I'm sure you'll be able to real soon." Dun slapped Gusee's back gently with his hub cap before he and Sun left to join the team.

San said goodbye to Lan and Baby Kal in the Ham Bat tunnel before he headed down to the Fig Wig Bin to visit Mat, Paz-ee and Jaz-ee. He leaned over Mat, who was still quite groggy. "Daddy, because of you'dl and your wonderful clumsiness, there is going to be a way to fight-ood'ly the drill bugs. I'll see'dl you soon, okay?"

"Okay," Mat whispered with a slight chuckle before he dozed off.

Mok and Kip entered Lil'la's room at the Bin. Lil'la was standing with help from Niv and Wit. Zin and Min took care of Fil, now in the feverish, delirious stage of his illness. Mok explained the bugs' apparent obsession with Kip's voice and his theory that she was the target of these attacks. He asked the Fig Wigs' permission to take Kip on the bait excursion, which would take her away from the bugs and hopefully keep her safe. Niv and Wit had a tug-of-war conversation with their eyes before Wit spoke up.

"We will support this, Mok, because we trust that you and the others will do all you can to protect our girl." Wit turned to speak to his niece. "You're obviously distressed, Kipee, and this environment is wearing you down even more. I say go. Be strong and helpful to Mok and the team. Your dad would say that the universe still deserves to hear your gift. I know you'll have a chance to share it again."

Kip nodded, tears streaming down her face. She silently hugged Wit and Niv, hugged her suffering father, and gave Lil'la's hand a sloppy kiss with her sweet yellow lips.

As Dr. Jon stood nearby, Mok sat in a chair next to old Dr. Jok's bed. He told his great grandfather all about the plans of the rescue team. Though barely conscious, Dr. Jok nodded at the news of potential help from little Fahbee Flingbee, Lek's sneaky limoncina find, and Mr. Huge Dude's emergence from silence and his willingness to help. Dr. Jok communicated his confidence in Mok's leadership abilities through a weak squeeze of his hand.

Mok leaned over and kissed him on his forehead. "I love you, G.G."

Dr. Jok again nodded.

Mok approached his father just as Dr. Jon heard someone call his name. Jon turned his head toward the kitchen, then back toward Mok. "I must go, son. Be careful out there." He turned and hopped off.

Mok hollered after him, "Love you, Pops."

As Jon hopped away without response, Mok simply

shook his head and moved on.

After spending a few silent moments at RJ's side, Mok escorted Kip to the main desk, then moved on to the Fog Bob Box.

In his lab, Dr. Pol busily mixed and measured and tested and scribbled notes, determined to find the correct ratio of gum to limoncina.

Mok observed for a moment, then placed a hand on his shoulder. "Papa Pol, I just wanted to let you know that we're leaving now. Nak and Bek should be getting a new supply of gum to you later this afternoon. As soon as we have new limoncinas in our hands, we'll contact Moms, so you can make production plans."

Dr. Pol stood and faced his grandson. "Take care, Mok-Mok. Thanks for doing this. I think this will work, and I have a few more ideas for capturing the bugs. I'll talk to you about it when you return."

"Okay Papa," said Mok as he gave Dr. Pol a big hug. "Thank you for all you're doing. We're all so lucky to have you. Love you!"

Dr. Pol shot him a shocked look. No one had said that to him in an exceptionally long time. "Love you too, Mok-Mok."

Pol returned Mok's hug before he turned and resumed his work. Mok closed the lab door, realizing he had never before known what it was like to say goodbyes to loved ones. Now, he needed to return to the tunnels to find his mother.

Roz, Wit, and Jes were reviewing the list of children and other folks to move into the Net Ken tunnel for hibernation when Mok arrived at the operations base. Roz stepped away from the desk when she saw him and pulled him aside to a more private space.

"Are you sure you're ready to do this, babe?" she asked of her son. She placed her hands on his cheeks and looked lovingly into his deep blue eyes. Her own eyes reflected her genuine concern as well as the motherly pain of releasing her firstborn to the greater world.

"I'm ready, Moms. We need to do this. If we all do our jobs, we should be back here in no time." He leaned toward her and gave her a hard hug. "And remember, Uncle Jake and Uncle Nick are on the other side. I'm sure they will do whatever they can to help us."

"Yes, I'm sure they will. I'm so proud of you, babe. You've taken on a lot of responsibility, and you're the right person to see things through for us. We'll take care of everyone here," assured Roz. "Keep in touch by radio as often as you can. And keep in mind wherever you are how much I love you."

"I will. I love you too, more than anything." Mok took her hands in his and leaned in to kiss her cheek. He turned and started to hop away but turned back one more time to wave. "Bye, Moms."

"Bye, son." Roz waved back and forced a smile. Both pride and pain tugged at her heart as her beloved Mok and his team moved on, the first Vowellans to ever venture out to the greater Heaven's Wait.

As a final stop at the north end of town, the rescue team stopped by the Ham Bat tunnels to say goodbye to the children. Mok assured the kids that everything would soon be fine and that, in the meantime, they were going to stay safe by taking a nice long nap.

Tok and Sil both hugged Mok's legs hard before they moved on to Mr. Huge Dude. They each took hold of one of his giant fingers.

"Mr. H.D.," said tiny Sil, leaning back as far as she could so she could see his face. "Stay safe out there. When you come back, we'll play again at the treehouse, okay?"

Mr. Huge Dude cracked a grin and nodded down to Sil. He placed a giant hand on each of their small backs and patted them gently.

Mok and his team headed north through the main tunnel toward Jimmy's Jungle in the vintage cars with Mr. Huge Dude following behind. New territory and new adventures sat in wait of their arrival.

CHAPTER 11

Jimmy's Jungle

The hunter green '56 Chevy Bucket and the powder blue '54 Chevy Two-Ten slowly drove up the recently completed ramp extending from the main tunnel to the wide central clearing the Vowellans had established within Jimmy's Jungle. Their headlights illuminated the otherwise deeply shaded portion of the jungle. Banana and mahogany trees, as well as coconut and oil palms, created a heavy canopy. It was impossible to tell if the drill bug cloud hovered this far north over the jungle.

On the west side of the clearing, a few narrow trails led to other clearings where the Vowellans maintained their coffee farms. On the east side, more trails led to the main waterfalls and fresh pools that supplied the town with water. To the north, the thick tangle of unexplored jungle sat in wait.

Lek, driving the Chevy Bucket, came to a stop on the right side of the clearing and yanked on the parking brake. Bek pulled up on the left side in the '54 Chevy, near the coffee farm trails. The Net Kens had been driving to this spot since the wide, extended leg of the underground tunnel had been completed. The construction had been long, hard, and tedious for the Rug Bums, the Net Kens, and their earth-digging pet rets. But the job had already proven to be worthwhile. Since the tunnel was large enough to accommodate the cars, it provided an alternate and sheltered route to the jungle. And to the Net Kens' liking, it offered more protection to the carefully maintained vintage cars, as well as more efficient access from the jungle to the storage areas of the tunnel system when time came to bring down crops and water.

Lek and his four passengers, Mok, Kip, San, and Dun, piled out of the Bucket, fully garbed in their protective overalls, head gear, and backpacks. They listened to the various jungle noises that surrounded them like a creepy symphony that both tempted the curious and hinted of dangers.

Bek, Sun, and Nak sat in the Chevy, trying to convince Jen and Nel that their reputations wouldn't be ruined if they were seen outdoors wearing the frumpy coveralls. Even image conscious Nak Ham Bat understood that vanity had no place in their mission.

"Look, girls, our job is to bring gum resin and limoncinas back to our crippled town-ood'ly. No one is going to see'dl you but us, and we look the same as you'dl," said Nak.

"Those purple legs are nothing to shout about anyway," chuckled Sun under her breath.

"You're no one to talk, Miss Shaggy Frump," snapped back Jen. A couple of her right facing red eyes gave a spin.

"Look, I promise I'll bring you girls back to the jungle for a special picnic date-ood'ly by the waterfalls once the town is free of drill bugs. Deal?" offered Nak.

Twenty red Net Ken eyes lit up on the girls' heads. "We're going to hold you to that, big Nak," said Jen in flirtatious fashion.

"Suit up then," replied Nak. He, Sun, and Bek left the car and joined the others while Jen and Nel squirmed into their overalls within the tight backseat space.

In the center of the clearing, Mok pulled everyone, including Mr. Huge Dude, into a huddle to explain his plan for getting the work done.

"Okay, you guys. Here's how I see it. We have two jobs to do. One, we gather as much gum resin as we can and get it back to town. Two, we chop a path through the jungle to get to the ponds by the airport at New Life City, where the limoncinas are. San, you and Fahbee need to be our navigators through the jungle. You're in charge of making sure the Net Kens work in the right direction. Bek, I assume you can establish the routine for the basic cutting operation."

"Absolutely," said Bek, who had done ample jungle cutting work since he had finished school.

"Good. Once you get Lek, Jen, and Nel going, though, I want you to come back so you and Nak can shuttle gum down to the town, since you know how to drive the cars.

"Mr. H.D., I'd like you to follow the Net Kens and clear away the debris they leave behind as they cut their path through the heavy tangle with their clippers.

"Dun and Sun, Kip and I will help you extract the resin. Nak, you're in charge of shuttling the gum back to Bek and the cars. Let's all grab containers. Let's go find Uncle Pun's secret gum tree grove.

"And Lek, use your two-way radio to keep in touch with me every half hour or so. We need to keep track of how each other is doing," instructed Mok.

"Yes, sir," said Lek with a grin. He beamed at the idea of being entrusted with something.

"Hey, dude, who put you in charge of this anyway?" Dun grouched at Mok. Rug Bums were unaccustomed to those outside their clan telling them what to do. "You're being kind of bossy, you know."

Mok looked at Dun and simply stated, "Mr. RJ. Now, let's go."

The scene at the main coffee farm pleasantly surprised Mok and his followers. Bright rays of sunlight beamed through the higher canopy, creating a mystical scene. Plump red cherries shone against the deep green leaves of the coffee plants like jeweled holiday lights strung in neat rows.

Mok examined the surroundings and the canopy above them. "Clear skies, you guys. Clear air. The bugs have not traveled this far north. I don't think we need to wear our protective headgear right now, except for you, Punkee. We'll be much more comfortable without it."

"Why except for her?" asked Sun. She stared at Kip with leery eyes.

"We don't want the drill bugs to know she is with

us," admitted Mok. He hadn't said more to the team before now. "They're attracted to her."

"You mean we're in danger because of her? Don't you think we should have known about this before now?" grouched Dun.

"No, Dun. It doesn't make any difference. We need to do this job whether you know this or not. I'm packing my headgear into my backpack."

"Are you sure, dude?" asked Dun. "I don't want any of those dang stings on my head like Uncle Pun got."

"Then pack it or not. I don't really care. We can always put it back on in a hurry if we need to."

After exchanging unsure glances, the others did as Mok did, even Dun. Kip watched in silence. No one was able to see the disgruntled, puckered face she made within her headgear.

The trail to Pun's gum trees was remarkably easy to find. Once Mok and his followers reached the main coffee farm, they spied a narrow trail that led southwest. They followed the bug juice jugs that Pun had hung from the plants along the way. How Pun had managed to maintain the sizable grove in the remote location without anyone knowing was a mystery. His usual daytime sleepiness and laziness were now accounted for.

"How long do you think Uncle Pun's been sneaking out here anyway?" asked Sun as she tromped along the trail behind Dun, pushing occasional branches out of her way. "What a stinker he is for not telling us. We could have been enjoying some good gum all this time."

"Aw, he was probably hoarding it for himself," rationalized Dun. "Considering what we're dealing with now, it's a good thing he did."

"I think it was his way of taking some time to himself with something he loved," offered Mok as he hopped along. "Think about it. If he had grown his own trees in the regular grove, would you Bums have left him alone to do his own thing?"

"Of course not, dude," answered Dun.

"Why would we? It's too much fun pestering him," added Sun.

"Well, you know what?" said Mok thoughtfully, "Mr. RJ once told me that we were all meant to do something meaningful during our lives. I think that tending to these trees was what was meaningful to Uncle Pun. But he needed time and space to do it on his own, without interference from anyone else. I think he deserved that."

"Always so philosophical, aren't you, brain man?" commented Dun as they finally spotted Uncle Pun's gum tree grove in the distance.

"No, I think I just pay attention." Mok shrugged as they reached their hidden destination.

Mok came to a sudden stop, his floppy feet firmly in place where the narrow trail opened to the gum tree grove. He turned his long torso and placed a finger to his lips, signaling the others to be quiet. He was the one who hadn't been paying attention as they neared the grove. Ahead of them, at least one hundred miniature monkeys hung from the branches of the gum trees and playfully chattered at each other. Having previously seen monkeys only in books, the team watched the live creatures in awed silence.

The monkeys were cute as could be and happy in their play. Mok wondered if they would still be happy if they knew that Vowellans stood nearby. He slowly tucked Kip behind Nak's much larger body, while Dun and Sun crept to the front of their small pack to shelter them with their hubcap armor.

A couple of monkeys caught flashes of light as scattered beams of sunlight, shining through the lighter canopy above them, bounced off the shiny hubcaps. One hundred little monkeys soon spotted the intruders and flocked toward them. Kip hurried to hide behind Mok, hugging his waist and pushing her face against his low back. Nak stepped up proud and strong, flexing his toned muscles, hoping the monkeys would simply run away. Dun and Sun crouched into attack stances.

The monkeys stopped short of the Vowellans. They leaned back as far as they could to examine Mok's face far above them. They cocked their curious heads to the side as they tried to figure out what this tall creature who looked like a tree yet wore a top hat was all about. A couple of monkeys bounced onto Mok's flat round feet, while a couple more lifted the round edges of those feet and let them slap back to the ground. Before long, monkeys were climbing up his coveralls, crawling into his pockets, and wrapping their curly tails around his skinny arms. They sat on his top hat, crawled down his back, and stopped to pick at the few random orange curls that had escaped the bottom of Kip's headgear as she continued to press her face against Mok's back. The monkeys playfully crawled and chattered and sniffed at their bodies until they were satisfied that Mok and Kip proved to be no threat to them.

They moved on to inspect Nak, Dun, and Sun. The tiny creatures were especially interested in Dun and Sun, most likely because they were used to their Uncle Pun's presence in the hidden grove. The Bums let the monkeys do their exploring without interference. The creatures crawled up and down the stout, muscular Rug Bum bodies, some cuddling into the crevices of their arms, some exploring the buckets they carried, others sitting on their wide, furry heads, biting at the bubbles that emerged from their suds spouts.

As Dun and Sun moved toward the gum trees, the monkeys scampered around their feet and clung to their legs. They were curious about every move the group made and were eager to see why the team had come to the grove.

"Well, these little dudes are going to slow us down," complained Dun as he tried to avoid stepping on a multitude of tails.

"Maybe not," said Mok. "I think they'll get used to us being here. The problem we may have, though, is that they might go after the resin once we tap it. I've seen these monkeys in books. They're called tamarins. Tree sap is a common source of food for them. We may have to figure out a way to pacify them while we do our work."

"I'm sure glad you know'dl so much, Mok," said Nak. "You're the right guy to get us through this."

Mok thought he saw Dun give a hint of a nod. "I'll

do what I can. Time will tell." Internally, Mok wished he believed in himself as much as others seemed to.

Dun took a hard look at the gum trees in front of him. Most looked robust, but some did not. "Hey dudes," he suggested. "Look at those scrawny trees over there on the left side. If these little critters need a little resin to keep them happy, why don't we tap into them first. The monkeys can work on them while we work on the bigger trees that look like they're just busting with the resin we need."

"Now you're thinking," complimented Mok. "Good idea, Dun."

As Dun strutted in a boastful circle, Mok was reminded that Pun hadn't suggested Dun for this job for nothing.

While the gum team dug into their task, the jungle team began the laborious process of clipping its way through the thick vegetation that lay ahead. Bek, having done this type of work many times before, taught Jen and Nel his special techniques for using his retractable clippers to hack through the jungle foliage and tangled roots. The girls tiptoed around on light feet, leery of potential creepy crawlers and unfamiliar noises. They moaned about their unstylish coveralls and flat work boots, which were so unlike the signature short skirts and spiky heels to which they were accustomed.

"Look, you two," said Lek, observing their discomfort as they approached the northern jungle wall of the clearing. "Get past your image issues. We need to focus on getting through the jungle in record speed."

Jen shook her head at her younger brother in snarky fashion.

"That's right," agreed Bek. "Think about Uncle Wes, my mom, and everyone else who is sick back in town. They don't care if you're hair gets messed up or if your heels aren't high enough. They care that we get back to them with help as fast as we can. We need to dig in and work hard."

"Yeah, yeah," moaned Jen. "Let's just get this over with."

The four Net Kens activated their clippers and dove into the jungle.

San, in the meantime, with Fahbee perched on his shoulder, tried to lead the crew in the right direction. Fahbee, who had arrived in Vowella via the jungle and spent many an entertaining evening attending flingbee social activities, knew exactly where the path had to be cut to achieve their goal. San's chubby body, however, was too wide to fit through the thick tangle that needed to be cleared. He had to follow the cutters while Fahbee shuttled ahead of the crew and then back again, making sure they were going the right way. Since San was the only one who was capable of hearing what Fahbee said, Fahbee flew back to San's shoulder to report directions. San announced the directions. Then Fahbee flew ahead again to scout.

"I'm sorry, Señor, but this back-and-forth stuff is exhausting," complained Fahbee after several runs. "Tell

Bek I'll ride on his shoulder and fly ahead when he needs direction. So sorry, Señor. I'm pooped."

"I get it, little buddy. I'll let him know'dl." San grinned at his friend. "You're do-d'ling great right now."

Satisfied, Fahbee flew on ahead. San made himself useful by helping Mr. Huge Dude clear away the chopped roots and rubbish that the cutters left behind them. The team worked efficiently for several hours.

Late in the afternoon, Mok radioed the jungle team to meet the gum team in the central clearing. As the Net Kens powered down their clippers, they realized that their tools had been drowning out the creepy jungle chorus of unknown creatures, who were lurking within the jungle's depths. There were screeches in the distance, croaks and gobbles closer by, intermittent yaps that sounded like laughter, and occasional hisses. Hot, tired, and a little freaked out, they followed Mok's order and straggled into the clearing.

The Net Ken girls had done well once they got the hang of clipping and buzzing through the tangled roots and vines, which had been their biggest obstacles along the route. Bek had thought it best to flatten the ground path as much as possible as they worked, in case they needed to use a wagon or other vehicle from Uncle Jake's place to transport the limoncinas back to the valley. During the afternoon, the jungle team had blazed a path that was about a half mile long and about four and a half feet wide. San and Mr. H.D. had efficiently cleared the rubbish behind the clipping Net Kens.

At the makeshift camp, a few stray monkeys scampered about, curiously exploring the resting jungle team. One climbed onto Nel's shoulder and poked at her rear-facing eyes while another climbed onto Jen's head, where it sniffed at her topknot of satellite-shaped ears.

"Eww, eww, get it off. Get it off!" screamed Jen. She batted at her head with her hands, her nets tangling into her topknot. Mr. Huge Dude stepped in behind her to lift the mischievous creature away.

"Don't worry. I've got him," soothed Mr. H.D. He lifted the monkey to his cheek and gently stroked its back. He allowed it to crawl around his upper body. It found a cozy nook in his neck and settled in for a nap.

"Augh!" screamed startled Jen. She whipped her head around to look up at Mr. H.D. with her front-facing eyes. "Don't ever sneak up on me like that again."

Mr. H.D. raised his flat hands and backed away from her. A wounded look washed across his face.

"Aw, relax, Jen," scolded Lek, who was also trying to adjust to the new Mr. H.D. "He's cool. You'll see."

"Yeah, well..."

Lek looked hard at Jen and Nel, who were pouting and picking leaf clippings out of their ragged hairdos. "Why don't you go over to the waterfalls, so we don't have to watch you take care of your stupid beauty needs. No one cares what you look like, you know."

Jen and Nel picked themselves up and sashayed down the trail to the waterfalls.

Plopping down in a circle, the gum tree teens peeled

back their protective gear and gobbled the snacks and drinks that San put out for them.

The gum team had done well. They had filled almost all of their containers with resin and had packed them into the '54 Chevy. The pesky monkeys had made it hard for the team to transport and pack the containers because they had swarmed both the resin and the teens. Kip had taken it upon herself to shoo them back down the trail while the others had done the transporting and the packing. Sun, not feminine in any way, had been an especially hard worker.

Bek turned toward San, who sat comfortably on a flat rock while Fahbee perched atop his orange fishing hat. Bek, a few years older than the others, didn't normally associate with San. "Tell me about Fahbee. Where in Heaven's Wait did you find him?"

"He found me," laughed San. "He was hanging out on my fishing hat-ood'ly at Lake Marie the day I found the limoncina."

"Did he live here in the jungle?" asked Mok. "I noticed several flingbees flying around today."

"No, he says he came from a land far to the north-ood'ly," said San as Fahbee nodded and marched around his hat. "He speaks with a Spanish accent, so they must speak Spanish-ood'ly where he comes from."

"What the heck is Spanish?" asked Lek while his eyes rolled with confusion.

"It's another language, dummy," Dun replied to him. "Don't you know anything?"

"They speak Spanish where I come from," announced Mr. Huge Dude, surprising everyone with his words.

Fahbee emitted a gasp that only San and Nak could hear. He left San's hat and flew onto Mr. H.D.'s unoccupied shoulder. He leaned back as far as he could to examine the giant face in front of him.

"They do?" inquired Mok. He scooted over to where Mr. H.D. sat. *If he's willing to talk, I want some answers*, Mok thought to himself. "Tell us, Mr. Huge Dude, where *do* you come from?"

"A big island that has a valley like yours," he said shyly.

"Where is it?" ask San curiously.

"I don't know," said Mr. H.D. with sad eyes. "I've been trying to find it for a long time now."

"You mean you're lost?" asked Mok. "How did you get lost?"

"I don't know," Mr. H.D. said quite painfully. "My brother and I were working in our backyard at home. The next thing we knew, we were in that forest where the limoncinas are. We were trying to find our way back home when I suddenly ended up in Vowella. I don't know what happened to him."

"Oh, Mr. H.D., I'm so sorry," said Mok with sincerity. "No wonder you were so terrified when you got here."

Fahbee decided he needed to enter the conversation. San had to translate for him.

"I come from an island too, Señor H.D. Do you

think we might come from the same island?"

"Why, I don't know. Do you know any other Huge Dudes? Do you know any Laim Branes or Frite Tykes?" asked Mr. H.D.

"No, can't say that I do. Do you know Maria Flingbee?" asked Fahbee.

"No, you're the only flingbee I know of."

Mok, fascinated by the conversation, jumped in. "Well, I want to hear more about all of this someday. Wouldn't it be great if you did come from the same place?"

"Yeah, yeah!" Dun couldn't help but interrupt. He was still cranky at the fact that this giant creature looked so much like a Rug Bum. "Someday. What I want to know is, what's your real name, dude?"

"Brune," Mr. H.D. said shyly.

"Brune! That's different. Brune what?"

"Brune Huge Dude," said Brune with a grin.

Dun jumped to his feet and marched in a circle, his arms extended above his head as though he were claiming a touchdown. He was the one who had given Brune his nickname. "See what I've been trying to tell you? Rug Bums don't call names. We only speak the truth."

"Oh, sit down, Dun," said Lek, annoyed with Dun's boasting and ready to test his bravery in speaking back to him.

Dun displayed one of his classic mean faces and plopped to the ground.

"It is pretty amazing, Dun, that you randomly landed on that name for him," said Mok with a shake of his head.

Turning to Brune, he asked, "I bet you miss home."

Brune's mouth drooped at the sides as he nodded.

"Well, thanks for putting aside your own worries to help us out." Mok noticed the sympathetic faces of the others. "Okay, gang. It's time to move on. Nak and Bek, are you ready to take the load of gum back to town?"

"Yep, let's do it," said Nak as he pushed himself up to his feet. He climbed into the '54 Chevy while Bek and the others attempted to load a few more containers into the Bucket.

When Bek tried to open the driver's door, the Bucket gave a loud honk. He tried again. The same thing happened. Bek climbed into the car and sat in the driver's seat. The Bucket sounded one loud, continuous honk until Bek climbed back out of the car. He plopped his hands on his hips and stared at the car. Mok hopped forward and gave the Bucket a hard look.

"It doesn't want to go right now," said Bek, who knew the cars very well.

"It does have a mind of its own, doesn't it?" said Mok, frowning at the green vehicle. "It certainly showed us that when it rode in Mr. RJ's parade without a driver."

"Yes. Before that, I had only seen it honk to music in the garage. I always thought there was just a short somewhere. I think it's best if I just go with Nak for now. We'll deal with the Bucket when we get back. We'll see you later tonight."

"Sounds good," said Mok, still puzzled by the car's behavior.

Bek and Nak turned the '54 Chevy around and drove down the ramp, disappearing into the main tunnel. Mok and the others readily returned to their work.

CHAPTER 12

In Town with the Gum

Bek and Nak pulled up to the cluster of desks that served as the operations base within Vowella's main tunnel to find Dr. Pol, Roz, Dok, and Jes in a heated debate regarding townsfolk going into hibernation. The emergency team failed to notice the car's presence.

Dr. Pol, with Jes on his side, argued, "I firmly believe that all the sting victims need to be put into the Net Kens' hibernation tunnel once they are well enough to be relieved of nursing care. Once the tunnel is sealed, they will safely fall into suspended animation. The ill folks will obviously be weak for a while. And if they stay here, they will be an added burden if the time comes that the Vowellans have to do all-out battle with the drill bugs. The healthy folks can't afford to be distracted by caring for the weak folks. They will need to concentrate their efforts on the battle at hand."

Roz, supported by Dok on the other hand, had another opinion. "I think a few key folks should be allowed to remain in the tunnels to give us advice, even if they're too weak to physically help the cause."

The decision was difficult because no one knew all they would have to do to eliminate the bugs. Also, the children, young teens, and their caretakers, as well as those wanting to go into hibernation to escape the stress of the situation, were waiting in the tunnels for the ill folks to recover enough to join them.

"I can tell you right now that you'll have one heck of a time getting Dr. Jok to go into hibernation once he's better," argued Roz. "He'll fight you every step of the way. He has more wisdom to lend to the situation than anyone, considering the fact that RJ is down and Mok is brand new at being a leader. I think his presence would be invaluable, as long as he's feeling okay."

"But see, Rozee, we shouldn't have to worry about whether he's feeling okay," said Dr. Pol. "Hibernation is such a great alternative. Look, he's my father, and I know how stubborn he can be. But he's just going to have to understand. We need the strong and able at a time like this."

"Remember, RJ told us to protect the Elders," added Jes. "They're very precious to this community. We can't take a chance on anything else happening to them."

"But we can protect them in the Fig Wig Bin," argued Dok who, though feeling he was overstepping his bounds with the adults, had to voice his opinion. "They could guide us from there."

"Uh, excuse me, everyone," interrupted Bek timidly. Their short time in the jungle had removed them from the dreary situation in town. "We wanted to let you know that we're back with the first batch of resin."

"Oh my goodness, son," said Dr. Pol with a jump. "I didn't even see you standing there. We weren't expecting you back so soon. Good job. Let's see what you have there."

The disaster committee huddled around the '54 Chevy to examine the load of resin.

"Wow, this is a lot," said Roz in a pleased tone. "Pun's trees must be at their best right now."

"They are," testified Nak.

Bek opened the trunk to display even more resin. "We actually had more to bring, but the Bucket was acting up."

"That's okay, Bek. This is fine for now," said Dr. Pol. "I'll experiment with what's here. We'll have to stockpile the rest anyway until we get our hands on more limoncinas. Just keep bringing it down."

Roz examined the diagram of the tunnel system that Dok had made for her. "Why don't you unload the containers into RJ's tunnel for now. It appears that's the only remaining available space."

"Will do, Mrs. Roz," said Bek with a nod. "We'll drop them off on our way back to the jungle. We probably won't be back again with another batch of resin until morning."

"Okay, honey. How is everyone doing? Do you think you'll all be safe up there overnight?"

"Yeah, we'll be fine-ood'ly," said Nak. "The jungle crew has made a good start at cutting a path northward. The gum crew is working hard, though they're dealing with some annoying monkeys. But as far as we know, the sky up there is free of bug-ood'lies. We can sleep in the cars, and Brune will stand guard for us."

"Brune?" said four voices at once.

"Oh...Mr. Huge Dude," said Bek with a grin. "He's openly talking to us now. It turns out his real name is Brune Huge Dude. How about that?"

"Yes, how about that!" echoed Roz, shaking her head in wonder. She remembered how Dun had randomly labeled the big guy and how little Sil Fig Wig had worked that label into her own name for him, Mr. Huge Dude.

"Well, tell Mok that we did some more tests on the drill bugs," informed Dr. Pol. "Our optimum ratio for effectively attracting them seems to be about fifty to one, which means that for every fifty pounds of gum we collect, we need one limoncina. The mixture will trap at least twice its weight in drill bugs. Tug and Gun have been monitoring the cloud hanging over the valley by peeking out the Rug Bum trap door. It appears to be a circle about 1300 feet across and about 1 foot deep. Considering that size, Dok and I have estimated that we need at least sixty limoncinas to make enough bait to eliminate the bugs. That is, of course, if no more drill bugs join their force. They've been just sitting up there since you left. That also means we need about three thousand pounds of resin. Is that realistic?"

"Possibly," said Bek with a nod. "We'll weigh what's here on the scales at the Ham Bat Pad before we store it. There are plenty of untapped trees at this point. Nak and I can keep making trips back while the others continue to cut through the jungle. Our only problem is with the crowd of little monkeys. They like to suck on the resin the way the Rug Bums do. All I can say is that we'll collect as much as we can, Dr. Pol. We'll give Mok the word on the limoncinas. And we'll see you again in the morning."

Dr. Pol nodded while Roz and Jes waved toward Bek and Nak like the concerned mothers they were. As Bek turned the car around in the rotunda, Roz called out to them, "Be safe."

The young Vowellans unloaded the resin into RJ's tunnel, then headed back up to Jimmy's Jungle, knowing there was still much work to be done.

CHAPTER 13

Back in the Jungle

Moving deeper and deeper into Jimmy's Jungle, the jungle team cut its way through the gnarled thicket. They appreciated the fact that the ground had remained surprisingly firm for them thus far, but they struggled to keep the trail's width consistent because massive roots grew upward, twisting around themselves as well as the trees from which they grew, complicating the removal of regular foliage.

Fahbee continued to serve as the team's scout and compass, making sure Lek, Jen, and Nel stayed on course. The Net Kens often stopped to not only unclog their clippers of chips and debris but to rest their weary arms, which had never had such a workout.

San perspired profusely as he gathered the cuttings the Net Kens left along the trail. He stuffed them as best as he could into the diminishing crevices along the heavy plant walls that were being established on both sides of him. He could almost feel his chubbiness melting away.

Brune spent much of his time taking up the rear,

stomping down the ground along the trail with his huge, heavy feet to keep the path's new surface somewhat smooth.

When the team came upon an unusually dark section of jungle, however, the team stopped to try to peek through the canopy above them to determine if a patch of drill bugs might be hovering. It was impossible to tell. The darkness suddenly burst above them, dumping heavy rain upon the Vowellans. Huge droplets fell from leaves and onto the heads of Jen and Nel, making them whine about their hairdos being flattened. Fahbee found himself having to zoom around to dodge those droplets, any of which would have knocked him flat to the ground. He managed to find his way to San's pocket, where he curled up, leaving the others to find their own way. The teens hurried to reattach their headgear so they could continue their work.

It didn't take long for wide, gooey puddles to surface, making all tasks almost impossible to complete. Brune watched far more gnarled roots appear and his flattening work all but disappear. With an unusual show of frustration, he attacked those roots, determined to get them out of the team's way. With strength he didn't know he had, he grabbed them with his giant hands and ripped them from their foundation. The teens watched in wonder as he yanked on the roots with great force, snapping them from their bases, releasing them from their entanglements. He bent the roots until they snapped and stacked them crosswise along the path, creating a crude, makeshift bridge as they moved forward. San and Lek, impressed with his handiwork, praised his efforts. All of them realized what a help Brune's newfound strength would be as they moved forward.

Just as suddenly as the rainstorm appeared, it disappeared. Random rays of sunshine shot through the canopy, which seemed less dense than before. The tropical heat quickly dried the drops from the leaves, as well as the teens' coveralls. The team was able to resume the routine they had established.

San's sensitive ears picked up a strange noise that was hard to identify above the racket of the Net Kens' clippers cutting through branches. When the Net Kens paused to clean their clippers, San was able to listen to and identify the noise. In the clearing behind them, the green Bucket performed an unrelenting song of honks.

"Lek, what in the world-ood'ly is going on with the Bucket? Do you hear all the noise-ood'ly it's making?"

Lek had to listen a little harder to hear the consistent honking. "I have no idea. Do you think someone back there is trying to get our attention?"

"I don't think so. We have our radios if they need'l us."

"Well, what we're doing right now is hard enough without worrying about that mind-of-its-own Bucket," complained Lek as he fired up his clippers again. "We'll deal with it when we get back."

The Bucket's crazy honks also reached the grove southwest of the main clearing, where Mok, Kip, Sun, and Dun continued to tap resin from Uncle Pun's gum trees.

Mok returned to the clearing to investigate the Bucket's strange behavior. He was shocked to discover that the vehicle had moved itself up to the mouth of the new trail the jungle team was blazing. The car tried and tried to fit through the narrow trail, but the harder it tried, the more its wheels spun, causing it to become lodged in a cockeyed position between the tall side walls of the path, where lighter branches became tangled around its front axle. It honked relentlessly, obviously irate at its confinement. Mok watched, stunned that the car had further acquired a mind and presence of its own and that it was so determined to catch up with the jungle team. *Are there more oddities in store for us as we venture beyond our little town of Vowella*, Mok wondered.

Mok approached the car and patted its left rear bumper as though the Bucket were a panicked child. "It's okay, baby. It's okay. Is this trail too narrow for you? You want to go through the jungle with us, huh? Is that what you're trying to do?"

The Bucket slowed its frantic honks as though soothed by Mok's words. While it had managed to get itself wedged between the thick plants on either side of the trail, it had also blocked the entrance to the path for the others. Mok assessed the situation on each side of the car before he pulled out his radio and called to Lek somewhere up ahead.

"Lek, come in, Lek," called Mok. "Lek, can you hear me?"

San's radar ears picked up Mok's voice coming through the radio above the noise of the Net Kens' clippers. He poked Lek's back and motioned to him to stop cutting. Once Lek cleaned off his clippers and they retracted back into his hands, he pulled the radio from his belt clip and responded.

"Hey, Mok. What's up?"

Mok explained the situation to him. "I need you to come back to cut the Bucket out of its trap because it's blocking our access to you."

"Okay, we'll be there as soon as we can," reported Lek. "We're quite a ways above the clearing now, so it will take us a while to get back to you."

"Okay. See you in a while. Over and out."

Just as Mok turned off his radio, Bek and Nak pulled into the clearing, having just returned from town. Nak followed Mok back to Uncle Pun's grove while Bek hurried over to the Bucket. Diminishing daylight filtered through the gum trees in the grove, so the gum team called it quits for the day and returned to the clearing with full gum containers in hand.

Lek and the jungle team eventually arrived back at the trail's entrance, which was obviously blocked by the wedged in Bucket. Bek had already managed to free up its tail end with his agile clippers but had waited on the front end because it was much more accessible from Lek's side. Jen and Nel, too tired and dirty to complain, took on the car's right side while Lek tackled its left side. He had to slither under the car and spend a fair amount of time clipping at narrow branches to free the axle of its tangle. Once the car was released from its bounds, it backed itself into the clearing, content to be surrounded by the

Vowellan teens. Bek shook his head, a couple of his red eyes spinning, at the hundreds of new little scratches that decorated the Bucket's hunter green surface.

"Ugh! Do you know how long we worked on this car to get it into perfect condition?" he moaned. "What in Heaven's Wait is possessing the Bucket anyway? What's it trying to do?"

Mok sat on the ground and stared at the vehicle. "I'm not sure, but for some reason, it feels the need to go with us."

"But should we let a *car* have its own way?" Lek pondered his words, knowing that having one's own way was such a Net Ken trait.

"I don't know," answered Mok with a puzzled look. "It must have a reason for wanting to go with us."

The teens took turns cleaning up at the waterfalls before reconnecting in the clearing to eat some food and figure out their sleeping arrangements. Mok suggested that Sun, Kip, Jen, and Nel share sleeping space in the '54 Chevy. Jen and Nel, too exhausted to argue, sighed deeply and rolled their twenty eyes at the notion. Sun made a grouchy face and called for the front seat. Kip shot Mok an irritated look. The plan suggested an awkward tolerance of vastly different personalities.

"All you have to do is sleep," reminded Mok as he examined the various expressions.

The guys were then left with the space within the Bucket, since it contained more room for their larger bodies. Dun, however, elected to camp out with Brune, who couldn't fit into a vehicle. Dun was accustomed to the sleeping conditions of the recently demolished Rug Bum Hut, which the Bucket couldn't provide. He also felt a sense of responsibility to stand guard for the group. He assumed Brune would help him with that chore.

As the young Vowellans settled in to spend their first night ever away from home, they wrestled with their own concerns and thoughts. They certainly wouldn't have chosen these circumstances for their first experience on their own. But they silently found their own peace with the situation, knowing that their efforts were all for the sake of their town and their clans.

Before drifting off to sleep in the driver's seat of the Bucket, Mok peeked out the front windshield at Brune, who was curled up in a huge ball on his side, peacefully snoring. Mok admired the persistent strength and patience that the giant displayed as he traveled his own journey with them. Mok would remember that strength in days ahead.

Mok dreamed that the sky above Vowella was raining little curly tailed monkeys, who then found their way into the tunnels by way of a broken window at RJ's place. His body jerked awake, causing him to ram his head into the overhead light inside the Bucket. He gave a low moan, removed his top hat, and rubbed his head. Looking out the windshield, he remembered where he was. *A new day,* he thought to himself, *in a most uncertain environment.*

He carefully opened the car door, slapped his floppy, round feet onto the ground, and stretched to his maximum capacity. Sleeping in a car was not the most comfortable thing for a tall Fog Bob to do. He scanned the scene, finding that everyone else was still asleep. It was no wonder. All of the teens had worked very hard the previous day. Looking up at the lush canopy of trees above them, he spotted slight beams of dawning light trying to slip through the ceiling's few openings.

Mok took advantage of the few moments he had to himself. He hadn't had much of a chance to think about the sudden role he had undertaken. He would never have imagined that he'd be leading a mission to find strange, squishy objects that could possibly save his town and his kind. There were so many unknowns ahead of them in their travels, as well as unknown consequences if the team was unable to find the limoncinas. And what if they got attacked by something out there in the mysterious world of Heaven's Wait? What would happen to the Vowellans then?

Mok's thoughts continued to wander while Kip slipped out of the '54 Chevy and approached him on quiet feet. The orange curls on her head created a wild, messy frame around her pale, delicate face. Her legs, weak from overuse the previous day, dipped unsteadily as she took her steps. Mok hopped to her side and wrapped a supporting arm around her tiny waist as he guided her down the coffee farm trail, to keep them from disturbing the others.

Kip yawned and pulled his shoulder down so she could whisper in his ear. "The sky above seems clear, Munkee. Do you think I can talk yet?"

In the middle of all Mok had been organizing and leading, he had forgotten that she had been mute since leaving town. He examined glimpses of the blue sky that hovered above the heavy jungle canopy. "The sky certainly seems clear of drill bugs here, Punkee, but I don't want to attract them here with your voice. Maybe you can try whispering just to me, and we'll see what happens. I always want to see that protective suit on you, though. Does that work for you?"

"Sure, Munkee," she whispered back. "Whatever you think is best. Is it still pretty early?"

"Yeah. You know me. I'm used to being up before dawn almost every day to do my chores. How did you sleep?"

"Not well. I've never gone to sleep without someone in my house giving me a kiss goodnight." Kip displayed a melancholy grin. "Besides, Sun's snores rattled the car most of the night. It must be awfully noisy in that Rug Bum Hut during the night." She thought for a moment. "Oh, poor Sun! There is no Rug Bum Hut anymore, is there?"

"I'm afraid not, Punkee. I guess I need to keep that in mind when I doubt my ability to get this job done. There's no time for doubt, is there?"

"How can you doubt yourself, Munkee?" whispered Kip as she gently stroked his upper arm. "We all know you're doing the best you can, which is far better than any of the rest of us are capable of. You have intuition, a sharp mind, and common sense, which makes you the right person to lead our mission. You have to believe that,

Munkee."

Mok affectionately pulled one of her kinky curls straight, then released it. "That's just why I brought you along, Punkee. I needed that little boost from you." He looked back toward the clearing. "Well, we'd better head back so we can start our day, huh?"

"Yes, I think so. The sooner we get going, the sooner we'll get through the jungle. I wonder how long it will take us to get to the end?"

"I wish I knew. But I do know one thing. Most of us will be going on to find the limoncinas, and it won't be practical for us to come back to this main clearing anymore. I've decided to leave a small crew behind to deal with the remaining gum while the rest of us move forward through the jungle. We'll just have to hope that the radios keep on working so we can continue to communicate with them and the folks back home."

"They will, Munkee."

As they headed back from the coffee farm, Kip gathered up her wild curls and twisted them into a knot on top of her head. She watched how closely Mok monitored her every move, seeming fascinated with her little routines. "Hey, this isn't a beauty contest out here. If the *fans* of my singing could only see me now."

Mok chuckled and wrapped his arm around her waist. Nothing but appreciation beamed from his eyes. "You look absolutely beautiful to me."

Mok and Kip's moment ended when they reached the clearing to find Dun banging on the windows of the cars. "Hey, dudes! Rise and shine. It's time for another day of down-and-dirty work. Yeah!"

Jen opened her car door and painfully rolled out onto the ground. "Ugh. You've got to be kidding me. Do you have any idea how much I hurt all over? Do you actually expect me to do more work today? Where's my hot tub?"

"Yeah," agreed Nel, dramatically imitating Jen's behavior. "How about a little massage, Kip?"

Kip's eyes widened as her yellow lips puckered.

"Good grief," interrupted Lek, emerging from his car with a few sore muscles of his own. "Each of us is as sore as the next guy, you spoiled brats. Get off your behinds so we can get going around here. Don't you know the folks back home are counting on us?"

Jen peered at her brother with resentful red eyes. "Yeah, yeah, yeah."

Sun climbed out of the Chevy ready to take on the world. "Hey, I slept like a baby last night. Sure was nice to get away from all that snoring at home."

Mok and Kip caught sight of each other's reaction and pinched their lips together to keep their chuckles silent. Mok asked everyone to sit in a circle in the middle of the clearing while Nak and San prepared their morning food. "Okay, you guys. Another day is upon us. Here's what I think we should do..."

He asked Nak, Sun, and Bek to continue the gum extraction until all the resin was delivered to town. At that point, Bek would leave Nak and Sun in town to assist Roz with whatever needs she had, while he headed north to rejoin the jungle team in the Chevy.

In the meantime, the other Net Ken teens would continue to cut through the jungle. Mok made an executive decision to widen the existing trail so that the Bucket would be able to accompany them. There was a reason the seemingly possessed Bucket was so determined to be with them. He told the others that he felt it was somehow serving as their guardian angel in Mr. RJ's absence. The youths liked the sound of his theory since none of them was used to being very far away from home.

The new jungle team, composed of Lek, Jen, Nel, San, Fahbee, Mok, Kip, Dun, Brune, and his cute little monkey, now named Scamper, gathered up its things, packed them into the Bucket, and headed out to tackle their first task of the day, widening the trail.

Once the Net Kens reached the end of their previous work and the Bucket was able to follow behind, Lek buzzed through the center of the projected new trail with Fahbee's guidance. Jen and Nel followed behind, widening the path on either side of him. Behind them, Dun, Brune, San, and Mok cleared the leaf litter, branches, and roots while Kip steered the Bucket. Since Kip was so short and needed a view through the Bucket's windshield, she sat atop the food basket in the driver's seat, her hands tightly clasping the steering wheel. It didn't seem to matter that her feet were merely dangling in front of the seat. The Bucket simply moved forward on its own, determined to accompany the team. Kip couldn't wait to get back to town to tell her grandma Lil'la about driving a car for the first time.

More than once, the Bucket came upon dips in the ground, where a tire or two got stuck. It honked its horn furiously as it sensed that the team was getting farther and farther ahead of it. Mok and Brune had to hurry back and pack clippings into the ruts and lay down crosswise lengths of branches and roots to smooth out the path. Mok decided that going forward, they would tend better to the path's smoothness for everyone's sake. The Bucket chugged along happily once that change was made.

While this routine continued, the folks back in Vowella tolerated their dreary underground existence. Roz and Jes continued their chores of manning the operations station and managing the various contact points within the tunnel system. Dok Fog Bob helped Dr. Pol prepare his lab for the work that would come once the limoncinas arrived.

The children in the Ham Bat tunnels drove their caretakers nuts with their overabundance of energy and loudness. The animals in the Net Ken tunnel displayed their restlessness at being confined. Several of the rets had to be put on tight leashes to keep them from chasing the hens, who were tense and laying less eggs than needed to feed the tunnel dwellers.

Small clusters of Vowellans huddled around candles within the occasional hollows that dotted the walls of the main tunnel. They held blankets tightly around their bodies to stay warm and tried to find activities to keep them busy despite the dim light. Rug Bums patrolled the tunnels and guarded both the operations station and the entrance to the Fig Wig tunnel and its access to the hospital within the Bin.

The Fig Wig Bin was the only home still occupied at this point. Dr. Jon hopped about, caring for stung Vowellans with the help of Niv, Pip, and several other volunteers. The drill bugs had been quiet in the sky since the teens had left on their mission, so the workload remained manageable for the hospital crew with no new sting cases.

Back in the jungle, the day wore on, and the teens kept at their task. A generation ago, when RJ's father's had struggled his way through the jungle, Jimmy PLOM had not known where he was going while looking for help after the storm that had brought RJ to Vowella. He had eventually found his way through but had gone in circles many times along the way. In contrast, the jungle team had the advantage of Fahbee's guidance and the established path to the first clearing that had been blazed by their relatives years previously. The team proceeded with confidence that they would succeed in their mission.

After spending a couple of late afternoon hours hacking through dark, heavy vegetation, the jungle team came upon a new clearing, where overhead foliage allowed stunning rays of pink-hued light to filter through. The colors and light transformed the otherwise dreary arena into a scene that spotlighted flowering vines, colorful birds, and a surprising number of animated flingbees.

Mok stood in awe of the storybook surroundings. Looking then toward his bedraggled crew, he found the decision clear. "Well, gang. This place is calling to me. Let's call it quits for the day and make camp."

No one was happier to hear the news than Fahbee Flingbee.

"Ay caramba, Señor," San translated Fahbee's reaction to the others while Fahbee marched around atop San's fishing hat, relishing the glorious sight. "Look at all the lovely ladies. I know I was here before, but never did I see so many beauties. I wonder where they were when I came through the first time. It seems they are having a party. You'll have to excuse me, Señor. I know the team won't miss me if I go have fun for a little while. Right, Señor San?"

"Right, little buddy," chuckled San as Fahbee hovered in front of his face, then flew away. "Go find yourself a sweet little lady and have a nice evening. I'll see'dl ya."

Lek, quite jealous that San had his own flingbee, asked, "Where's he going? What's he going to do?"

San scanned the wondrous surroundings and grinned. "He's going to try to find the love of his life."

CHAPTER 14

Another Night Away

"Moms! Come in, Moms. Can you hear me?" Mok hopped around the new clearing to find a spot where the radio would pick up a signal as he tried to call home. "Moms! Come in, Moms."

Broken static replied to his request until he paused at the far western side of the clearing. His mother's voice responded but in broken sentences. "I hear ...babe. How is ...Over."

"Pretty good, Moms. Making our way through the jungle. We've stopped for the night now. How are things there? Over."

"Fairly .... The sick folks ... Rug Bum. Gun ... bait. Over."

"Moms, I can't hear you. What did you say?"

Mok frowned at the radio in his hand.

"Sorry, Moms. There's no reception here. I'll try to contact you once we're free of the jungle. Love you, Moms. Over and out."

Mok exhaled a frustrated sigh. *What about the bugs? Which Rug Bum was she talking about? Why isn't this darn radio working?* With a growl aimed at the radio, he hurried to join the others.

The young jungle team found a new waterfall and pond nearby, where they washed away the grime from their day. They dangled their tired feet in the coolness of the water that lapped against the smooth boulders on which they sat.

Mok and Kip cozied together on a rock, discreetly pressing the backs of their hands together. Their simple contact made their chests tickle inside. They gazed into each other's eyes with deep affection.

Their flirtation did not go unnoticed by Jen Net Ken, whose many curious eyes detected the subtle gestures. She watched them for a few moments, her calculating mind planning her next move.

One of San's duties for the day had been to scout out fruits and berries along the cutting trail. He had been quite successful in his hunt so, upon arrival at the new clearing, he had begun organizing the team's evening meal. Kip left Mok's side and walked ahead of the others back to the clearing to assist him.

Upon Mok's return, he settled onto a downed tree that sat off to the west of their evening campsite. He noted the unique antics of several odd-looking creatures. He identified them as flatbirds and smiley kooks from the lore of Pa PLOM's (RJ's father's) journey through the jungle a generation earlier. The flatbirds were chartreuse and royal blue creatures with yellow feet like those of a chicken. They stood a good six inches tall with red plumes sprouting from their heads. When Mok viewed one flatbird straight on, he was able to verify the story that its body was only as wide as a pencil, as though someone had smashed it in a heavy book. The bird became uncomfortable with Mok's staring and screeched "miahh" at him before scooting under some nearby ferns.

One of the smiley kooks, the oddest creature Mok had ever seen, crept up to his round, flat foot to investigate this tall, log-like being that was imposing on its environment. The kook was much larger than the flatbird, with a wide, smile-shaped body that was a semi-transparent, iridescent shade of orange. It had a grinning turquoise mouth that was just as wide as its body and eyes that were bright green. A fringy purple skirt hung from the bottom of its body, mostly hiding its white webbed feet.

"You're a smiley kook, aren't you?" asked Mok with a chuckle.

The kook's green eyes shone at Mok, and its smile widened. Before it scurried off into a thick patch of fern, it proclaimed as though it were a parrot, "Smiley kook, smiley kook, ha-ha!"

Mok watched other colorful birds play while he contemplated his situation. *Look at this place,* he thought to himself. *It's a wonderland of color and sparkling water and nature. Why can't Moms and G.G. and the other Vowellans be here enjoying all of this instead of dealing with stress and misery that they didn't ask for? Why did this happen?*

Jen, sitting with Nel a short distance away, caught sight of Mok in his contemplation. Her many eyebrows rose as she couldn't help but notice the weight he carried in trying to lead this mismatched group of teens. *Hmm. I must admit, he's got a lot of responsibility on him right now,* she thought. *Maybe he needs a little comfort from someone like me, who knows how to treat a boy much better than that curly-haired freak of a girl, Kip. He does have pretty blue eyes behind those eyeglasses, and his top hat is to die for. I think I can help him out.*

She rose from her seat and headed in his direction.

"Jen, what are you doing?" asked Nel in a loud whisper.

"Never mind, Nel," snapped Jen, waving her netted hand behind her back. "I'll be back."

Nel, wondering what her best pal was up to, watched her to see what would come next.

Jen strutted over to Mok, her hips swinging from side to side within her frumpy coveralls. When she reached him, deep in thought on the log, she bent from the waist and, with no hesitation, planted a sloppy kiss on his surprised lips.

Mok didn't hesitate to back away from her intrusive purple face. He cringed and rose so quickly that he almost knocked her over. He wiped his lips with the sleeve of his grimy coveralls. "What the heck are you doing? Get away from me, and never do that again."

"But you looked so sad. I was trying to cheer you up.

Didn't that make you feel better, Mok?" Jen frowned all around her head, seeming genuinely shocked at his bad reaction when she thought she was doing him a favor.

"Absolutely not! What made you assume it was okay to do that?" Mok again wiped his mouth with the back of his hand while his face wrinkled into a puckered grimace. His gaze shot to Kip. He was relieved to see that she hadn't seen what happened.

Lek, huddled with San and Kip, their backs to the incident, sensed the commotion and hurried to Mok's side. "Hey, what's going on? What did she do now?" His many eyes shot Jen multiple dirty looks.

Mok glared at Jen in disbelief. *Had she actually done that?* "Nothing. A big fat nothing." He hopped over to Kip.

Kip glanced up at him, then looked a little closer at the troubled look on his face. "Munkee, what's wrong? You look shaken."

"Nothing. It's nothing." Mok took a deep breath, then grinned down at her. "I just don't get how others' brains work sometimes."

"Yeah, me either." Kip studied him for a few more seconds before returning to her dinner prep work.

Lek continued to shoot dirty looks at Jen while she lifted her nose in the air and sashayed back to Nel with a shrug of her shoulders. Lek shook his head, knowing that Jen had definitely been up to no good.

San, Kip, and Lek presented quite a feast to the young crew, which was more than ready to spend some time relaxing. San's jungle finds complemented the items he had brought from home. While Kip tended to the fire, San sat on the ground, leaned against the center log, and munched on a generous slice of a purple jungle fruit that had the shape of an eggplant but the taste of a melon.

He laughed at the aerial show the flingbees were performing in the clearing's airspace right above them. The colorful creatures swooped back and forth, doing love dances while they sang little flingbee songs that only San could hear. He recognized Lucinda Flingbee amongst the air dancers. Fahbee had schooled him on distinguishing the females from the males of the species. The females were solid in color, while the males were striped. Lucinda was bright pink with lavender wings and teal eyelashes. Fahbee was orange with red and lime green stripes, lavender wings, and a mostly green curlicue tail. San was happy to see that Fahbee had a fine selection of females with which to mingle.

Within the flingbee airspace, Fahbee fluttered amongst the lovely females, not yet having noticed Lucinda's presence. He flirted with many a lady, showering each of them with compliments that he considered romantic, while Lucinda, well aware of his presence, subtly watched his antics with curiosity.

Once Fahbee realized Lucinda was one of the air dancers, he swooped to her side, leaving the entranced lady flingbee with whom he had been flirting behind.

"Oh, my dear Lucinda! You look especially beautiful tonight. Perhaps you would dance with me?"

Lucinda frowned at him. "Now, why would I want to dance with you, Señor Fahbee, when you are so free with your flirtations with others? I fear you are too mischievous for my liking."

"Why, I would never flirt with another if you would only allow me to love you," said Fahbee, trying too hard to be convincing as he fluttered in front of her, his tiny claws clasped, his wandering eye struggling to focus.

"I'm sorry, Señor. I will only love someone who is sincere inside and out. And you are not that someone. Good night!" Lucinda flew off to join some lady flingbees in a sweet circle dance.

Fahbee lowered his crooked beak in a pout before heading toward another cluster of female beauties.

Lek plopped down next to San to watch the flingbee show. "Looks like they're having fun up there, buddy. What do you think they're doing?"

"Oh, that's right-ood'ly. You can't hear them, can you'dl. Fahbee just made a fool of himself trying to get the attention of his favorite girl flingbee, Lucinda. It's such a laugh-ood'ly that he thinks he's a romantic expert. The males and females are dancing and flirting with each other. The males are singing that they've traveled far to find a love-ood'ly. The females are pretending they don't care-ood'ly. They are playing cute game-ood'lies with each other."

Mok, intrigued by the tiny creatures, joined them when he caught part of San's narration. "They're really singing, San? What does their music sound like?"

"Mostly Latin or opera style. Funny, isn't it? It seems out of place-ood'ly here in the jungle."

"Interesting," commented Mok as he glanced over at Brune, who was preoccupied with his little monkey, Scamper. "Odd, isn't it, that both Fahbee and Brune come from places with Latin influence. I think we need to ask a few more questions of them."

Mok's attention shifted to the others in their camp. His eyes inconspicuously observed the behavior of each of them. San continued to be entertained by the lively flingbees. Brune sat against the '54 Chevy, making deep giggling sounds as Scamper crawled up and down his body. Dun and Sun sat cross-legged by the fire, chomping bananas while polishing their hubcaps with their furry forearms. Lek, losing interest in the flingbee show, pulled messy handfuls of sticky notes from his pockets with hopes of sorting them into categories. Kip busied herself by tidying up the camp after the evening meal, as she would have done back home. And Jen and Nel sat facing each other on the ground, fluffing each other's droopy black hair, the goop that held it spiky having long ago melted away.

Mok's body gave a mild shudder as Jen's awful kiss flashed through his mind. *Should I tell Kip? Does it matter at this point? No! Because Jen doesn't matter. What matters is that I'm in charge of these young Vowellans, and I have to somehow lead them in getting what we need so we can do battle with the drill bugs. That's all that matters now.*

The tired teens gradually settled in for the night. The girls retired to the Bucket. The boys stretched out around the dwindling fire. The flingbee party raged on, and Brune Huge Dude dozed off with Scamper cuddled safely around his neck.

CHAPTER 15

Stolen Hat

Kip awoke to the discovery that nothing but gray appeared through the windows of the Bucket. Puzzled and disoriented, she rubbed her eyes and looked again. Scanning the inside of the car, she examined the well-polished interior and witnessed the vain Net Ken girls slumped together in the back seat, looking their worst ever. Their hair stuck out on one side while it lay flat and damp on the other; their coveralls were askew and rumpled; and their many eyelids lacked their usual caked makeup.

Gazing back toward the window, she witnessed nothing but a wall of gray staring back at her. She gradually came to the realization that the pretty clearing that the jungle team had so much enjoyed the previous night was very heavily fogged in.

Quietly opening the door, she slipped off the seat and onto the ground. There was no way to tell where the camp's firepit and the sleeping boys were, though they should have theoretically been within a few yards of her.

She shivered in the dampness, pulled her blanket from the car, and wrapped herself tightly in it to warm up.

Cautiously moving forward, she stepped toward what she thought was the direction of the campfire area. Sliding her feet forward, one at a time, she eventually bumped up against something with her right toe. Dropping to her knees, she felt around with her tiny hands to discover what it was.

San was sleeping on his back. Kip's discovery of his ample, squishy midsection gave way to his identity. San exhaled a contented sigh before he rolled onto his side. Kip couldn't remember how the boys had settled in the previous night or where Mok might be in relation to San. She knew, though, that she had to find him to make sure he was wearing his top hat in the fog. Fog Bobs, after all, were extremely allergic to fog, and exposure of their scalps to such dampness caused serious reactions.

On her hands and knees, Kip scooted to the left of San, blindly feeling for another body. As fortune would have it, she came upon one of Mok's flat, round feet, cold and upright below his blanket. There was no question it was his foot. She carefully slid the backside of her hand up his right side before settling in next to his right shoulder. She tugged on his arm as she tried to wake him.

"Munkee," whispered Kip. "Wake up. Munkee, can you hear me?"

His body shifted as he gave a slow groan.

"Munkee, you need to wake up. It's really foggy out. Do you have your hat on?"

Mok groaned a little louder and said, "Wha-a-at?"

Kip felt around his head, not finding his top hat to be anywhere nearby. She touched his hair, finding it dripping with moisture. She searched the ground beyond his head with her hands. Scooting around him on her knees, hoping to come upon the hat somewhere within the surroundings, she found nothing.

"Munkee, what happened to your hat?"

His words dragged out as though he were running on dying batteries. That was the usual effect of fog reaching his unprotected scalp. "Uh, I don't know."

Kip crawled back over to San and shook him awake. "San! San, wake up."

"What? What's go-d'ling on?" San sat up with a start and rubbed his eyes. Fahbee popped his head out of San's jacket pocket.

"Look! It's so foggy, I can't even see you. Mok's top hat is off of his head. Will you help me find it?" Her tone was close to that of panic.

"Of course," said San, alertness slowly creeping into his brain. He rolled onto his hands and knees and felt his way around the ground beyond where Kip searched.

"We have to find it," urged Kip, "so he can think straight again."

"I know'dl. He can wear my fishing hat-ood'ly if he wants."

"But doesn't it have air vents in it?"

"Yeah. I guess that wouldn't be much help."

"Hey, what's going on?" asked Lek, a voice coming from the other side of the fire pit. "Where are you guys?"

"Over here," called Kip. "Come help us."

"Need a ha-a-a-t," moaned Mok, adding to the plea. "Sa-a-a-ve the town. Dril-l-l- bu-u-ugs."

"I know, Munkee," said Kip in a testy voice. "We're trying to find it for you. Would it help if I wrapped my blanket around your head?

"Ya-a-a," Mok continued to drawl.

"Hold on, Kipee." said Lek. "Keep talking so I can find you. I'll use my clippers to cut a bandanna for him out of the blanket." Also on his hands and knees, he fumbled over Dun's feet.

"Hey dude! What the heck are you doing? Can't a guy sleep in peace?" Dun, having awakened with a start, was of course grouchy.

"Not right now," slapped back Lek. "We're having an emergency."

"Emergency? I'm good with emergencies."

Lek and Dun followed Kip's voice until they reached Mok and San. They spread out Kip's blanket, felt their way over it, and cut a large triangle out of it. Kip, in the meantime, shivered as she sat by Mok's side, her side fins bristling up and down. Dun lifted Mok's drippy head while Kip and Lek first rubbed his hair as dry as they could with the blanket, then carefully tied the large blanket bandanna around it. They pulled up the hood on Mok's coveralls and cinched the drawstrings tight into a bow below his mouth.

"What's going on over here?" asked Brune, his looming body barely visible through the soupy air. "Is there a problem?"

"Yes," explained Kip through constant shivers.

"Mok's hat is missing, and he's sick because of it. This darn fog is keeping us from finding it."

"Well, let's just see if I can help." Barely able to see the others, he faced them, sucked a deep, deep breath into his giant lungs, and began to slowly blow. A warm, steady breeze washed over the teens and the immediate area, melting a hole in the pesky fog. The kids were soon able to see each other.

"What the heck, dude," said Dun, trying not to allow his expression to reveal that he was impressed. "How did you do that?"

"My brother and I used to play hide and seek back home on foggy days. That's how we would find each other. We got to be good at it." Brune shrugged, seeming surprised that the others didn't know that trick.

"I'd say so." San, now able to see a little of the camp, grabbed the blanket he had been sleeping on and wrapped it around Kip's tiny, shaking body. He placed his wide, chubby hands on her shoulders and rubbed up and down her arms. Lek and Dun knelt on either side of Mok to tend to him.

Brune took another deep breath and slowly exhaled as he turned himself in a circle. His technique, to everyone's amazement, cleared the fog away from a wide, circular area. As he continued his task, the little camp gradually showed itself.

The gentle giant knelt next to Mok when he saw that he was still lying flat in a stupor. Brune again started blowing, hoping to expose the top hat, which certainly had to be lying somewhere near Mok. Brune blew and blew, and the teens earnestly searched the area, but no top hat was to be found. As the camp cleared, they realized that the hat, for whatever reason, was gone.

"Where the heck could it be?" grumbled Dun. "Whoever took it deserves a good rug snapping."

"Wait-ood'ly!" exclaimed San, who stopped moving and put a finger to his lips to cue the others to quiet down. "Do you hear that? Someone is laughing."

"What are you talking about, fat boy?" Dun caught the dirty look that Kip shot his way.

"Come on, you don't hear that?" San listened harder, encouraging the others to do the same.

"Remember, dude, we don't have your ears," Dun stated to San.

"Well, someone is definitely laughing. We're not missing anyone, are we?"

"No, we're all here," observed Lek. "The other girls are still in the Bucket. Where's Fahbee?"

"He's asleep-ood'ly in my pocket," said San. "Too much late-night partying for him."

Little Scamper began to chatter. She scurried up to the top of Brune's head and pointed a fuzzy finger into the fog toward the east. She screeched and pointed again. Brune turned to face the direction of Scamper's finger. He sucked in a huge breath, held it for a moment, and blew it out long and hard.

His fast-moving breath made a hole straight through the fog, which exposed a couple of tall trees. To their great surprise, a good-sized ape-like creature sat on a high, sturdy branch with a grin on its face and Mok's top hat on its head. He leaned back and laughed at the onlookers.

"Oh, no!" cried Kip. "What is that thing? What do we do now?"

The creature laughed again. It plucked the hat from its head and waved it at them to show off. With its backside secure on the branch, it waved its feet at them in a further attempt to annoy them.

"Now that is an ugly dude if there ever was one," stated Dun, his mouth dropping at the sight of the strange creature.

"Wha-a-at does it lo-o-ok li-i-ike?" asked Mok, who struggled to comprehend the conversation while still lying flat out on the ground.

"Dude, it's kind of like a black gorilla, but it has tall ears like a rabbit and big, round, flat feet like yours. Who ever heard of a creature with so many weird features?" asked Dun with a shake of his head.

"You mean like us Vowellans?" interjected Lek with a nervous chuckle.

"Gor-r-r-abobbs-s-s-s," said Mok in reply to Dun. "Pa PLOM's gor-r-r-abobbs-s-s-s."

"Yes, Mok," agreed San with a nod. "Remember the stories about Pa PLOM-ood'ly and his adventures in the jungle back in his day-ood'ly? He was captured by gorrabbobs."

"Well, whatever it is, why did it have to take Mok's hat?" asked Kip. "What does he need it for?"

"To harass us, to laugh at us, to show us he's boss," answered Dun confidently. He was particularly good at such behavior.

"But how will we get it back?" asked Kip, distress making her voice shake.

"Let me see what I can do," offered Brune.

He lumbered off toward the gorrabbob's tree and started talking to the frisky creature in a soothing voice. The gorrabbob cocked its head to the side and listened intently to Brune's deep, slow voice. Brune reached his long arm up into the air and nicely asked the creature to come down and give him the hat. For a moment, it seemed that the gorrabbob was going to move toward Brune. But it stopped, pointed a hairy finger at him, and laughed out loud before it turned, swung away on a vine, and disappeared into the jungle. Brune returned to the others, his head hanging low.

Mok, whose senses were gradually returning to him, sat up and held the sides of his head with his hands. "It's okay, Brune. I'll be all right."

Kip placed her tiny hands over his, turned his head toward her, and looked into his eyes, trying to determine his true state of alertness. "Are you sure, Munkee? Is the bandanna working?"

"Yeah, I think so. I just need more time to recover. We can always call back to Moms and have Bek bring me a new hat when he returns later." His words were less and less slurred the more he spoke. He gazed back into her eyes with increased focus. "Punkee, you need to help me be the leader now, until I'm fully recovered."

"What? I don't know how to do that."

"Of course you do." Mok's mouth spread into a confident grin. "You can do anything you set your mind to. I just need you to be my eyes and help me think things through for a while in case there are decisions that need to be made."

"Okay, Munkee, whatever you say." Kip's eyes widened, then settled into a determined stare as she assessed the status within the clearing. "The fog is still clinging to the outskirts of our space, but it seems to be dissipating some. Sun and the Net Ken girls are still in the Bucket. The guys are waiting to hear what they should do next."

"Okay. Lek and Dun," said Mok, "would you please get the girls out of the Bucket and help me into it? I'll recover faster if I'm in an enclosed space."

"You got it," answered Lek, ready to help. His left side eyes flashed a glance toward Dun who, surprisingly, nodded his head with no objections.

"San, please prepare some food for us, so we can get our day underway," added Kip.

San responded with a thumbs up and scurried over to his backpack.

Bending way back to look up at Brune's kind face, Kip asked, "Brune, would you please blow more fog away from the outer edges of the clearing for me?"

"You betcha!" said Brune with a wide grin. Kip grinned in return, knowing he was proud to have been given a useful chore.

Lek and Dun helped Mok to his feet and guided him to the Bucket, where they sat him down to lean against the right front tire. Taking this prime opportunity to pester his sister, Lek opened the rear right door and commenced poking Jen on her purple forehead with his right index finger. Jen frowned with all her brows in half-sleep before jumping to a fully awake state. Her jerking body popped Nel, whose head rested on Jen's shoulder, out of her sound sleep. Once Lek explained Mok's situation to them, they groaned but slid out of the car. Their grouchiness persisted throughout the day.

Mok spent the remainder of the day with Kip in the Bucket. While she manned the driver's seat, his mind slowly cleared. The dense fog, however, did not. Brune blew his strong, warm breaths in the direction of Fahbee's trail so the jungle team could proceed with their work. They moved through the unexplored jungle at a steady pace. The pesky fog, like an eerie and unwelcome shadow, relentlessly followed the tail end of the Bucket as it crept forward along the new path.

By early evening, the fog finally melted away. Mok emerged from the Bucket wearing his unfashionable new bandanna. The Net Ken girls, still so fashion conscious, snickered at his appearance.

"Well, Mok, poor fashion choice," giggled Nel. "Your top hat looks much cooler on you than that bandanna."

"Although the bandanna does keep your ears from flapping," added Jen, joking but at the same time being factual. "I guess that's a good thing."

"Good grief!" hollered Lek. "No one gives a nanaberry about your stupid opinions."

Mok and Kip couldn't help but laugh and shake their heads at the Net Kens' unbreakable ways.

Within minutes, Bek, driving the '54 Chevy, pulled into their new evening campsite. The Vowellan teens told Bek about their annoying fog adventure. And Bek assured them that everything back in town was as they had left it. Mok hadn't been able to reach Roz on the radio about a new top hat, so he continued to sport his bandanna. The team spent the rest of the evening putting the fog incident behind them by playing a silly guessing game based on the messy pile of sticky notes that Lek kept stuffed into his deep pants pockets. The mood was good. The relaxation was needed.

As the young Vowellan kids retired to their sleeping places for the night, Mok and Kip hung back, sitting close on a log, to chat for a few moments.

"Long day, huh Munkee?" asked Kip as she straightened the left side of his blanket bandanna for him. "Are you sure you're okay now?"

Mok had to think about his answer for a moment. Leaning his head against hers, he tried to explain what he was suddenly feeling inside.

"Yeah, I'm fine, Punkee. I guess I'm just a little scared. I think we were lucky today that the gorrabbob was content to just take my hat. Back in Pa PLOM's day, the gorrabbobs held him captive for quite a while. We just don't know what dangers are here in this jungle. What if something worse happens? What if we're not able to get back to town to help everyone? We have a big responsibility on our shoulders. I just want everything to turn out okay."

Kip placed her hand over his, giving it a couple of soft

pats. "It will, Munkee. I know it. We need to believe it, to carry a positive attitude with us no matter what we encounter. Come on, Munkee. We can do this."

Mok pinched his lips together, looked deeply into her sparkling turquoise eyes, and nodded. "Thanks, Punkee. I needed that. See? That's just why I wanted you to come along. Come on, we'd better get some sleep."

Mok rose and extended a hand to pull her up from the log. After a warm hug, they retired to separate cars to sleep, their minds a little more unsure than the words they had spoken.

CHAPTER 16

The Other Side

Within Fahbee Flingbee's most colorful morning dream, Lucinda Flingbee flitted through the bright jungle clearing while fluttering her long blue lashes at him. *Is she really flirting with me*, he thought? *Should I fly after her and blanket her with my romantic charm*, he wondered. He approached her with his curly tail posed in a heart shape, his eyes focused from their usual wandering. As he neared her, her lips puckered. Her long lashes swept her cheeks. Just as he was about to swoop in for a kiss, he was jolted awake and onto his back within San's jacket pocket, her image shrinking to a size of a pinhole.

Fahbee's attention quickly returned to the jungle. The sound of clippers buzzing through tree branches filled the air. He rolled onto his tiny claws and climbed to the top of San's pocket. He was groggy from three nights of flingbee partying, so it took some time for the scene before him to register. He watched Lek and Bek buzz their way through the thicket, even though he was not ahead of them to guide them. He groomed himself with his snake-like tongue and flew from San's pocket to the rim of his hat.

Hanging from the rim with an upside-down view of San's eyes, he asked in a wounded tone, "Hey Señor, what's going on? Why did they start without me?"

"Oh, everyone thought you deserved some extra sleep-ood'ly. You've been working and playing really hard-ood'ly, you know."

"Yes, I know," confirmed Fahbee. His position of being the team's scout had become quite important to him. Even though he was tired, he certainly didn't want to lose that position. "But how do they know where they are going?"

"Well, Bek examined the trail behind us-ood'ly and figured out that for the most part, we're moving forward in a straight line. So he and Lek thought they'd get an early start continuing the line-ood'ly. Bek's been itching to get back to cutting, now that all the gum-ood'ly has been delivered to town."

"Oh, I see." Fahbee's head dipped with sadness.

"Don't worry, Fahbee. We still need youd'l," assured San. "How long do you think it will be before we reach-ood'ly the end of the jungle?"

"Hmm," Fahbee contemplated. "Perhaps by the end of tomorrow? That's my guess."

The noise of the clippers came to a halt. Bek and Lek took a few moments to remove accumulated leaf litter from their handy tools.

San hollered to them. "Hey guys, Fahbee thinks we might get-ood'ly to the end of the jungle by tomorrow night."

"Wow, that would be great," answered Mok, who was picking up after Bek. "The sooner we can get some limoncinas in our hands, the sooner we can get back to town. But I must say, I can't wait to also see all the things that Mr. RJ told us regarding New Life City. It will be interesting to see how they compare to the pictures I have of them in my head."

"Yeah, dude. I'm with you," said Dun with a nod of his head while he stuffed branches into the nearby thicket. "It all sounds too good to be true, doesn't it?"

"Not at all, Dun," said Mok "I believe Mr. RJ has always been honest with us. And books have shown us that other places exist outside of Vowella. It's simply hard to imagine because all we've ever known is Vowella."

"Well, I can tell you that other places do exist because I come from one of those places," interjected Brune, who was bringing up the rear of the work team. He was a creature of few words, but he now spoke when he had something of value to express.

"Yes, you do, don't you," said Mok as he eyed Brune curiously. "And we sincerely thank you for helping us get to those places." Mok paused, his mind turning. "Tell me, Brune, what is the name of the place that you come from?"

"Vocalla!"

"Vo-ky-a," Mok repeated phonetically, his brows wrinkling into a frown. "Hmm. Distantly similar to Vowella."

"What? Vocalla?" shouted Fahbee, quick to circle

Brune's head and land atop his ample nose. "Then we do come from the same island."

San had to quickly translate, since Fahbee's sudden intrusion startled Brune and Scamper.

"Well, then," said Brune as he gently swatted Fahbee away from his nose so he could better see him. "We have much to talk about later."

"Indeed!" replied Fahbee through translation.

The conversation quickly died when Lek and Bek once again fired up their clippers. Further revelations would have to come later.

The male team members plowed forward while the girls cleaned up camp and loaded the cars. Kip took a hard look at the cars in these unlikely surroundings. Having both in the jungle now was of comfort. They made it possible for seven of the eight Vowellans to sleep indoors while providing storage space for their provisions. Dun chose to sleep outside with Brune to guard their camp. Kip knew everyone felt much safer sleeping in a protected place, especially after Mok's stolen hat incident. As she glanced from car to car, she wondered if the '54 Chevy would prove to be as self-motivated as the Bucket.

With all packed up and ready, Kip climbed into the Bucket, while Nel and Jen manned the '54 Chevy. Nel took the Chevy's driver's seat since Bek had been teaching her how to drive in recent weeks. Jen shot her a snobby look with three of her left-facing eyes to let her know that this move didn't mean Nel was cooler than she was. The Bucket, of course, took the lead and headed north along the new path that the boys were in the process of cutting. The Chevy did indeed follow the Bucket's lead without Nel having to do much to guide it.

Jen and Nel resumed their side clipping chores behind Lek and Bek. Fahbee returned to his scouting routine while San, Mok, Dun, and Brune Huge Dude continued the heavy rubbish cleanup behind the cutting crew. Kip manned the '54 Chevy, taking up the rear of the caravan behind the self-steering Bucket. With everyone now focused on the major chore at hand, the path-blazing project through the jungle proceeded at an efficient and much more rapid pace.

In a sudden turn of events, however, Dun stepped into what he thought was a tangle of roots that the cutters had neglected. His left foot and ankle became clamped within that tangle. He tried and tried to free his foot from the knotted maze, but the more he pulled, the more the tangle pulled back and proceeded to squeeze his lower limb. Dun hollered and cursed at his trap, but it did not free him. Instead, it sent out tentacles that slithered around his stumpy leg and up toward his crotch. The creepers were one inch thick and twisted. They were pale brown in color yet riddled with deep green gashes that resembled question marks. Fortunately, Dun was clothed in his protective coveralls and boots. He hollered again and pounded against a creeping tentacle with his left hubcap. The pounding did nothing to hinder its progress.

"Help! Help me, will you?" he hollered to the others. "These dang roots are attacking me. Dudes, give a Bum a hand."

Mok waved down the Net Kens, signaling them to stop clipping while Brune hurried to Dun's side. It wasn't long before San also hollered for help. Squeezing tentacles crept up his coveralls and squeezed his chubby legs as well. Mok rushed to his side to investigate the problem. He soon became a victim too.

Realizing that the tangle was not composed of roots at all, Mok hollered to the others, "Holy Jungle! Snakes! We've stepped into a bed of snakes. They must have been buried under the roots we cut."

"So what do we do?" yelled Dun, who was heading toward a panic attack. Rug Bums weren't used to being victims.

Kip, at the caravan's rear and curious as to why everything had suddenly come to a halt, hopped out of the Chevy and hurried to stand by the Bucket. She didn't quite understand what she saw. "Munkee, what's going on? Why did you stop?"

"Punkee, get back in the car now! HURRY!" Mok shouted at her, knowing he would not be able to help her if she also became entangled.

"But," pleaded Kip.

"GO! NOW!"

Kip ran back to the car, climbed inside, and shut the door. She stood on the driver's seat and pressed her face against the windshield to try to discover the source of the problem. The Bucket blocked her line of sight. Frustrated, she turned the vintage handle to roll down the window, hoping at the least to hear what was going on.

Without hesitation, Brune jumped into the snake bed, determined to stomp on as many of the slithering snakes as he could with his huge, heavy feet. Brune grunted and yelled at the creepy creatures, hoping to shoo them into the thick jungle on either side of them. Several of the snakes indeed scattered and slipped into the side walls that the Net Kens had established.

In the meantime, on the path just north of the trouble, the Net Ken girls did all they could to climb up the leaf-covered bodies of Lek and Bek. They screamed non-stop, losing their senses completely. The boys had to wrestle them to the ground in order to free themselves of the girls' grasps, an act that drove the girls into greater hysteria, since the ground put them in even closer proximity to the slithering invaders. Once Bek scolded them and convinced them that they would be freed if they would just shut up, Jen and Nel slowly managed to compose themselves. The four Net Kens rose from the ground and gazed in silent horror at the dismal situation.

High above Brune's head, camouflaged in the thick branches that canopied the snake bed, a giant snake, a good ten feet long and six inches in diameter, slithered along the branches, observing the scene below. Its purple skin, inlaid with yellow diamond shapes, shimmered in the filtered light, while its long red tongue snapped in and out of its ample mouth.

Kip spotted the frightening intruder from the front window of the Chevy. Her eyes bulged as she gasped for a breath. She rolled down the side window, pulled herself partway out in order to plant her feet on the windowsill, and further pulled herself up onto the roof of the car. She spotted the top of Brune's head as he stomped and stomped on the bed of snakes.

"BRUNE! MUNKEE! Watch out," she shouted toward them. "There's a giant snake on the big branch above you. Brune, do you hear me?"

Brune glanced toward her with a puzzled expression. Kip repeatedly pointed her index finger toward the sky above her head. Brune examined the airspace above her and frowned as she continued to point. Kip realized she should change the direction of her action, so it was directed above Brune's head.

"Look up, Brune, look up!" she shouted. She pulled at the wild orange ringlets that hung around her face while she panted with fear.

Brune changed his focus to the large branch above him and flinched at the sight. He froze in place, as did the others in the snake bed, as the giant snake proceeded to hang its head and slowly work its way downward toward him.

The trapped Vowellans froze where they stood as well. As small snakes continued to sneak up and around their bodies, the giant snake drew nearer and nearer to Brune. Kip watched in horror from the roof of the car while the Net Kens shook in their coveralls on the opposite side of the snake bed.

When the distance between the giant snake and Brune's head reached 3 feet, the creature opened its mouth wide, flapped its red tongue, and released a hiss that rattled the leaves of all the trees surrounding them.

The Vowellan kids, from their various locations, squeezed their eyes shut, panting where they stood. But Brune, in a moment of sheer bravery, stared the creature in the eye, refusing to be the first to look away.

The giant snake paused and stared back at Brune. It pulled its head back, then shoved it forward again, releasing one more rattling hiss. The small snakes that had entrapped Mok, Dun, and San wasted no time in retreating, freeing the Vowellan teens from their bondage. The small snakes slithered into the jungle walls and disappeared.

Brune stared down the giant snake until he broke the creature's concentration. The snake retreated to its tree branch and gradually turned and returned to the deep jungle like the others.

Mok breathed heavy sighs of relief. San wept while Fahbee flew around his head to comfort him. Dun moved onto more solid ground near the Net Kens and had himself a little stomping fit. Brune bent from the waist, placed his hands on his knees, and shook his head. Sweat dripped from his head fur, concealing the tears of relief that fell from his eyes.

Mok observed each of their reactions. He especially studied Brune with deep admiration for his bravery. Because of Brune's shy nature, he assumed the gentle giant would not later want to be singled out as a hero. Mok proceeded to take a count of his teammates and grinned at the sight of Kip climbing back into the Chevy through the open window. With a final sigh, he spoke. "Is everyone all right? We should move on right away, before they have a chance to return. Can you all do that for me?"

The shaken Vowellans and a certain Huge Dude nodded, tossed the incident behind them, and returned to their duties.

The efficient team made such excellent progress that Mok urged them to plow forward for an extended period, which would delay their much-needed lunch break. The team members, aware of their unusual momentum, readily agreed. They cut and sweat and cleared and disposed until they were about to drop, the vehicles rambling along behind. It wasn't until Bek and Lek came to a dead halt, their clippers rapidly winding down, that the momentum suddenly changed.

Jen and Nel slowly caught up to them, as did the cleanup crew. Fahbee fluttered onto San's shoulder. Catching up to the others, the Bucket came to a stop and shut down its engine. The Chevy did the same. Curiosity brought Kip out of the car. She hurried to join the rest of the jungle team. She found them stretched out in a horizontal line, frozen in place, eyes northward. Kip rushed to Mok's side.

The innocent, hard-working team had reached the end of the jungle.

While the young Vowellans, as well as Brune, stood amazed at the sight that lay before them, Mok's mind absorbed the visual information at a furious pace. During their many intimate talks, RJ had described to him the world that existed beyond the jungle in great detail. But his physical descriptions didn't compare in that moment. Miles of flat, dusty space and clear blue sky stretched ahead of them. In the far distance, the flat horizon was dotted with what looked like boxes stacked to varying heights and perhaps a tall, narrow triangle or two. Far to the east and west of them, strips of green suggested boundaries of more forests or jungles.

Mok's eyes welled with tears when he realized what the magnificent sight before him meant. The structures in the distance were those of none other than Heaven's Wait's majestic capitol, New Life City. The surrounding areas and their significance were a blur in comparison. New Life City was where Uncle Jake and Uncle Nick lived. It was where the mysterious Lady Wisteena resided, as well as the Troubled Young Angels and the earthly folks who were waiting to go to Heaven. Mok understood that he and the others were that much closer to reaching help for their town. But he also realized that they, mere teens from a little town called Vowella, were now witnesses to the fact that new and different places did exist in their larger world. These places were now available to them, beyond what was written on a page or told in a story. Mok knew in that moment that life would never be the same for him. He would learn about those places and the folks who lived within them. He would discover all there was to know about the greater world of Heaven's Wait.

Kip gently tugged on Mok's arm until he snapped out of his thoughts. A hot tear dribbled down each of her cheeks. "Munkee, isn't this amazing? I'm so glad I get to share this moment with you."

Mok's jaw rose and fell a couple of times before he was able to speak. "Uh, yes. Totally amazing. I can't even describe what I'm feeling right now."

"I can't either." Kip leaned against his left arm as she slipped her tiny fingers between his. "So now that we're here, what do we do next?"

Mok tore his gaze away from the landscape to look at her. "Wow. I didn't expect to be here this soon. Let me think."

He again surveyed the new environment, looked to the jungle trail behind them, and then to the raggedy crew that had worked so hard to get to this point. Mok knew that Uncle Jake's place was somewhere in the distance, near the spot where Lek had collected his limoncinas in the past. Mok's right hand shook as he pulled the radio from his back pocket and fumbled with the buttons and dials. "I'll try to reach Uncle Jake to let him know where we are."

Kip rubbed his forearm to soothe him. "It's okay, Munkee. You're doing fine. We've gotten through the hardest part. Now, let's go find those limoncinas."

Brune and the other Vowellan teens chanted in, "Yeah! Let's go! We're ready! Let's do it!"

Mok grinned at the lot of them and pushed a button that would allow him to transmit. "Uncle Jake! This is Mok Fog Bob speaking. Come in, Uncle Jake. Can you hear me? Over."

Everyone listened eagerly. There was nothing. He

repeated his message. Again, they listened. Just as Mok flashed them a disappointed expression with sad eyes, a familiar voice answered him.

"Come in, Mok. I hear you, son," said the welcomed voice of Jake. "I've been worried sick about all of you. Where are you? Over."

Much relieved, Mok answered. "We just broke through the jungle on your side. We came for help. How do we get to you? Over."

"You mean you worked your way through Jimmy's Jungle? How is everyone? Over." Jake shook his head in amazement.

"We'll explain when we see you. Have you spotted any drill bugs on this side, Uncle Jake? Over."

"No, and I haven't heard any reports of them being here in New Life City," assured Jake. "Over."

"Good," said Mok with a breath of relief. "Well, we need to get to your place. Over."

"Okay, just stay where you are. I'll head south till I reach the east side of the jungle, then I'll head west till I find you. I'll bring the flatbed truck to pick you up. How many are with you? Over."

Mok quickly counted heads. There were nine of them including Brune. "There will be five of us, six including Mr. Huge Dude. But we have the Bucket with us. If we start driving due east, should we be able to find you? Over."

His teammates gave him a puzzled look.

"Yes," answered Jake. "It's so wide open out there, we should have no trouble spotting each other. Over."

"Okay, Uncle Jake. We'll see you in a while. Over and out."

Mok hopped away from the others for a moment. He pushed a radio button, turned a dial, and pushed another button, as he tried to connect with his mother.

"Moms, are you there? Over."

All he was able to hear were loud, crackly, staticky sounds.

"Moms, we made it through the jungle," Mok said anyway, just in case she was able to hear him. He fought back the emotion that was trying to force its way out. "Uncle Jake is coming to get us. Over."

The crackly sounds continued. There was no response.

Kip crept behind him and slipped her arm in his. She stared at his frowning face and attempted a bit of speculation. "It's most likely, Munkee, that the bug cloud is totally blocking your radio reception. Try to trust that everyone back home is fine. The best thing we can do is to keep moving forward, so we can get back there as soon as possible."

Mok nodded and patted her hand on his arm. "You're right, Punkee. You're right. Why are you always right?"

Kip flashed him a wide grin with her puffy yellow lips. She was relieved to see that a touch of Mok's unworried self still existed somewhere within his tense, determined body.

Returning to the others, Mok turned to Bek and the Net Ken girls. "I'm sorry, you guys, but I'd like you to return to town now. All three of you have been invaluable in getting us through the jungle. We wouldn't be here without you. But, at this point, I think you could be of more value back in Vowella. You could use the Chevy to shuttle water back there and to fetch more gum if needed. And we can try to radio you if we need help getting back through the jungle. I think it's best if the rest of us go on. We need Fahbee for direction, which means San needs to come with us. We need Lek and Brune to lead us to the limoncinas. I'd like to keep Dun as our guard. And the longer we keep Kip away from the drill bugs the better."

"You're right," agreed Bek. "We are needed back home. There is much to do since so many folks are still sick. We'll stop along the way and bring as much fruit and water back to town as we can." He stepped forward to shake Mok's hand. "By the time you get back, we'll have the gum all ready for you to mix with the limoncinas. Maybe then we can end this nightmare. You've been a good leader, Mok. I'm proud of you."

Mok grinned at Bek, then turned his focus to Jen and Nel. The look of relief on both of their purple faces was undeniable.

"Thank goodness," announced Jen. "Now I can go home and fix my hair and change my clothes. I never want to do this again."

Mok cocked his head to the side and flashed her a sad expression. "Well, hopefully, you won't ever have to." He then spoke to all three. "Have a safe trip back. With any luck, we'll see you back in town in a couple of days."

Jen and Nel climbed into the Chevy while Bek gave

hugs to the remaining team members. He hopped into the Chevy's driver's seat and made a wide U-turn in the expansive flat space before heading back into the jungle. Mok and his friends waved and hollered their thanks as the three drove away.

Mok turned toward the city in the distance. His fresh frown revealed his concern for the unknown challenges that were bound to present themselves when they reached Uncle Jake's. But he climbed into the passenger seat of the Bucket and directed Lek to drive them eastward to meet up with Uncle Jake. Brune plodded along behind like an obedient soldier.

CHAPTER 17

Limoncinas

The welcomed sight of Jake's flatbed truck rapidly approaching the Bucket from the east excited its Vowellan passengers. Though they had never seen a flatbed, they readily recognized its owner. The vehicles came to a hurried stop facing each other. Jake rushed from his truck to embrace the teens, who had wasted no time evacuating the Bucket. Jake couldn't help but chuckle at the animated, overlapping chatter that tumbled from each of the Vowellan mouths.

"You should have seen the big ape-ood'ly that had the nerve to steal Mok's hat-ood'ly," spewed San.

"Do you have anything I can use to sharpen my clippers, Uncle Jake? That jungle sure beat them up," complained Lek.

"Those dang drill bugs ate our house. Can you believe it? They want war? I'll give them war. I'm gonna snap them with rugs and smash them in my hub caps when I get back," announced Dun.

Jake's head snapped when Brune, who had been mute

as far as he was concerned, blurted out, "We came across a giant snake that dared to stare me down. I took care of him." Brune nodded with pride at his accomplishment.

"There are so many sick folks back home, Uncle Jake. We really need your help," pleaded Kip.

"Uncle Jake, there's something important I need to tell you. It's about Mr. RJ," expressed Mok in a gentle voice.

Jake vigorously waved his hands in the air and gave a big whistle through his teeth to silence the chatter. "Hold on, hold on. I can't listen to all of you at once."

The teens quieted, and Mok hopped forward. "There's so much going on back home, Uncle Jake. We really need your help. Our town is in great danger. And Mr. RJ..."

"Yes, I know, son. I had a brief conversation with your mother a couple of days ago on the radio. I can't get through to her now. And I can't believe RJ and the entire council are out of commission. You kids are so brave to have ventured out to find help for everyone back home. Come on, let's get you back to my place where you can freshen up, get some food, and tell me more about what's been going on. Just follow me."

Jake turned toward Brune, with whom Jake was now more intrigued since he had chosen to speak. Jake grinned at the tiny monkey that sat on Brune's shoulder. "Hop onto the flatbed, Mr. Huge Dude. I'll bet you could use a rest."

Brune issued a wide grin, nodded, and did as Jake said.

The Bucket followed Jake's flatbed northward along the right side of the vast flat space, close to the wall of lush forest that extended to New Life City and beyond. The vehicles headed toward Jake and Bessie's place, a bungalow within an airplane hangar that sat in the southeastern corner of New Life City's airport. The area was called the Materiality Zone. The paved land within the Zone was dotted with numerous large warehouses, where "stuff" from Earth that had been discarded and recycled for use in Heaven's Wait sat in storage. Many of the things RJ bought in New Life City for the Vowellans came through the Materiality Zone, then were passed on to the many shops within the city.

Lek drove while Mok occupied the front passenger seat with Kip squeezed between them. San and Dun, with their broader bodies, occupied the back seat. All were fascinated with the view through the windows. The skyline of New Life City grew and grew as they moved closer and closer to their destination. Along the way, Lek tried to explain to them all that they would see, but his words did nothing to convey what seeing the city was like. Glossy buildings of various shapes and sizes arose from the landscape, gleaming in the sunlight like giant versions of the jewels they had been told had once occupied the caves back home. The buildings' architecture fascinated everyone, even Dun, who had never given thought to the fact that buildings could be beautiful. Mok and Kip looked at each other with jaws dropped and eyes filled with wonder. No words were necessary.

Lek also tried to explain to the others that the

PLOMs (Posthumous Legends or Mentors) of New Life City didn't all look like Mr. RJ, Uncle Jake, Auntie Bess and Uncle Nick, though they were all former earthlings. PLOMs came in all shapes and colors and sizes, just like Vowellans. Dun and San couldn't imagine that, while Mok and Kip agreed that they had to see some PLOMS for themselves while they were there.

When the caravan reached the airport hangars straight ahead of them, Jake led the vehicles to parking spaces that were tucked behind his hangar, near a forest entrance. Lek recognized the very spot because of the short stowaway adventure he had experienced on RJ's plane in the recent past. Jake explained to the kids that it was best to keep their presence in the city a secret for the time being, since he, Bess, and Nick were the only ones who knew the Vowellans even existed. RJ had shared with Jake on numerous occasions his concerns that the PLOMS would be overly fascinated with the Vowellans, which would likely overwhelm the naïve teens. RJ had also wanted to protect them from any other beings that perhaps lived on the outskirts of New Life City, beings that had subtly been suggested by Lady Wisteena.

The teens filed out of the Bucket and into the large hangar by way of a back door that, luckily, was tall enough for Brune to squeeze through. Lek paused before entering to look toward the forest that sat just to the east of them, across a short stretch of asphalt. A slight chill passed through him as he remembered how scared he had been the last time he had visited that forest. Inside, Auntie Bess enveloped each of them in a comforting hug. She passed a mountainous plate of fresh doughboys, her delectable, fried, cinnamon-sugared bread puffs, which were vigorously gobbled down. Dun, in a surprise move, took it upon himself to make sure Brune got his fair share too. San tucked a small doughboy into his pocket for Fahbee to enjoy. Fahbee emerged a short while later looking like a sugared Hallie-Day cookie. Uncle Jake and Auntie Bess rolled with laughter at the sight.

    Mok reviewed the disturbing events in Vowella that resulted in them having to cut their way through the jungle to get to the New Life City side to hunt for limoncinas. Jake and Bessie displayed their serious concern for the ill and especially the Elders and RJ.
    "I'm confident RJ will be fine once the sun is able to shine on him again," suggested Jake. "Our Pa made it through, and he will too. My deepest concern is for the Elders. Their fragile bodies deserve to be well again."
    "Yes, the poor things," sighed Bess. "I wish I was there to help."
    "If we can get those limoncinas back to town and rid ourselves of those awful bugs, I think there's a good chance they will be okay," said Mok, more hopeful than sure. "We just can't afford to let any of them get stung again."
    "That's for sure," agreed Jake. "I don't know of these limoncinas, but if Lek says they're somewhere in the forest right behind us, we have to do a search. It sounds like Vowella depends on finding them."

While Jake and Bessie packed some supplies into backpacks for the next part of the Vowellans' journey, Mok joined Kip and Lek at the wide front windows of Jake's office. They marveled at the sight of the numerous planes that landed and took off from the many airstrips.

"Munkee, look at all those planes, so much bigger than RJ's," noted Kip. "Why haven't we ever seen any of them fly over Vowella? Why haven't they seen our town? Doesn't that seem odd to you?"

"Yes, as a matter of fact. I'll have to make sure to ask RJ about that sometime," replied Mok, his mind working overtime to take snapshots of all he was observing. "I'll bet Lady Wisteena knows the answer to that."

Mok eyed the numerous PLOM workers who walked the airstrips, guiding planes with their flags and unloading cargo from the planes' cargo bays. Lek had been right. There were more varieties of PLOMS than Mok could have imagined. He was disturbed when he realized how young some of them were.

"Uncle Jake," called Mok as he turned away from the window for a moment. "A couple of those PLOMs out there don't look to be any older than me. Why is that?"

"Well, Mok, unfortunately, illnesses and accidents sometimes take young people before their time. Most of the young ones stay here and wait for their parents to come. Uncle Nick does a lot of work for the youth program in the city," explained Jake. He joined Mok at the window. He grinned when he saw an old battered '68 Ford van pull up to the office's front door. "Speaking of Uncle Nick, here he comes now."

Spotting familiar faces through the window, Nick hopped out of the van and hurried through the door. He eagerly greeted each teen and Mr. Huge Dude as well. "Boy, am I glad to see all of you. We've been so scared since we couldn't get the plane through that nasty bug cloud. I'm glad you found a way to get to us. How's RJ? How's Pun? How's dear Lil'la doing?"

RJ had managed to communicate with Jake and Nick about Lil'la and Pun before he had gotten stung.

The Vowellans again started chattering at once. Jake had to wave his hands to get them to stop. Mok once more took the lead and explained everything there was to know about the disaster in Vowella: the sick, the plan to put folks into hibernation, RJ's deep sleep reaction to his bug sting, Dr. Pol's antidote, and the gum-limoncina bait that they hoped would rid their town of the evil drill bugs.

"What if we take a huge vacuum cleaner back to town and suck those monsters up?" asked Nick as random ideas popped into his head.

"That would be great if we were assured that the bugs died in the process," explained Mok. "Papa Pol says that their venom is so lethal that we need to make sure the bugs are either eliminated for good or that they're somehow driven away so they never come back. So far, the gum-limoncina bait is the only method we've come up with. Speaking of which, maybe we should try to search the forest for the ponds and limoncinas that Lek found while there's still some daylight. What do you think?"

"I'm ready," announced Dun as he banged his hub caps together like cymbals. "I can't wait to get back to town and do battle with those nasty suckers. Nobody messes with my family or my home, and they did both."

"I'm really sorry about that," said Jake, shaking his head in disgust. "Let's go see what we can find."

Jake and Nick followed the determined Vowellans and Brune out the back door, where Lek and Brune took a hard look at the forest that stood directly to the east of them. It was different in nature than the jungle had been. It was drier, airier, deeper green, with firm ground and taller trees. It still looked to be dense in spots, however. Lek nodded his head, recognizing the surroundings.

"Yes, this is where I entered the forest last time," confirmed Lek as he marched across the asphalt.

"And I recognize this area too. I was wandering around in there before I was suddenly taken to Vowella," added Brune. "I never came out of the forest, though. I saw these buildings from the trees, but I was too scared to step out onto the flat space to see what the area was all about."

"Follow me." Lek focused his three center eyes on the forest and marched forward with Brune. Scamper clung to the back of Brune's neck, sneaking a peek ahead now and then. Mok, Kip, Dun, and San followed closely behind. Fahbee Flingbee curiously watched from the top edge of San's coat pocket. Jake and Nick took up the rear.

Lek readily led the search team to the pond where he had first spotted the limoncinas. He crouched down and pushed aside several water lilies with his left net, searching the edges for the yellow squishy balls they so yearned to find. Colorful fish swam about, and to Fahbee's delight, numerous flingbees lounged on the rocks that edged the pond. No limoncinas, however, were to be found. Lek moved on to another nearby pond he had previously visited. There was nothing.

"I don't get it," lamented Lek. "There were big bunches of them when I was here before. I was too scared to take more than two, especially once I saw that face in the water that looked like Brune. "I didn't want anyone to know I had been here, and now they're gone."

Brune leaned over Lek, his face reflecting in the water. Lek jumped and turned, the scary flashback running through his mind.

"Jeez, Brune. Don't do that. You freaked me out."

"I'm sorry, Lek. I didn't mean to scare you. I just wanted to say that I think there are more up this way." Brune pointed northward. "I remember wandering through this area before. I know there are more ponds."

"Yes," agreed Fahbee, telling San in his tiny voice that he agreed with Brune's assessment.

Jake watched in amazement. In all his years in New Life City, he had never really paid attention to the forest behind his building. Though he had spent his career in forestry back on Earth, all he had attempted in this new world was to grow a small vegetable garden at the edge of the pavement with some of the recycled seeds that had come through the Materiality Zone. Jake watched Brune move about and wondered how long he had wandered around in his own backyard before he had landed in Vowella.

Nick was also fascinated by the scene. The Vowellans were looking for mysterious squishy yellow balls. How these objects could possibly save the folks of Vowella was mind-boggling to him. Nick had come from Earth, where science and problem solving was so much more sophisticated. He followed them through the forest to see what else might reveal itself.

Brune led them to a wide clearing where numerous ponds, all within view of each other, dotted the forest floor. They were hard to see because lush ferns and water grasses camouflaged them quite nicely. Lek hadn't ventured this far north on his "city day," so he was equally fascinated by the new territory before them.

The team spread out within the clearing and headed toward the various ponds. Mok and Kip wandered to the east side while Dun and Brune headed west. Nick and Jake hung back on the southern side to observe and add their assistance if needed. San and Lek worked their way around the ponds on the north side, where Fahbee settled onto a nearby flat rock that just happened to be occupied by a handful of lounging female flingbees.

"Aah, what beauties I see here. How fortunate to have happened upon you. May I join you, dear ones, on this lovely day of relaxation?" inquired Fahbee of the huddle of colorful creatures. He approached them, his stride accentuating his stick figure legs, his crooked beak, and his googly eyes.

A snobby female, brilliant in her flamingo pink body and her chartreuse beak and tail, pushed her beak upward and turned her head away from him. "I don't think so, sir.

You speak strangely."

Another flingbee, of pale blue and bright orange colorings, watched his wandering eyes and shook her head. "Oh, no. You make me dizzy just looking at you. Go away."

Her tail rolled into a tight pinwheel, then sprung back to its gentle curve before she turned away from him.

"Fine, then," stated Fahbee, not shaken by their insults. He flew off knowing more sweet ladies were soon to be found.

San chuckled as he listened to Fahbee recite his flirtatious lines as well as the discouraging comments the rude little ladies had thrown his way. San decided Fahbee needed a refresher course on being romantic. The flingbee's current methods simply weren't working. Lek, having become a recent flingbee gossip fan, quizzed San about the details of the exchange and agreed with San's assessment.

San and Lek searched foliage from the pond that sat farthest north, hoping this would be the one that hid the precious limoncinas. As they leaned forward and saw their reflections in the water, a huge face showed itself between theirs. Suddenly seeing creepy eyes staring at him, Lek again jumped back and turned, anger bubbling up inside of him.

"Brune, I told you not to do that anymore. You're more than freaking me out." He took a hard look at the giant body that stood next to them and let out a curdling shriek. "AAUUGH! THIS TIME IT REALLY IS THE GIANT RUG BUM!"

San took one look at the giant figure and screamed too.

Hearing the urgent commotion, the others left their positions and rushed over. Everyone stared in awe at a big stranger who looked just like Brune but wasn't Brune. Brune was the last to arrive. He looked at the figure and ran toward him. The two wrapped giant shaggy arms around each other and sobbed on each other's shoulders. While Lek and San backed away from the surprising reunion, Mok, Dun, Kip, Jake, and Nick watched in wonder.

"Oh my goodness, oh my goodness," blubbered Brune repeatedly. "Oh my goodness."

"Dude!" hollered Dun, rushing to Brune's side, his hub caps in attack position. "Dude, what's wrong? Who is this?"

"He's my brother," sobbed Brune, his head still buried in his sibling's shoulder while Scamper scurried over, under, and around their heads.

Everyone closed in. Kip placed her tiny hand on Brune's calf. "Brune, are you all right?"

Brune, still leaning on his brother's shoulder, turned his head to look down at her. "Yes, I'm all right. I just need a minute to get past this surprise."

"Surprise, indeed!" Mok shook his head with eyes wide. He examined this new giant with great curiosity. He had never seen a being that looked exactly like another being. The only things distinguishing them were their loincloths. Such identical beings didn't exist in Vowella.

Brune detected the shock on the faces of his traveling

mates. He separated himself from the other giant, looked him straight in the eye, and let out a long, deep chuckle. He received an identical wide grin in response.

Putting his long arm around his brother's shoulder, Brune pulled him close and spoke. "Everybody, this is my brother, Krune. Krune, this is everybody."

Krune looked each individual up and down with a combination of shock and curiosity. Obviously, he had never seen creatures like the Vowellans. He was particularly drawn to Dun with his short stout body, blue fur, big muscles, and hub cap armor. He bent over Dun and gently poked at his suds spout. He pulled at the shaggy fur around Dun's ankles, which was blue instead of gray like his own. All he managed to respond with was, "Hmm." He examined Jake and Nick as though they weren't quite as strange to him.

"Krune," said Mok, taking the lead. "I'm Mok. It's so nice to meet you. Brune told us he was with his brother when he was suddenly taken from here. Have you been alone in this forest since then?"

Krune lowered his droopy eyelids and nodded sadly.

Brune again pulled him closer, his eyes still misty. "It's okay, Kruner. They don't bite. It was a long time before I felt like I could speak to them, but I'm good with it now."

Krune shot him a wounded, puzzled look. He opened his mouth, but nothing came out on the first try. On his second try, he spoke in a low tone to Brune. "Where have you been? I looked everywhere for you. How could you disappear on me like that?"

Lek and San scooted behind Jake and Nick to protect themselves from the new giant. But everyone listened closely to the conversation.

"I had nothing to do with it," said Brune with a sigh. "I was with you, and then suddenly, I was in Vowella with these nice folks. They were scary to me at first, but they've taken very good care of me. Have you been alone all this time?"

Krune nodded. "Except when the apes come around. I've been really lonely here."

Brune embraced him again. "I'm so sorry, Kruner. But I'm here now. We're all here. And you can stay with us now, right Mok?" He turned to the young Fog Bob for a reply.

"Of course," replied Mok with no hesitation. "You're welcome to join us. And perhaps you can help us with our mission."

Krune shot him a bewildered look. Brune chuckled and said, "Don't worry, Kruner, we'll tell you all about that."

"Wait, dudes," interrupted Dun as he stomped back and forth, his natural defense instincts kicking in. "We don't know him. You're just going to assume it's safe to travel with him?"

Lek vigorously nodded his head, agreeing with Dun. What? Lek was agreeing with Dun?

Brune approached Dun, towering over the feisty Rug Bum as his own protective instincts showed their face. "He's my brother, 'dude', and I say it's safe."

"All right, all right, that's enough," Mok scolded.

He directed everyone to take a break to recover from the great surprise. The team sat in a small clearing beyond the pond at which they had been standing. Brune introduced his team mates individually to Krune. Brune wanted his brother to feel as comfortable around them as he felt.

The team members had a million questions to ask Krune, but Mok reminded them of their current priorities and promised that there would be time later to discover all there was to know about the Huge Dude brothers. He suggested they report back to the ponds to which they had been assigned to resume their hunt for the limoncinas.

Jake and Nick crouched down next to the southern pond. They weren't quite sure what they were looking for, except that the objects were round, squishy, hairy, and yellow. They had yet to see a live limoncina. Nick thought he spotted something hiding under a lily pad in the northwest corner of the pond, but as he headed around the left side, something clicked somewhere above him. He stood and searched the branches of the tall trees that towered over them. He thought he saw a furry hind end slip behind a large branch.

"Hey, Brune," Nick hollered to Brune, who was searching on the west side. "Where's your little monkey?"

"She's wandering around on Krune's shoulders," Brune replied. "Why?"

"Oh, I thought she might have been up in a tree over here. I thought I just saw a monkey butt up there. Oh, wait. This butt didn't have a tail. Your monkey has a tail, right?"

"Yep, a real curly one."

"Okay, never mind." Nick turned back to the pond.

With fanned ears suddenly standing at attention, San straightened his back from its curled pose at the northern pond that he and Lek were investigating. Muffled laughter filled his ears. "Who's laughing?" he hollered to the others.

"Nobody here," hollered Mok from the east side. He frowned at the question. "Do you really hear laughing?"

"Yeah, I do'dl. It's coming from the trees above us. Do you see anything up there now, Uncle Nick-ood'ly? I have no view-ood'ly from where I'm standing."

On the west side, Krune flashed Brune a puzzled look and asked, "Why does he talk like that? Is there something wrong with his tongue?"

Brune chuckled. "No, it's just a Ham Bat thing. They all talk with ood'lies."

Krune stared at San with curious eyes. "Okay, then."

Nick moved and strained to see beyond the crisscrossed branches above him. "Wait, I do see something. There is some kind of creature way up there. Oh, wait! I might be seeing things, but it appears to be wearing a hat."

Mok's ears perked up, and his eyes widened. "Does it look like a top hat?"

"I think so, as a matter of fact." Nick shook his head. Jake shook his as well. They were reminded that Heaven's Wait was amazing in so many ways. There was usually sense to be made of things in this land, though it often came about in the oddest of ways. But they wouldn't have thought that a creature wearing a top hat in a forest would be part of their PLOM experience. Such behavior belonged in fantasy novels.

Dun, who hadn't been paying much attention to the conversation, suddenly called out, "YO, DUDES!"

He ran back and forth at the edge of the large pond on the west side, clanging his hub caps, to express his excitement. "Bingo, baby! I found some limoncinas."

Except for Nick, the search team rushed to the pond where Dun celebrated. Nick stayed back to keep an eye on the hatted creature, who was suddenly less important.

"There they are!" yelled Lek, excitement spilling from his three words.

"Yep, there they are," repeated Brune. He clapped his giant hands together and belted out a deep laugh that the others had never before heard from him. Krune followed suit.

Mok bent his knees to sit on his heels, his round flat feet keeping him in balance. He exhaled a sigh of relief as he witnessed dozens of limoncinas in clusters at the pond's edge beneath the surface of the water. They were plump and healthy looking, hairy for sure, and bright yellow in color. They bobbed and floated, as water balloons would.

Mok's emotions flooded him when he realized that the odd objects that could possibly bring about the solution to the Vowellans' greatest challenge were actually sitting in front of him.

"Oh my, oh my, oh my," he couldn't stop saying. A tear ran down his right cheek. In a whisper, he confirmed to himself, "We found them, Moms, Papa Pol. We'll be back with them real soon."

Kip, with radar on his emotions, hurried to him to provide some comfort. But Mok breathed deeply to gather his composure, rose to a stand, and switched back to leadership mode.

"Okay, guys. This is what we came here for. Dun, do you have the cases we brought with us?"

"Right here, boss," said Dun. He pulled a handful of softly padded woven pillowcases from his backpack. The cases were what Kip's mom usually used as laundry bags. Niv had suggested to Mok that they use them to cushion the limoncinas during the transport process.

Lek and San pinched their lips together to keep from giggling when they heard Dun call Mok "boss." They had never thought they would hear that word come from a Rug Bum's mouth.

The comment slipped right by Mok, whose brain was working at a most efficient pace. He turned his attention to the fidgety Net Ken, who was just itching to get to work. "Lek. Are you ready to do some dipping and scooping?"

"Yes, sir," answered Lek enthusiastically. He gave Mok a funny looking salute with his netted right hand. "I'm all about dipping and scooping, you know."

"Yes, I know." Mok turned to Kip. "Punkee, would you please help me transfer the limoncinas from Lek's nets to the cases?"

"Of course." Kip smiled up at Mok with her puffy yellow lips. "I knew we'd find the limoncinas."

"Yeah, I did too." Mok grinned back, catching a brief glance at her kaleidoscopic eyes.

"Uh-oh," interrupted San, his fanned ears flapping back and forth. "The laughing is coming back-ood'ly. Uncle Nick, is that top-hatted thing-ood'ly coming closer?"

"No, he's still sitting in the same spot in that tree up there," hollered Nick as he pointed toward the east, where the creature had yet to move.

Jake hurried over to Nick.

"Whoa," warned San. He covered his ears with his chubby hands. "I hear a lot of laughing, and it's getting closer."

Mok turned and searched the canopy above them. "I think we should get these limoncinas out of here as fast as we can. Come on, Lek. Start scooping."

Lek knelt at the pond's edge and dipped and scooped at a rapid pace. The limoncinas easily detached from their vines. Mok and Kip hurriedly emptied his limoncina-filled nets into the cases. Dun, Brune, and Krune moved in behind them to stand guard. They watched the surrounding trees and listened intently.

The laughing was eventually audible to everyone. San lifted the earmuffs from around his neck onto his sensitive ears. Lek, Mok, and Kip stayed on task while the others cautiously watched and listened. The original laughter from the east was joined by separate laughter from the west and by even more laughter from the north. Soon, a chorus encircled the pond area and closed in on the search team. Jake gasped when he spotted three very large gorilla-like creatures sitting together high in a tree on the west side of the pond, limoncinas in hand. He gasped again when he spotted five more in the north side trees, also with limoncinas in hand. All the creatures comfortably lounged on high, sturdy branches. All of them wore top hats of different sorts. All of them curiously watched the team at work while pointing fingers at them and laughing out loud.

"What the heck?" Jake observed the scene in disbelief. He spoke in a soft voice barely audible to Nick. "In all my years in New Life City, I've never known these creatures were here. They look like gorillas, but they're different. Their faces are shiny black, and their bodies are furry like gorillas. But their feet are flat and floppy, kind of like Fog Bobs."

One of the creatures on the east side removed his top hat to scratch the top of his head. Nick joined the conversation in a whisper. "Yeah and look at that one. His ears are tall and pointy like a rabbit's."

"Yes, they're gorrabbobs, like in the old stories about Mr. PLOM," added Mok, who spoke while he continued his work. "We came across one in the jungle. It stole my top hat."

"Yes, these guys are Pa's gorrabbobs," decided Jake. "Pa told us he had been captured by such creatures when he got lost in the jungle so many years ago. RJ and I thought he was delusional after his difficult journey. Wow, looks like they were real after all."

"But that's impossible," hollered San from his position. "There's no way-ood'ly that the gorrabbob-ood'ly that took your top hat-ood'ly could be here. We would have seen it on the flat space."

"And why would it leave the jungle for wide open space anyway? This is really odd," remarked Mok.

"And what about the other top hats?" whispered Nick. "How would they ever get their hands on those unless they sneaked into the Top Hattery in New Life City? This is odd for sure."

"I wish RJ were here to see this," added Jake.

"So do I," interrupted Mok as he carried a full pillowcase over to them. "What do you think, Uncle Jake? Do they seem aggressive?"

"I don't think so," interrupted Krune with a surprise response. He shot the gorrabbobs on the west side an intent stare. "I've been dealing with them while I've been here in the forest. I think they are harmless for the most part. You just have to show them who's boss."

Krune faced the west side creatures, took an authoritative stance, and placed his hands on his hips. The gorrabbobs stopped their laughing, cocked their heads to the side, and stared at him to find out what might come next. When Krune turned toward the creatures on the north side, they stopped and stared while the west side creatures resumed their pointing and laughing. "I think they're all talk and no action. Just don't mess with their top hats," Krune added.

"But look-ood'ly," added San, who had simply been observing the scene. He pointed out the gorrabbobs who were clutching yellow orbs. "They have their own stash-ood'ly of limoncinas. The nectar takes you to a happy place. And they're in a happy place-ood'ly right now. Let's be glad about that."

Mok observed the scene in amazement. "Well, as much as I'd love to stay and discover more about these creatures, I say let's hurry and finish up here, just in case they do decide to act. We need to get back to Vowella." He turned toward Kip. "Punkee, how many limoncinas did Bek say we needed to bring back?"

"Sixty," Kip was quick to reply. "How many do we have so far?"

"Seventy," offered Lek while he kept at his task.

"Okay, a few more won't hurt," decided Mok. "Let's wrap things up."

"Just a few more," Lek picked up from the conversation. "Just a few more. Just a few more."

Lek continued to dip and scoop until Mok and San had to physically stop him by grabbing his arms and pulling him away from the pond. Lek's obsessive-compulsive tendencies, a little less prevalent these days, had hit high gear.

While the team worked at wrapping up their tasks, the gorrabbobs, from high in their trees, continued their seemingly harmless harassment. But when Mok and his crew started to move southward, away from the pond clearing, three of the nearest gorrabbobs climbed down from their trees and rapidly approached the group. They ran circles around the team while grunting and chattering at them. Krune, more acquainted with their behavior, spoke to the team in a low voice. "Just be still. Let them do what they want to do. They'll soon back off and go away."

But they didn't go away. They zoomed in on San and approached him with curious, quite mean-looking eyes. Fahbee shriveled into a ball within San's pocket, deeply hoping not to be discovered.

San's eyes bulged when he noticed the long, razor-sharp nails at the ends of the gorrabbobs' ugly black fingers. He trembled like he had never trembled before.

One of the gorrabbobs stood eye to eye with San, his foul breath, much like the Rug Bums' bug juice breath, washing over San's face. The creature inspected the jungle-stained fishing hat that sat on San's head. It cocked its head from side to side, as though deciding whether to confiscate it or not. It finally nodded a "yes" to itself and snatched the hat from his head with one of its mean nails. It backed away from San, and the three satisfied gorrabbobs hurried back to their trees. Their mission was complete. They had secured a unique addition to their hat collection.

And so stood San, shivering and standing embarrassed because he had wet his pants during the confrontation. He peeked over at Lek, who had done the same. They could do no more than notice and grin at each other. The others, more concerned with the trees filled with gorrabbobs, gave a collective sigh of relief and quickly moved southward, away from the ponds.

CHAPTER 18

Ready to Go Home

Mok stared through the window of Jake's office at the shiny city standing so majestically in the distance. Kip stood by his side, looking up at his face, wondering what was going on in his head.

"We did it, Munkee," she said in a quiet voice as she slipped her tiny hand into his. "We finally have the limoncinas in hand. You should be so proud. You've been a great leader, and we got the job done. Now, it's time go home and help our kin."

Mok continued to stare at the city. "Yes, we did well. But Punkee, look at that out there. I need to know more. It's difficult to think we're leaving New Life City without having a chance to explore all of the wondrous things that undoubtedly happen there. Returning to the valley is paramount, but I need to learn what else exists in the world of Heaven's Wait. Did you see how hard it was to drag obsessive-compulsive Lek from the limoncina pond? I feel like you need to drag me away from this place. Reading about foreign places like this just won't do it for me anymore. I want to find out why limoncinas grow in those ponds. I want to know why the gorrabbobs in the forest are wearing top hats. I want to explore places like this city in person. I want to meet the folks who live there. I want to learn about new environments and how things work within them."

"I know, Munkee. And you will someday. I know it." Kip leaned her curly mop of hair against his arm. "We can come back with Mr. RJ when the trouble has passed. But for now, we need to concentrate on our return trip. We can't help the folks back home until we get there."

Mok looked down to her and listened to her sensible words. "You're right, Punkee. Of course, you're right, as usual. Promise me you'll come with me to explore new things someday?"

Kip spread her puffy yellow lips into a happy grin. "I can't wait."

Mok glanced around at his teammates. He was pleased that they were able to return to the valley with an abundance of limoncinas. He hoped that, once the bug problem was eliminated, there would be extra limoncinas, so all the townsfolk would have a chance to spoil their taste buds with the heavenly flavor that San and Great Grandpa Jok raved about.

Jake decided he should stay in the city with Auntie Bess. "You know, at my age, I don't know how much I can do to help the cause in Vowella. And it won't help matters if I get stung and end up in a deep sleep like RJ. I think I'll take on the project of studying the gorrabbobs' behavior after you all leave, especially since they're not that far away. I can get help from some of my buddies in the city. Krune was right about those top-hatted critters that interrupted our work. They made a lot of noise, but they really were no threat to any of us. They just wanted a new hat."

San and Lek shot them looks that questioned Jake's analysis.

"Well, Uncle Jake, I promise that someday I'll return to the forest too, to find out why the gorrabbobs wear top hats. It's such a Fog Bob thing to do, and I need to make sense of it." Mok was adamant about his commitment.

"Not me," offered San.

"Me either," added Lek.

Jake's face wrinkled into a frown as he looked from young face to young face. "I can't lie. I'm worried about you kids. I want you to take every precaution there is and remain strong. As with any major challenge, you have to work your way through the hard parts and, eventually, there will be an end to it. I believe in all of you. And when it's all over, Auntie Bess and I will fly to the valley with fresh batches of doughboys and limoncinas, now that I know what and where those squishy yellow things are."

Each teammate grinned at the thought, even Krune, who wasn't quite sure he understood all that Jake meant.

"Don't worry, Uncle Jake. We Rug Bums will fight those dang drill bugs with everything we have," proclaimed Dun. "The sooner we do it, the sooner we'll get doughboys again."

Everyone chuckled at Dun's end goal.

"Well, I'm going with you," announced Nick to the

teens. "I want to do what I can to help. Now that a decent trail runs through Jimmy's Jungle, I don't need to concern myself with how Pa PLOM aged during his time in the jungle way back in his day. And besides, I think I need to witness the battle against the drill bugs using limoncina-gum, of all things. So, hold tight and wait for me. I'll be right back."

Nick hurried out the office door and hopped into his van.

Mok and Lek tried to chase after him, knowing this would be a chance for Mok to see the city up close and for Lek to get an eyeful of the collectible "stuff" that was surely there. But Nick was too quick for them. He zoomed off toward the city to take care of a few details, since there was no way to know how long he would be gone.

He reappeared about 45 minutes later with several items he thought might be useful: new rolls of wire mesh, several bolts of Teflon-coated fabric (so protective suiting could be made for Brune and Krune), several more pre-made Teflon overalls and hoods for the Vowellans, a pile of shiny new hubcaps for the Rug Bums to use in battle, and two sets of giant hubcaps from monster trucks for the Huge Dude brothers. Nick had also managed to collect a dozen new sets of earmuffs for the Ham Bats, a file to sharpen Lek's worn clippers, a new blanket for Kip, a new fishing hat for San, and two stylish new top hats for Mok. Nick felt that the official "captain" of the team deserved to be properly attired in Fog Bob fashion, even though he knew that "proper" was way down the list of priorities these days. Mok promptly shed the soiled bandanna that had protected his scalp through the latter part of their journey through the jungle and plopped a shiny new blue silk top hat onto his head. He expelled a relieved sigh that made everyone grin.

Nick had also remembered to grab some gallon containers of gasoline for the vehicles that were to make the return journey. Jake suggested that Nick drive the flatbed truck back through the jungle to Vowella. "That way, there will be plenty of room for supplies and the Huge Dudes."

Brune and Krune, who would otherwise have to walk the entire way back to town, nodded approval of that suggestion.

Once the Bucket and the flatbed were ready to leave the airport, Jake leaned in the right front window of the Bucket, where Mok sat. "Give that brother of mine a big hug for me when you see him. When he hears about the fine job you've done, he'll be so proud. You're a good one, Mr. Mok. Good luck to you all. Let me know when it's over."

Mok grinned at Jake and nodded. Signaling Lek with his left index finger, he and the team began their trip back to Vowella and the great challenge that surely awaited them.

CHAPTER 19

New Jungle Challenges

Traveling back through Jimmy's Jungle was a new experience for the young Vowellans and the others. As they rode along in the Bucket, they admired the high, straight walls of foliage they had carved on either side of their freshly blazed path. The fairly smooth ground, now free of gnarled roots and packed with cuttings that Brune had stomped into holes and crevices to reduce the ruts, carried the vehicles quite easily. Lek and Nick had to carefully navigate the vehicles through the deserted snake pit section of road, however, since the team had not lingered to fix the path after their scary snake episode. Mok eyed their progress and determined that, at the rate they were going, they would be back home in a few short hours.

Mok tried his radio as they rode along, but only static came back at him.

"The airspace must still be too crowded with drill bugs to let the signal through, Munkee," said Kip in an advising tone. "Just put the radio down. We'll be there soon enough."

He frowned at her and tried a few more times before relenting and placing it on the floor by his feet.

"I don't know about you guys, but I'm kind of freaked out right now," confessed Lek, fidgeting in his seat. His long purple fingers clenched the steering wheel, causing him to over-steer and occasionally bump up against the jungle walls. "What if the bugs have attacked more folks? What if they've destroyed our stuff? What if they've gotten into the Fig Wig Bin? How is this silly Limoncina juice going to save our town?"

"Aw, get it together, eyeball man. You're losing it, and your crazy driving is freaking ME out," hollered Dun from the back seat. "I need to get back to Uncle Pun and the other Bums."

"Come on, Lekee," added San, while Fahbee's head poked out from his pocket. "I'm already worried about Jaz-ee and Pazee and my dad-ood'ly and everyone else-ood'ly. You're not helping matters with your fidgeting."

Kip, from her position between Lek and Mok in the front seat, placed a calming hand on Lek's right arm. "You know what, Lekee, we're going to be back home before we know it. You'll be able to see the situation for yourself. We can't change anything from where we sit. The best thing you can do is keep on driving and remember we're bringing back help for our families and our town. You're doing great."

"Okay, okay, you're right. I'm getting ahead of myself. I'm sorry, guys," said Lek with a deep sigh. He relaxed his fingers around the steering wheel. "You know me and my obsessive brain. I'll do better now. I promise."

Mok grinned at Lek and then at Kip. He was glad she had handled the situation because deep inside, he struggled with his own fears. He was the one everyone was looking to for answers. He was supposed to be the leader, the strong one. But deep inside, he knew he was just an inexperienced teenage boy, his mother's child. And this had been his first journey away from home. He couldn't wait to get back to her.

The team rolled into the clearing that had been their last campsite before breaking through the jungle. There was nothing special about it, so they moved on.

Before long, they came upon the magical clearing, the one that had been full of colored sunbeams, partying flingbees and eventually, dreaded fog. The space seemed strangely lifeless. It made Fahbee stand up on San's shoulder in the backseat of the Bucket and take notice.

Fahbee paced back and forth before coming to a stop. "Something's not right here, Señor. I don't know what it is, but I don't feel good about it."

"Mok," San called from the backseat. "Fahbee thinks something's not right here-ood'ly. Does anything look weird-ood'ly from up there?"

"It's hard to tell," replied Mok. His feeling of urgency to get back to town battled his curiosity. "Lek, pull over to the left here for just a minute. We'll quickly look around."

He and Dun hopped out of the Bucket. Nick and Brune joined them from the flatbed. Krune stayed on the bed, feeling unsure about these new surroundings. The jungle was quite different from the forest in which he had been living.

"What's up?" asked Nick, concern all over his face.

"I don't know," Mok said as he scanned the area. "Fahbee has a bad feeling about this place. It was a great stop for us the other night, but something does seem a bit off."

"OH NO," yelled Fahbee right in San's unprotected ear. "Look, it's Lucinda. See, on the ground over there?"

He left San's shoulder and flew out the open car door, landing at her side. She lay still in a ball next to several other limp flingbees.

"Oh, no, Señor, what has happened to them?" he continued to holler.

San scooted out of the car and hurried to Fahbee's side. "Hey guys, look at this!"

The others had already exited the vehicles. They crowded around the disabled flingbees.

Mok crouched down and gently scooped tiny Lucinda into his long fingers. She looked like a precious flingbee doll, sleeping in a fairytale. Mok lifted his open hand to his face and examined her through his spectacles. Her tiny legs gave a couple of barely visible twitches and her belly's slight movements provided some proof of life.

Fahbee flew onto Mok's hand and settled down next to Lucinda. He stroked her colorful body with his delicate wing and spoke to her softly. "It's okay, my precious. You'll be okay. I'll take good care of you."

"She's still breathing," said Mok to the concerned flingbee. "We'll take her and the others back with us. I'll have Papa Pol take a look at them. Hopefully, he can help them."

"Oh, thank you, Señor Mok. I am most grateful." Of course, San had to relay Fahbee's response to Mok since all he could hear was a buzzing sound.

While that scene played out, Dun and Brune tromped around the clearing, hoping to figure out why the place seemed so different.

"Hey, Mok!" hollered Dun from the west side. "It's like there's no life here anymore, dude. There are no birds singing, no monkeys calling, no bugs buzzing."

"Yes, and it looks like all those pretty flowers that were here have been drained of their moisture. They're limp on the ground," added Brune.

"It's just dead here," Dun continued to report. "What do you think happened?"

"Do you think the drill bugs have been here?" asked Brune without hesitation.

Mok's body stiffened, and he handed Fahbee and Lucinda over to San. He hopped over to where Dun and Brune stood. "Why do you say that, Brune?"

"Well, I get the feeling they want to destroy anything that's pure or beautiful," said Brune thoughtfully.

Mok's eyes widened with acknowledgment. "Yes, what could be purer than a thriving jungle, a native flower, an innocent flingbee, an isolated community or Kip's beautiful voice? Well, if that's the case, we should get back to the cars and make sure your coveralls and hoods are zipped up tight. San, you're in charge of the flingbees. Punkee, it's time for you to go silent again. Dun and Lek, see what you can do to wrap that Teflon fabric around Brune and Krune to protect them. Uncle Nick, you'd best suit up and lock yourself in your truck until we find out what's going on for sure. Keep Scamper inside with you. Who knows what else those nasty critters may be able to do to harm us."

"Don't worry about me now, Mok. Let's just keep going and see what we find." Nick kept a calm sense of adventure about him.

Once they felt that the Huge Dudes were sufficiently protected in the open bed of Nick's truck, the caravan resumed its journey. The Bucket paused twice along the trail to pick up colorful clusters of limp flingbees that Mok spotted on protruding palm leaves.

Mok could feel his body tensing as they made their way closer to Vowella. He hoped he was strong enough to handle what might lie ahead. From the seat next to him, Kip sensed his stiffness and reached up to massage his taut shoulder.

"Munkee, keep your focus now. We're almost there. You know I'm here with you every step of the way," Kip said in her quietest whisper. Her turquoise eyes sparkled at him. Her yellow lips spread into a comforting grin.

Mok turned and returned an understanding grin. He leaned in and whispered to her, "I know, Punkee. That's just why I brought you with me. Somehow, you know the right things to say. Look how you helped Lek. You know that the unknown is the scariest thing. And the unknown ahead of us is huge. I guess all we can do is dive into it headfirst and deal with the consequences once we get there."

"That's right, Munkee. One step at a time. My papa always told me, 'Don't project an outcome. It's a waste of time and worry. Tackle the challenges as they come and manage the consequences when the need arises.'"

"Very wise words, Punkee. I'll remember that." The tender look between each other expressed a deep love that was steadily growing.

As the caravan pulled into the familiar home clearing of Jimmy's Jungle, the team was shocked to find the '54 Chevy sitting quietly in the center, its doors wide open. Again, the surroundings were dead quiet. Again, there were no signs of movement. Mok, stunned and confused, stared at the Chevy and thought hard.

"Okay, you guys. If you get out of the car, be careful until we figure out what's going on here," warned Mok. "Punkee, you need to stay inside. And continue to be silent."

Kip's eyes widened as she nodded her agreement.

"Hey, boss, I'm going to run out to the gum trees to see if Bek is there," announced Dun. "I'll take Brune and Krune with me."

"And I'll head over to the waterfalls," suggested Lek. "Maybe Jen and Nel are there making themselves beautiful."

Nick climbed out of the flatbed, appropriately suited in a set of protective overalls from his New Life City purchase. "Hold on, Lek. I'll go with you."

I'll stay here," suggested Mok. "Give a holler if you find anything."

As the others took off toward their respective destinations, Mok hopped over to the Chevy to check it out. San stayed in the Bucket with Kip to keep an eye on the flingbees. He had made them a cozy home within the bandanna Mok had worn when his top hat had been stolen. The flingbees still lay limp and practically motionless. Fahbee moved from flingbee to flingbee, gently stroking them with his translucent wings and humming soothing arias.

The Chevy was fully intact. Nothing was out of place. There were no signs of damage, but Mok found it odd that the car doors were wide open. He inspected the surrounding airspace. There was no indication that drill bugs were around. As he looked up farther through the canopied trees, however, he did notice that the sky seemed to be darker than it had been previously. He shivered at the thought that the drill bugs had found their way this far north. Mok's attention turned to the west when he heard Dun suddenly call out.

"Boss, boss, we're coming back. We have Bek." Dun's voice was tight with anxiety.

"What do you mean, you have Bek?" Mok hollered back.

Brune broke into the clearing in a run, holding Bek, limp and draped over his arms. Dun followed behind with something in his arms as well. Brune gently placed Bek on the ground in the clearing next to the Chevy. Mok knelt over him and examined him. Bek's forearm was badly swollen, as was the back of his normally thin neck. He was not wearing his protective gear.

"Those drill bugs got to him, didn't they?" Brune tilted his head back and sighed in frustration.

"It appears so," said Mok with a similar sigh. He stood and faced Brune. "Please get him in the cab of the truck, Brune. We need to get him home."

Brune hurried to obey the order, carefully lifting Bek and placing him in the flatbed cab.

Mok then looked toward Dun, and a wave of sadness washed down his entire body. Dun held a lifeless gorrabbob in his arms, the very one that had stolen Mok's top hat. His hat sat on the creature's chest.

"He's gone, dude. Look! There are five drill bugs stuck in his butt. Poor bugger! I wouldn't wish that on anyone." Dun expressed more compassion than Mok had ever known him capable of.

"That is very sad," said Mok. "Dun, will you stay behind and bury him? I don't want him to be left out for the drill bugs to further pick at. One of us will wait for you at the tunnel entrance."

"Will do! I'm protected. I can easily walk back to the tunnel entrance and meet you back in town later." Dun extended the body and the top hat toward Mok. "Here, take your hat back."

"No, please bury it with him," said Mok as he turned away. "It was important to him."

Dun nodded and headed back down the coffee tree trail.

"Hey, Mok!" yelled Nick from the opposite

direction. "Come quickly. We have Jen and Nel over here."

Mok and Brune hurried to the path that led to the waterfalls. They found Nick and Lek halfway along the path. Brune rushed to relieve Lek of Nel's weight. Lek had barely been able to manage her tall, rubbery body. Brune ran back to the clearing with her, while Krune took Jen from Nick. Both girls were unconscious with swollen stings on their legs. They were also without their coveralls.

Lek stood over the two Net Ken girls. He stomped his feet three times. "They just assumed it was safe out here, didn't they? Darn girls and their need to be beautiful!"

"Listen! I'll ride back in the flatbed so Jen and Nel can fit into the Bucket." Mok paced a few seconds, then continued. "We need to leave now. There's no telling how long Bek and the girls have been out here like this. Even better, let's squeeze Bek into the Bucket too. That way, Lek, you can get Kip, San, and the three of them back to town for treatment while the rest of us make a stop at the tunnel entrance to wire it up."

"Good idea, boss," said Dun, glad to rejoin the group before they departed. "I was going to tell you. There were hundreds of drill bugs stuck in Uncle Pun's gum trees where we found Bek. Those nasty things are definitely around."

"Yeah, well, let's hope they haven't already found their way into the tunnel," said Mok with a deep frown. "We'd better get going."

Brune and Krune loaded the Net Kens into the back

seat of the Bucket. Kip scooted next to Lek in the front seat to make room for San to squeeze in. Brune had to use more force than he anticipated in order to close the car door, due to San's wide body.

Mok hopped around to the driver's side to speak to Kip, who was squashed between Lek and San. "Punkee, we won't be far behind you. Get Bek, Jen, and Nel to my dad and your mom right away. Make sure my mom gets the limoncinas and bring the flingbees to Papa Pol. Once we cover the tunnel entrance with wire mesh, we'll be right down, okay?"

Kip nodded, her eyes shining at him. In her softest whisper, she mouthed, "Be careful, Munkee. I need you, you know."

"I need you too." Mok fought to swallow the lump in his throat. They squeezed each other's hands as Lek started up the Bucket and slowly rolled away with their terribly ill friends.

"Come on, Mok," hollered Nick from the flatbed. "Time to get that tunnel covered."

Mok nodded. He and Dun hopped into the cab of the truck while Brune and Krune jumped into the flatbed. Nick headed toward their next chore. It was more than time to be back home, and it was finally time to face the enemy.

CHAPTER 20

Revisiting the Plan

Mok, Dun, and Nick rode in the flatbed's cab while Brune and Krune walked behind them. The tunnel's ceiling wasn't tall enough to allow the Huge Dude brothers to ride on the truck's bed. Nick was struck by the overwhelming sense of gloom within the tunnel, which had become the unintended home of the Vowellans. Mok and Dun also felt the gloom. Clusters of folks huddled together along the sides of the main tunnel. Sparse lanterns lit the passageway. The air was heavy with a stale, damp smell. It felt as though someone was trying to suffocate them with a thick, black blanket. The team had just visited an amazing new world, where they had witnessed wondrous sights. Now, to return to the reality of the Vowellans' present existence, which was so far detached from the colorful, animated life they were used to, was both heartbreaking and frightening.

When the flatbed reached the operations station, Mok jumped out of the cab and hugged his mom for a long time. Dun headed toward the Fig Wig Bin to visit his family members. Brune took Krune to the guard post at the school tunnel, where the town's animals seemed to be unattended. Mok and Nick settled in at the operations table to catch up on the current status in Vowella.

"It hasn't been an easy time since you left, babe," started Roz. "The many folks who have been stung are taking so long to get to the point where we can put them into hibernation."

"You mean no one has been put into hibernation yet?" Mok's disappointment was all over his face.

"No, babe. We need to do it in one shot. Once we seal the Net Ken tunnel, we can't reopen it until it's safe outside. Otherwise, folks will be going in and out of consciousness, and that's no good."

Nick nodded at the logic of it all. Mok tipped his head back and sighed.

"There are still dozens of folks being cared for in the Fig Wig Bin. Your dad, Niv, and the other caregivers are finding it difficult and exhausting to keep up with it all. We were counting on Bek, Jen, and Nel to help when they got back. But now, with their new stings, we've had to add them to the caseload. Jes left her post here as soon as the Net Ken kids arrived. They're her family, and they're likely to need intense care for quite a while, considering the unknown length of time they were lying untreated in the jungle.

"And when you left for the jungle, Dok, Kan Ham Bat, and Bun Rug Bum were strong and able. Dok was a big help here at the desk. But they're all down now with stings too. A few stray drill bugs found their way into the main tunnel through the jungle entrance this morning before you had a chance to secure it. As a result, I've been here alone at the desk; Jan Ham Bat is alone to prepare food; and the Rug Bum guards are short another body."

"Well," Nick added. "Chances are, there are a few more of those clever bugs hiding in dark corners somewhere, waiting for a chance to pounce on new victims."

"And what about the bug cloud, Moms? I assume it's still hanging thick over the valley," asked Mok.

"Yes, Tug and Gun have been checking on it regularly through the Rug Bum trap door," advised Roz. "No one down here has done anything to cause a fuss, so the cloud is just sitting in wait."

Mok nodded and took a seat behind the command desk.

Ahead of Roz's Vowella update, Kip had returned to her nursing duties at the Fig Wig Bin, her voice silent, her mouth pressed shut. San and Lek had hurried the limp flingbees to Dr. Pol's lab for examination. He had determined that the tiny creatures were mainly suffering from exhaustion and that a good dose of sleep would cure them. They hadn't been stung, and Lucinda had regained partial consciousness. Therefore, San and Lek had brought them to the Ham Bat tunnel to be cared for by a couple of able Ham Bat teens. Fahbee had stayed on with the recovering flingbees, insisting that he serve as their personal guard. Once San and Lek had had a chance to visit their ill relatives at the Fig Wig Bin, they had returned to the Ham Bat tunnel to help Jan with community meals.

Nick moved on to take care of storing the flatbed, which he loaded with various supplies. He drove it back to the north end of the main tunnel, so it would be out of the way. He then returned to the central station on foot and from there, he moved on to the Fig Wig Bin. Nick put a smile on many a groggy Vowellan face within the Bin. He sat with the deeply sleeping RJ for a short while, then checked in with Niv to see how he could be of the most help.

Somewhat encouraged by the progress of his ill Rug Bum kin, Dun left the Bin to run down to the Rug Bum tunnel to catch up with his clan regarding battle preparations. He also recruited a few Bums to sweep the tunnels another time for stray bugs.

The research lab was dead quiet. Aside from a couple of lamps to illuminate the room, no clues suggested it was operational. Shadows filled the corners. Heat failed to flow from the vents. Only the figure of Pol Fog Bob leaning over his desk, picking at a drill bug carcass with a pair of tweezers, animated the room, which was heavy with a skunk-like smell.

"Papa Pol, it's so good to see you." Mok hopped up to his grandfather's desk and affectionately patted him on the shoulder with one hand while he covered his nose with the other. Roz came around Pol's other side and patted him as well.

Upon Pol's realization that Mok was standing next

to him, he surprised them both by popping out of his chair and wrapping Mok in a huge bear hug, which was so uncharacteristic of him. Pol held him long and tight before releasing him and saying, "Oh, ho, ho, good to see you too, Mok-Mok. I'm so glad you're safe. You did a fine job of getting those limoncinas back here intact. Looks like we have more than enough to mix with the amount of gum we now possess."

"Thanks, Papa." Mok stood stunned at his grandfather's gesture. Never in his lifetime had he seen Pol demonstrate any affection toward anyone. He had always been so serious, distant, and buried in his work. Mok fought back the tears that were burning his eyes and took advantage of the moment to hug him hard in return.

Roz's hand flew to her mouth as she witnessed the unexpected exchange. Moisture glistened in her eyes as well.

Mok's thoughts suddenly returned to the present, and his brain spun with questions. "So, you have the formula down for the gum and limoncina. You've calculated how much bait we need to attract the mass of bugs in the sky. How are we going to handle the actual mixing of all that bait? By the way, can you tell if the bug cloud has grown at all?"

"I don't think it has. Tug has been keeping a close eye on it. He sneaked out to the tennis court site yesterday and grabbed several surveying tools that Nick left there. The cloud may have even shrunk a little. While you were gone, we captured a substantial number of bugs with the bait from Lek's two limoncinas."

"But not enough yet, huh, Papa?" asked Mok.

"Not enough, Mok-Mok," agreed Dr. Pol.

"Well, the cloud may also seem a little smaller because of the drill bugs that found their way into the jungle."

"True." Pol went back to picking at his sample drill bug. "Since you've been gone, the Rug Bums have been hand-mixing the bait in their bug-stomping barrels, but the process is slow. And it takes a lot of strength. That resin is tough to stir."

"Hmm. I wonder if the PLOM fruit machine could handle the stress?" said Mok, thinking out loud. "It would certainly speed up the process and save the Bums' strength."

"Well, talk to Pun. He is amazingly alert now," suggested Roz, who had simply been listening to the conversation. "His body is still quite weak, but he's certainly the guy to ask about the machine. That's one of his 'babies,' you know."

"Yeah, I know. I'll go find him right now and see what he says. Then, we need to figure out a better way to use the bait. This cookie sheet method we're using is so inefficient," said Mok with a shake of his head.

"You're right, son," agreed Dr. Pol. "If we stay on the current production pace, we could be setting bait for the next two years."

"No, that will never happen." There was no hesitation in Mok's reply. "We'll think of something."

Mok squeezed his mother's hand and instead of patting Pol's shoulder as he usually would, he stole another hug while Pol was still in the mood. He told them he would return shortly, before turning and hopping away.

The eerie quiet and dreary sight of so many disabled Vowellans within the Fig Wig "hospital" once again stunned Mok. He closed his eyes, took a deep breath, and reminded himself that he needed to stay strong and committed to the cause. He thought about Brune, who had also stayed committed. After finding Krune in the forest, Brune could have left them with the limoncinas and moved on with his brother to try to find their way back to their home. But Brune had put his personal needs aside to help the Vowellans and their cause. Mok knew that he now needed to put *his* needs and apprehensions aside and continue to serve the Vowellans to the best of his ability.

"Hello, Pops, Mrs. Jes." Mok approached Bek's cot, which sat adjacent to the center fire pit of the main room. Dr. Jon hovered over Bek while Jes sat on the ground next to him, holding his hand. "How is he doing?"

"Not good, son," answered Dr. Jon, not bothering to look up to acknowledge Mok's presence. "It's a good thing you found him when you did, but he has three stings, and he's barely breathing. It certainly would have been better if he had been treated immediately. Time will tell whether he will make it or not."

Jes lowered her head, the sides of her mouth dipping low.

"How are Jen and Nel?" Mok was afraid to ask.

"They're in better shape than poor Bek," explained Jes, "since they were each stung only once. They're pretty out of it, but they'll be okay. Lol is tending to them in Kip's room right now."

Mok shook his head at the irony of the situation. Of course, it was Lol who had to care for her perpetual tormentors.

Kip approached Mok from the rear and placed her tiny hand on his right forearm. Relief beamed from her face. She pulled a notepad and pencil from her apron pocket, quickly scribbling notes for Mok to see.

Lilla's okay now. She's waiting to go into hibernation. Papa's better too. Just talked to him.

Mok leaned down and gave her shoulders a gentle squeeze. "I'm so happy for you, Punkee." His eyes scanned the Bin before asking, "Do you know where Uncle Pun is? I hear he's alert. I need to talk to him."

In Uncle Wit's room with Lil'la and others on list for hibernation. It's the holding room for now. G.G.'s there too.
Kip's puffy yellow grin expressed her pride at being able to share the news with Mok that Dr. Jok was better.

Mok's eyes widened. He now gave her arm a gentle squeeze. He hopped off toward Wit's room, calling behind him, "Thanks, Punkee. I needed to hear that."

Kip hurried back to her room to help Lol take care of the Net Ken girls, Dok, and Kan.

Mok entered Wit's room to find Tug Rug Bum arguing with Pun and Dr. Jok. Pun sat in a chair while Dr. Jok leaned against a dresser. Tug faced his father. "Daddy,

I don't care what you say. The rules are the rules. Once you're well enough to leave here, you go into hibernation. Ol' Jud, Granny Zen, and the other Elders are willing to go. You two need to go so we don't have to worry about how you are now that we'll be busy getting rid of the drill bugs. There aren't too many of us left to take care of things."

"That's why we need to stay out, you young whippersnapper," argued old Dr. Jok. "I can help with the strategic elements of your plan, and you know darn well that your daddy knows everything there is to know about how everything works around here."

Tug's arms flew above his head as he hollered at them. Bubbles spewed from his suds spout. "Hey, I'm just doing what I'm told, and I'm telling you, you two are going into hibernation as soon as it's ready."

"Now, that's ridiculous," Pun hollered back. "That's my gum you're using out there, and there's no way I'm going to sleep through all the action. You have a few screws loose if you think that's the case. Now, I can see where ol' Jok here needs to go because he's an Elder and all and needs to be protected, but--"

"Don't you try to push me into hibernation, Pun Rug Bum," yelled Dr. Jok. "Yes, I'm an Elder, the oldest one to be exact. If anyone deserves to determine my welfare, it's me."

"I have to argue with you on that one, G.G.," said Mok, finally entering the exchange. He hopped up to Jok, slipped his arms under his armpits, gave him a healthy bear hug, and swung him around before placing him back on the bedroom floor. He felt incredibly grateful that his great grandfather was back to his feisty old self. "Because you're the oldest and inarguably the wisest, you are the least disposable individual I know. We need you to be around for a lot longer."

"And I will be," said Dr. Jok to everyone as he lowered his extended arms to press down the tension in the air. "Listen. I understand where you're coming from. But if I'm the wisest, then I need to stay awake so I can impart my precious wisdom upon all of you." His eyes darted from Mok to Tug to Pun. "Besides, I don't want to miss all the action either."

All Mok could do was chuckle at his dear G.G.'s fortitude.

Ol' Jok looked up at his able great grandson and grinned. "Word has it that you have been a great leader, Mok-Mok. Just like your old G.G., huh?"

Mok lowered his head and shook it from side to side. "If I could be half the leader you've always been, I'd be doing well. I've been doing the best I know how. We all have."

Mok turned toward Tug. "Tug, I'm sorry to interrupt such a good argument, but I need to ask Uncle Pun a couple of questions."

Tug, who normally would have scowled at Mok to display his tough side, simply nodded and backed away so Mok could move closer to Pun.

"Uncle Pun," asked Mok as he placed a hand on Pun's shaggy blue arm. "We're thinking about using the PLOM fruit machine to mix the limoncina nectar with the gum. Do you think the machine can handle the stress? We have lots of gum to process, and it's so tough to work with. We can't continue to mix it all by hand. Nobody knows that machine better than you do."

Pun stared at Mok's hand on his arm and thought about the question. He looked up at Mok's face, his mind still trying to figure things out. "Whoa! That's a tall order for that old machine. I don't know. Let me think about this for a minute." Pun scratched at the itchy bump that still protruded from his head. "How many pounds per hour are you cranking out right now?"

Tug stepped forward with the answer to that one. "I'd say about ten, for about ten hours a day. That stuff is tough, Daddy, and we're not used to mixing something into it."

"Yeah, I know," said Pun with a shake of his head. "At that rate, it'll take us too long to get the bait ready."

"That's what Papa Pol and I thought too," added Mok. "That's why we wondered if the machine might do better."

"I guess we can give it a try," said Pun. He shot Tug a hopeful glance. "But it will be a great strain on the machine. I want to be right next to it in case there are problems."

"Jeez, Daddy, you're just itching to be a part of this, aren't you?" Tug, now calmer than at the peak of the argument, had to chuckle.

"You bet!"

"And so am I. Mok-Mok, tell him you need me to help out," pleaded Dr. Jok. "I am not going into that hibernation tunnel. No way!"

Mok rubbed his forehead. He and Roz were the only designated decision makers at this point. "Okay, Tug. Let G.G. stay out for now. I'm sure my mom needs a bit of a break at the operations base. With him there, I'll be free to help you out at the machine, Uncle Pun. I was there when Mr. Mat got stuck in the bin, remember? I think I know a little about it."

"Ha! Yeah, I remember. Let's hope that gum doesn't give us as much trouble as Lan's purse did that day. Yep, I could use your help, especially since I'm still pretty weak."

"So, see what I mean, Daddy?" Tug's spout spewed bubbles as his stress again started festering. "Mok here doesn't need to be babysitting you."

"He ain't going to be babysitting me, boy," declared Pun. "I can take care of myself."

"Yeah, well, let's see," Tug offered. "Okay, if you two stubborn dudes won't cooperate, I'm going back to the Bum tunnel. I hear Uncle Nick brought some new hub caps that might need polishing. I'll tell the Bums to start hauling the gum up to the workroom so you can try the machine."

"You do that," hollered Pun as Tug stomped through the bedroom.

"Tug, wait!" said Mok, somewhat afraid to say his next words.

"What?" snapped Tug, stopping and turning toward Mok.

"Before you do that," said Mok hesitantly, "I need you to carry Uncle Pun down the Fig Wig ladder, then take him up to the workroom to get him situated."

Tug's brows tangled into a knot on his forehead, and a new round of bubbles shot from his spout. He turned and returned to Pun's side.

"Unbelievable!" he shouted for all in the Bin to hear.

CHAPTER 21

Strategy

From his post at the school tunnel, Brune watched Pun Rug Bum's transfer from the Fig Wig hospital to the main tunnel's floor. He watched Roz push a wheelchair from the command desk to Pun's position. He rushed to relieve Tug from his chore.

"You go on, Tug. I have him from here," Brune offered.

Tug shot Brune a tentative look, then nodded. "Thanks, dude, but we need to get him into the Ham Bats' workroom. Can you help me lift him up the ladder and all?"

"Sure thing," assured Brune.

Though it was somewhat of a struggle handling Pun's bulky body on the vertical steps, they made sure Pun became comfortably situated in the Ham Bat's workroom. The windows had been covered with protective storm panels. Tug placed him in a comfortable chair next to the PLOM fruit machine's control panel before returning to the tunnels.

Pun and Mok gave the entire machine a good greasing before they ran it through a series of mechanical tests. Were the gears turning smoothly? Did the elevator work correctly? Was the top bin free of PLOM fruit and miscellaneous debris? Was the weighing mechanism performing accurately? All of those elements mattered during the big job that was ahead of them. Pun was suddenly eager to push the machine to its limits. If everything worked as planned, he would have something to be proud of besides his secret gum tree grove.

Tug and a few of the other Bums began moving containers of gum from RJ's tunnel to the workroom, while Sun Rug Bum took on the assignment of handling the limoncinas and assisting Pun. Before Mok left Pun and Sun to do their work, he wrote them the recipe for the drill bug bait. He then set up a schedule for the Rug Bum boys to follow so that ingredients would be delivered, and bait would be picked up in a timely manner. Mok was disappointed that the forklift was still parked outside because it would have been useful in hauling their "weapon" back and forth. He advised Tug to use the Bucket, which easily fit in the main tunnel, if hand delivery became too cumbersome.

Mok made his way to the operations base in the underground rotunda in front of the Fog Bob ladder, where he found Roz, Dr. Jok, Nick, and Dr. Pol waiting for him. The time had come to make final decisions about how to best use the bait to eliminate the drill bugs.

"Please fill me in," requested old Dr. Jok, who rested in a cozy tub chair that Lek had brought to the base from the Net Ken Den. This new disaster team felt reassured to have an Elder back in the loop. "I know I missed a lot while I was sick. I know about the gum-limoncina bait. Tell me your strategy for using it."

"We have developed a few options so far," Dr. Pol told his father. Pol had spent all his time contemplating such a strategy. "What we know for sure is that the drill bugs need to be killed or driven away as quickly as possible. And though the cookie sheet method of drill bug capture works, the process is much too slow.

"While Rozee and I were here by ourselves, we experimented with another form of the bait. The Rug Bums were already catapulting huge gum balls of dead drill bugs from their trap door to the land outside. So, we tried sending clean, softball-sized balls of the mixture outside. Gun carefully peeked out of his trap door and observed the drill bugs' heavy attraction to the bait. They swarmed the balls in masses and because of the depth of the balls, their stingers penetrated much deeper than they did with the bait set in flat layers. The balls eliminated any chance that the bugs could escape the gum. We only encountered a couple of escapes with the cookie sheets, but a couple is too many. And we found that the bugs attacked the balls while they were airborne, so the probability of them approaching the trap door was significantly lessened. Gun retrieved a couple of the balls. One ball was 99 percent infested by the time it hit the ground."

"So, in theory, we could shoot bait balls straight into the bug cloud, and significant numbers of bugs would be captured before the balls returned to the ground," said Mok as his brain processed the information. "What kind of catapult mechanism did Gun use to hurl the balls?"

"At this point, it's a simple catapult with a deep cup at the end to house the balls. The Bums have been keeping the cup greased with koolibarba oil to keep the sticky balls from adhering to it. The oil doesn't seem to affect the limoncinas' potency. Once again, the method is effective, but it's much too slow," explained Dr. Pol. "Therefore, last night I designed a huge slingshot using a rubber and gum formula that I have confidence in. I have yet to test it out. If it works, I could easily make more slingshots, so we have more weapons to use for our attack."

"Well, let's test it out," suggested Nick, nodding his head enthusiastically. "I used to love firing things from slingshots in my younger days. We can practice right here at the Rug Bum end of the main tunnel. What can we do to imitate bait balls?"

"How about bags of grain, so you can add or subtract to determine the ideal firing weight for the balls?" suggested Roz.

"Yes, that's a smart approach." Nick nodded, liking how the plan was progressing.

"Before we do that, though, I think there are other factors we need to discuss," said Mok, who, along with Dr. Jok, was always looking at the bigger picture. "How quickly can the bait balls be made? From which locations should the slingshots be fired? How do we keep the stations well supplied with bait? How do we defend the stations while we are exposed? How many of us are actually available to carry out such an attack?"

"You're thinking, Mok-Mok," said Dr. Jok, nodding in agreement. He was gaining more energy by the minute as the potential battle plan was being formulated. "Thank goodness for your attention to detail. Nicky, why don't you grab Tug and Gun and do your slingshot testing? Mok, take Nak Ham Bat and scout out potential firing stations. Rozee, you and I will work on protective gear for our 'warriors.' Pol, why don't you go ahead and make us a few more slingshots? Let's meet back here in an hour."

The ever-evolving emergency team went about its business and returned to the operations base 60 minutes later with much more information in hand. Nick, Tug, and Gun determined that the slingshot was most efficient when it was hurling three-pound sacks of grain. The weight would be easy enough for the Vowellans to handle, and the spring action of the slingshot would certainly allow the gum balls to travel the distance to the ugly bug cloud. Dr. Jok and Roz redesigned the Teflon suits by adding face screens made of Nick's fine wire mesh to the hoods. Roz rushed a prototype of the hood to Niv and Wit, who took on the job of making enough face screens for the Vowellans who would do battle with the drill bugs. Niv also whipped up custom coveralls for Brune and Krune with the new Teflon fabric Nick had brought from New Life City.

Since the bug cloud hovered over all but the outskirts of the valley, Mok and Nak calculated the best vantage points from which to fire gum balls: from the south through the trap door of the flattened Rug Bum Hut, as had already been done; from the east through Lek's second story bedroom window at the Net Ken Den; and from the north, from the bedroom courtyard at the Ham Bat Pad. They estimated that falling gum balls would land in crop locations or open fields, rather than atop structures. Gum balls would have to be handed to the slingshot teams at the stations and quickly slung in methodical fashion. Otherwise, the drill bugs would surely swoop down on those vantage points to attack any exposed bait, placing the warriors themselves in serious danger.

The locations would have to be closely patrolled if they were to fend off stray drill bug intruders. Mok suggested to Gun and Tug that they keep gum-coated hubcaps at their stations to deter crafty bugs that tried to sneak by the guards. According to their calculations, the supply of resin and limoncinas was more than enough to do the job.

Sun reported from the workroom that the PLOM fruit machine would be able to handle 40 pounds of gum at a time and that each batch of bait would take ten minutes to process. And just a touch of koolibarba oil added to each batch made the mixing much easier for the machine to handle. According to Dr. Jok's calculations, the contraption could produce 80 gum balls per hour, which meant it would be a good 12 hours until the Vowellans were well supplied with their first stockpile of ammunition. He thought that was reasonable. After all, the bugs had been hanging in the sky for days anyway. A few more hours wouldn't hurt. The other committee members agreed. They felt it was worthwhile to wait until they were amply prepared before they began their attack on the drill bugs. Dr. Jok suggested that, in the meantime, everyone should take turns sleeping.

Mok asked Sun to send San and Lek down from the Ham Bats' makeshift kitchen when she returned to the workroom. When they arrived, he gave them an affectionate grin and spoke to them as their ongoing leader instead of as a friend and schoolmate.

"I need to have you guys report to the workroom with Nak to make our ammunition for us. The drill bug bait needs to be weighed, formed into balls, and wrapped in wax paper. If you can't keep up with the machine's production, bring in more help, anyone who can spare the time."

"Yes, sir, Captain Mok." San grinned back at Mok. "You're doing great-ood'ly with all of this, you know."

Mok lowered his head and shook it. "I'm trying. I guess that's all any of us can do."

Lek's left front eyes noticed Mok's hands fidgeting within his pockets. "Remember what you always tell me. Just focus moment to moment, one foot in front of the other. The cracks don't matter."

Mok looked up at Lek and chuckled. "You're right, Lekee. We'll get past the cracks."

Lek turned to walk away with San, but Mok stopped him.

"Just a minute, buddy. I have something else I need to talk to you about."

"Sure, what do you need?" Lek was quick to reply.

"Your bedroom window at the Den is a prime location for us to use to attack the drill bugs. I know your room is filled with all your important stuff. I need you to go there and clear it out, so we can use it as a firing station. I'm sorry we have to do this. I know it will be hard for you to move things from their designated spots, but we need that room. Can you clear it for me?"

Lek's ten eyes rolled in their sockets. He paced back and forth in front of Mok, stepping on a tunnel floor crack without even noticing.

"Come on, buddy," said San. "Let's go. I'll help you'dl."

Lek came to a stop and thought for a moment. "Okay. I'll move everything into Granny's room since she's in the hospital anyway. I'll make it work. Don't worry, Mok."

Mok exhaled a sigh of relief and nodded. Lek and San took off for the Net Ken Den.

While the gum balls were being prepared under Pun's supervision, Mok joined Dr. Pol in his lab. The two of them worked hard to make the slingshots they needed, 15 to be exact. They calculated that with five at each of the three locations, they could fire constant streams of gum balls into the bug cloud. They stretched the rubbery material into flexible bands and whittled apple wood branches, which had been packed away to make canes for the elderly, to make the mechanisms they needed. They chatted and collaborated like they had never done as grandfather and grandson. When they finished their task, they stood back and admired their accomplishment.

"Thanks, Papa, for all you do for everyone in this town. You're really selfless, you know." Mok's face beamed with admiration for his brilliant grandfather.

Pol shrugged his shoulders and grinned. "Aww, you know me. My brain always needs to be working on something new. There's no time to be idle when there's always an invention on the horizon. But you, Mok-Mok. You have an intuition that I'll never have. Guard it well. It is more valuable than you know."

Mok admired their work one more time. "Well, Papa, I really should get back to the station. Thanks for these slingshots. If you come up with any more ideas, let us know."

Pol stepped forward to embrace Mok for the second time in a day. Mok hugged him back before loading the slingshots in his arms and leaving the laboratory.

Dr. Jok and Roz pored over their list of healthy Vowellans to determine who would be stationed where, who would serve as guards, who would handle the gum balls, and who would man the slingshots. Nick split his time between helping Niv and Wit prepare the protective gear and visiting the ailing Vowellans.

Several able Rug Bums, when they weren't patrolling the tunnels, prepared their ample supply of hubcaps in case they were needed to smash drill bugs during the gum ball attack. They were just itching to get out there and finally have a chance to get even with their enemy, the dark and evil shadow that had destroyed their home and had dared to hurt their family, and yes, their friends.

In the meantime, Tug, Gun, Brune, and Krune moved the children, the weak and recovered Vowellans, and those who didn't have essential battle duties into the hibernation tunnel. All who required additional doses of the antidote were inoculated. When it was determined that all were safely settled within the tunnel, Tug and the boys sealed the entrance off with school chalkboards they had cut to fit and plenty of duct tape. They hoped the folks inside would easily drift off into extended sleep.

Mok hopped over to the Fig Wig Bin to spend a little time at RJ's side and even more time with Kip. RJ continued to lie in deep sleep, unaware of all that was about to happen around the valley he loved so much.

Kip took a break from her nursing duties to sit with Mok against the wall of the massage studio. The patient load diminished greatly when hibernation was put into place. Fortunately, there had been no loss of life. Hun and Pun, the worst cases that had been dealt with, were slowly on the mend. Only those who had most recently been stung remained in the Fig Wig hospital under Dr. Jon's and Niv's tireless care.

Kip leaned her damp curly head against Mok's arm. He explained the plan to her so she would know where he was during the upcoming attack.

"We'll all be well protected, Punkee. Don't worry about that. Our only concern is that stray bugs might sneak into Lek's room or through the Bums' trap door. But the Bums should be able to handle those breaches.

Just stay silent and do your good here where you're needed. Give your mama a break here and there. I'm sure she'll appreciate it."

Kip looked up at him with her sad but adoring turquoise eyes. She nodded and pressed her head harder against his arm.

Mok leaned toward her and sprinkled several kisses across her forehead. "Take care, Punkee. Love you."

She pressed her puffy yellow lips into a forced grin and nodded. She cleverly hid from him the worry that twisted and knotted within her tiny body.

CHAPTER 22

The Battle

The defensively clothed and determined warriors took their places at the three battle stations, where Brune and Krune had delivered their allotments of bait balls. They kept the bait behind closed doors until it was needed. The unit at the Rug Bum Hut was led by Gun, just about the strongest Rug Bum in town, who served as lead gumball slinger. His unit included Sul, Sun, and Nak as backup slingers and guards, Dap and Zin as gumball suppliers, and Dr. Jok as radio contact. Brune had carried Dr. Jok and his tub chair to a strategic location within the Rug Bum tunnel.

Dun led the unit positioned in Lek's bedroom. His unit was composed of Lud, Lum, and Tak Ham Bat as slingers/guards, Lek and Sis Fig Wig on the gumballs, and Mok on their radio. Dun and Lud cautiously removed the heavy storm panels from the two windows in the room, hoping like heck the drill bugs wouldn't break through the glass before the unit was ready.

Lastly, Tug took charge of the unit in the Ham Bat

courtyard. Behind him were Mun, Auntee Gus (combat boots and all), and Van Ham Bat, with San and Jil Fig Wig as gumball handlers and Dr. Pol on the radio. The unit huddled in San's room and waited for the call to begin their attack.

Roz manned the operations base with the help of Jes and Nick, while Brune and Krune guarded the tunnels and floated between the stations. The Huge Dude brothers looked mighty Rug Bum-ish in their new Teflon suits with their giant, shiny monster hubcaps strapped to their elbows.

Gun and his unit at the Rug Bum Hut knew they were at a disadvantage. Since the Rug Bum Hut was a pile of sawdust, he could not check the initial status of the drill bug cloud without opening the trap door. The other units, in contrast, were able to see the cloud from Lek's bedroom windows and San's oval courtyard window. Gun and his unit knew that when it was time to attack, they would have to emerge to ground level, which would fully expose them to the bugs and their potential wrath. He, therefore, had his unit double suit and double mask for extra protection. Gun also realized that it would be hard for them to keep a constant supply of bait balls at ground level because of the vertical ladder below the trap door. Dap and Wit would not be able to do the job by themselves. Nick volunteered to help them relay the bait, since no one else was available.

Mok, who was given command of the attack because his natural leadership and intuitive senses, took a moment to examine the sky from his vantage point in Lek's bedroom. He was glad that the hovering cloud of vile bugs had no clue that it would soon be punctured by gumballs that would, if all went as planned, dissolve its very core. Mok was prepared for the challenge and determined to end the Vowellans' nightmare.

"Let's do this thing, boss," said Dun to his commander as he stood at Mok's side and stared at the black cloud. "It's our turn now."

"It certainly is," agreed Mok, his voice strong and steady. He lifted the radio to his mouth and stated with conviction, "Vowellans, take your positions and wait for my command."

The battle units boldly emerged from their cover. Gun and his crew filed out of the Rug Bum trap door and reclaimed their recently violated home ground. Dun opened the two double casement windows in Lek's room and banged out their screens. Tug and his unit charged into the Ham Bat courtyard and took their positions. Mok stuck his head out of one of Lek's windows and inspected the battle stations. He backed up to give Dun and his boys access to the windows and proclaimed into his walkie-talkie, "FIRE NOW!"

From the three stations, bait balls flew through the air with force and remarkable speed. Mok had instructed the slingers to fire their bait balls in a timely and methodical fashion. He didn't want them to rush because he wanted each sling to be as effective as possible. The Rug Bums displayed their full physical strength as they pulled on the high-tension slingshots, allowing the balls to make their way to the looming bug cloud.

The homemade ammunition punched holes in the cloud's black density, just as the Vowellan army had hoped, forcing the drill bugs into unexpected alertness and agitation. The ugly critters scrambled to focus their attention on the intrusive bait balls that were suddenly invading their self-proclaimed space. The previously solid black cloud morphed into angry clusters of smaller clouds that were determined to attack the foreign orbs that had entered their airspace. The Ham Bat warriors paused to push their earmuffs closer to their sensitive ears as the frantic, twitching behavior of the hard-bodied drill bugs raised the noise level within the valley.

Through the high-powered binoculars Mok had borrowed from RJ's belongings, he observed the consequences of the bait ball invasion. He watched dozens of drill bugs pounce upon each bait ball as it flew. The bugs zoomed toward their airborne enemy and aggressively drilled their lethal stingers into its core, only to find themselves stuck and helpless as a result. Bait balls heavy with captured drill bugs began to drop into the community fields and orchards and to bounce off the town's rooftops and into their respective yards, playgrounds, and paths.

But the bugs became wise and suddenly divided their forces. While the majority of bugs continued their attack on the constant stream of bait balls that flew through the air, others gathered themselves into ribbon-like formations that swooped down like slithering snakes toward the exposed units. A black ribbon of bugs wove itself around the protected bodies of Gun's crew at the Rug Bum Hut station, interrupting the steady firing of bait balls as they swooped between the Vowellan warriors' legs and around their arms. While Gun ignored the scary distraction and continued to fire when able, Sul, Sun, and Nak, who were each armed with gum-slathered hubcaps, waved their armor into the bugs' paths. The Vowellans were not afraid, determined to out-fight their enemy. Their protective gear held strong, to their great relief.

Another single ribbon of drill bugs blasted through the stationary window of Lek's bedroom. The bugs, swooping past Mok and the slingers within that battle station, tried to pound their way through the bedroom door to gain access to the bait that Lek and Sis guarded in the hallway on the other side. Luckily, the steel door was impenetrable. So, they made Mok their target.

"Dudes! Protect Mok!" hollered Dun above the unbearable racket of the clashing hard-bodied bugs.

Angry bugs banged against the Mok's face shield, trying with vigor to reach his face through the wire mesh with their venomous stingers. Mok pulled his head back within his headgear as far as he could, just beyond reach of the stingers. The screw-like points of the stingers banged against his glasses yet, by some miracle, did not break them.

While Mok stood frozen in place, Dun, Lum, and the other slingers surrounded him, shielding him while waving their gum-slathered hubcaps to bash the aggressive intruders, who couldn't resist the lure of the limoncina-infused bait. They drew the focus away from Mok's head and eventually eliminated the last of the stray bugs. Using steak knives they had previously retrieved from the Net Ken kitchen, they scraped the bug-infested bait from their hubcaps while leaning outside the open window, allowing it to drop into the richly flowered garden below them, while Lek and Sis quickly opened and shut the door to shove more bait balls into the room. Dun went about resurfacing the hubcaps with fresh bait.

Mok pressed his Teflon-gloved hands against the sides of his similarly protected head. "Think! Think, Fog Bob! This wasn't in our plan."

Within the Ham Bat courtyard, a small swarm of bugs attacked Auntee Gus's combat boots with vigor, trying to drill its way through their dense leather. The boots' thick composition, along with her angry stomping and cussing and hollering, discouraged the enemy, so it instead moved on to other potential targets within the unit. All it found was more bait-slathered hubcaps, which it couldn't resist. The swarm was wiped out in no time. The unit had to re-bait its hubcaps too, while still trying to sling a steady flow of bait balls into the sky. From his safe viewing position inside San's room, Pun marveled at Gusee's spunk and did all he could to stay in his wheelchair while his insides itched to participate in the momentous battle.

Gun and his team, back at the Rug Bum property, fought the issue of keeping gumballs in supply from the underground. The process was slow because of having to open and reopen the trap door, pushing out only a few balls at a time. And each time they did reopen, they exposed the tunnel system to danger. They worked desperately hard at ground level to sling the balls into the air before the bugs swarmed them. Dr. Jok, observing the situation from the Rug Bum tunnel below, radioed to Roz, requesting that Brune come to assist, hoping he could use his giant hubcaps to smash stray intruders who made it past the workers on the ladder above them. Brune, itching to do more for the cause, hurried to help.

When Gun felt the coast was clear, Sun pounded her foot on the trap door, signaling Dap that it was safe to open the trap door and push new bait out to ground level. In bucket brigade fashion, Nick passed bait balls up to Zin, then on to Dap, who then pushed them out to Sun, before slamming the trap door shut again.

Nick, looking straight up the ladder from the tunnel floor, waiting for the next signal, didn't realize that his face mask wire mesh pressed against his nose and lips. He was also unaware that a drill bug had managed to slip through the trap door just as it had closed after the last pass. Before realizing what happened, Nick had a nasty sting on a portion of his lip that protruded the mesh.

"Oh, no!" Nick, frustrated, spit through the mesh and swatted at the mask with his gloved hand.

"What's wrong there, Nicky?" asked Dr. Jok from his chair in the tunnel.

"One of those buggers just got me on my lip. Unbelievable!"

"Take that, you ugly varmint," hollered Brune as he squashed the culprit between his giant hubcaps.

"Darn it anyway," growled Nick. "I should have been paying attention. I know better than to have my face up against the mesh."

"You mean his stinger went right through the mesh and got you?" quizzed Dr. Jok.

"No, my mask fell against my face, and my lip poked through just enough for it to get me."

"Well, then, get up to the Fig Wig Bin right now," insisted Dr. Jok. "Have Jon give you some of the antidote. I'd better warn the others, so the same thing doesn't happen to them."

"I'll go," agreed Nick. "but I'm coming right back. This station needs me."

He left the Rug Bum tunnel for aid.

Mok alerted the battle stations about the danger of getting one's face too close to the mesh mask. The troops now had something else to think about while they did their vigorous work.

After almost 30 minutes of methodical bait slinging, long lost patches of blue sky began to peek through the slowly diminishing cloud of bugs. The Vowellans had made major strides during their battle against the enemy. Ugly gumballs, heavily blackened by trapped drill bugs, lay everywhere on ground that was usually perfectly manicured.

From his lookout position at the Net Ken Den, Mok noticed that the most recently slung bait balls were no longer collecting the same volume of drill bugs as they had at the beginning of the attack. He shook his head at the realization that the nasty opposition was now widely disbursed instead of hovering in its previously tight cloud. The bugs' positions made it less likely that the bait balls would attract them as they flew through the air. And the significant number of remaining bugs were highly agitated after the shock and damage that had been done to their mighty pack. The battle was not over by any means. Mok slammed Lek's bedroom windows shut, repositioned a storm plate over the broken window, and ordered the outdoor units to retreat from their positions to safety behind closed doors once they left some tempting bait balls out for the bugs to attack.

The bait balls certainly attracted a good number of drill bugs while other bugs zoomed frantically back and forth and up and down, looking for something new to attack. Since the sky was still full of threat, something else needed to be done.

Mok dreaded the reality that faced him, the implementation of Plan B, which now seemed inevitable.

Before the battle had begun, while the Vowellans had been waiting for the bait balls to be made, Mok had been part of a private meeting with his grandfather, Dr. Pol, and his great-grandfather, Dr. Jok, in the research lab. Dr. Jok had come up with the idea of allowing the Rug Bums, and whoever else could maneuver the hubcaps, to use the restricted gum hoppers, the springy footgear that Dr. Pol had developed for the purpose of helping the elderly get around town with more ease. The two doctors, as well as others from the early morning gang, had recently thrilled the townsfolk with an aerial display, which they had performed at the parade to honor RJ. With Rug Bum hubcaps strapped to their elbows like wings, they had been able to jump high enough on their gum hoppers to reach drafts in the airspace above them and fly in formations within those drafts.

So, theoretically, the warriors could hop up to and sweep the drill bugs' airspace with their baited armor. Once old Dr. Jok had heard how well the bait, which had been spread on the cookie sheets and hubcaps, had caught the demons during the testing period, he had envisioned himself saving the town by single-handedly swooping through the air, eliminating any and all drill bugs in his path. The three of them had decided that sky sweeping would be their backup plan if the bait balls were unable to clear the valley of all the drill bugs.

Implementing the plan would be a risky move on their part. They would be putting inexperienced fliers right in the middle of enemy territory. The seniors had essentially been the only ones who had had any flying time. The youngsters who would do battle had only learned of the flying maneuvers at the parade. Previously, the hubcap flying had only occurred in the early morning hours, long before the younger generation was out of bed. Jok, Pol, and Mok knew that if they used this plan, however, they would make more efficient use of the remaining bait. The fliers could continue to circulate through the sky until the hubcaps were sufficiently loaded with trapped bugs. The unknown variable in the Fog Bob theory was the extra weight of the gum and bugs. How much weight would the fliers be able to carry before they were dragged back down to the ground?

The impending end battle had somehow landed in the hands of the future generation of Vowellans because of unpredictable circumstances. The young people had avoided being previously stung or placed in hibernation because of their potential to aid the cause. Except for a few Rug Bums, they had not volunteered for such a mission. Making the final decision to proceed to Plan B was too much for Mok to make on his own. He was a member of that future generation, but he was just a boy underneath it all.

The young Vowellans appreciated the temporary pause in the battle. They took time to rest, clean up some, and scrape the dirty, bug-infested bait from their hubcaps. Tug slung as much of it as he could through the Rug Bum trap door when all seemed safe, so they wouldn't have to look at the ugly reminder of their dark situation.

Mok called for a meeting at the operations base. Roz and Jes, already there, stood on duty, tracking the overall positions and conditions of the Vowellans. Dr. Pol left his research lab and descended the vertical ladder from the Fog Bob Box. Brune carried Dr. Jok to the meeting from his post in the Rug Bum tunnel. Tug threw Pun over his shoulder and delivered him to base while Krune trailed him with Pun's wheelchair.

Mok investigated each of the faces that surrounded him. He pushed aside his urge to retreat from the position with which he had been charged and spoke with authority. "The time has come to move on to a new strategy. The bait balls served us well, but a good many drill bugs continue to occupy the airspace above us. We won't be safe until they're gone. G.G. came up with an alternate plan that we think will work, but I want to make sure that its implementation is agreeable to all of you."

He went on to explain the plan to Pun, Roz, and Jes. Roz and Jes stood shocked at the idea. Pun fully supported the idea but was spitting mad that he, like Dr. Jok, wasn't strong enough to participate.

Roz's face went dark with worry. "Son, you and the others would be at great risk. You could be swarmed in the air. You could easily fall from the sky. None of you has experience using the gum hoppers, and few of you know how to maneuver the hubcaps."

"None of them know how to maneuver them, Rozee," corrected Dr. Pol. "These young Rug Bums have never been exposed to these flying techniques. They'll have to be trained. But let me tell you, Father and I had no trouble whatsoever learning how to use them. Even RJ and old Paz-ee were quick to learn. It's really just a matter of using the gum hoppers to jump up to the air drafts. The hubcaps on outspread arms take over from there."

"We can do this, Moms," explained Mok. "It's the most efficient way to get rid of the rest of the drill bugs. They're not going to go away on their own." He was now entirely committed to the cause, having grown up considerably because of his recent responsibilities.

"And we can't go on like this forever, Rozee, with most folks in hibernation, a limited food supply, and an ongoing lack of fresh air and sunshine," added Dr. Jok.

"It's no way to live."

"I realize that, and I know that, logically, it's the right move. But I'm always going to be a mom about the welfare of our young people. They are our future, and I want to protect them." Roz placed her fingertips on her temples and massaged them in circular fashion.

"And I love you for it," said Mok soothingly as he hopped around the desk and wrapped his twiggy arms around her.

"Don't worry, Rozee. I'll take good care of them. I'm going with them," Dr. Pol announced.

Bewildered eyes shot toward Dr. Pol in an instant.

"What? You can't do that," exclaimed Roz, as her hands dropped to her sides. "You might get hurt up there."

"Papa, no!" Mok's face reflected the shock of hearing his grandfather's bold statement. The others look as surprised as Mok.

"Look, I'm the most experienced. I know those gum hoppers inside and out. I can teach our warriors how to use them and how to maneuver the hubcaps. No one else from the early morning gang is here to help. I'm going," Pol proclaimed. "Besides, the gum hoppers and the bait are my creations. It's time I stepped out of the lab and into the action. I deserve that privilege, don't you think?"

"I think so," agreed old Dr. Jok. "I know I'd be fighting to go if I were stronger. I'm proud of you, son. You deserve to reap the benefits of your hard work. You're a Fog Bob through and through."

"Thank you, Father." Dr. Pol flashed him a gentle

grin that reflected his emergence from a recluse to a team player.

"Well, this is getting exciting," said Pun from his wheelchair, suddenly more animated. "I need to watch *this* show."

"Me too," added Dr. Jok. "Let's find a place where we can all watch."

Mok scanned the faces of the committee members. He felt confident in their decision making. He was once more ready to take the lead. "We'll get you both up to the Rec Hall. Moms, you and Mrs. Jes should come too. As long as everyone is wearing protective gear, we should be able to take the storm panels off of the southern doors. Then, you can all watch us practice by the Council Porch and have a front seat view once we're up in the sky."

"Can I go too?" Brune asked timidly from behind Dr. Jok.

"Of course, Brune," answered Mok. He turned toward Krune, who was minding Pun. "I think both of you can fit into the Rec Hall.

"No, I mean, can I fly with you guys? Do you have any gum hoppers that are big enough for me? I want to help," said Brune in his deep, lazy voice. He spoke in such a gentle manner that the committee members couldn't help but feel their hearts melt.

"Hmm," responded Dr. Pol. "You do have those giant hubcaps now, don't you? Let me see if I can come up with something."

Brune and Krune flashed each other excited grins.

"Gee, thanks," said Brune. "I love to jump, and I've

never been able to fly before."

"Well, neither have the rest of us," said Mok with a slight chuckle. "Hopefully, you can learn just like us. Thanks for wanting to help."

Brune and Krune wriggled with enthusiasm.

Roz and Jes assisted Dr. Pol in making modified sets of gum hoppers for the Huge Dude brothers. Mok directed Lek and San to collect all other sets of gum hoppers from the homes around town, while Dun made sure the Rug Bums polished up all available hubcaps ahead of their flying instruction and the application of fresh bait.

Though Fin Fig Wig kept a watchful eye on the sky from the Rug Bums' trap door while the others prepped for Plan B, it took him a while to realize that the black dots in the sky were gradually increasing in number.

Mok returned to the Fig Wig Bin for a final dose of encouragement from Kip and to look upon peacefully sleeping RJ. As Mok sat and took RJ's still hand in his, he somehow felt courage passing from RJ's body to his. "We're almost there, Mr. RJ," he whispered as he leaned in toward RJ's ear. "Next time I see you, our town will be free again."

He thought he spotted a hint of a smile pass over RJ's sleeping face.

"Do you think that's true?" whispered Kip, who suddenly stood behind Mok's right shoulder.

"Yes, I do, Punkee," said Mok with total conviction as he stood, faced her, and placed his hands on her tiny shoulders. "This is the final battle. Then, the town will be ours again. The Vowellans will wake up to a new day. And we will be able to listen to your beautiful voice again."

As Mok took her hand and led her out of the room to a quiet spot near the Massage Studio, Kip lowered her head and nodded in an attempt to compress the worry that fought to choke her throat. She wrapped her tiny arms around Mok's log-like body and squeezed hard. She lifted her hooded turquoise eyes and looked directly into his.

"I love you, Munkee!" Her eyes adored every aspect of his most familiar features: his deep blue eyes behind distinguished glasses; his straight, narrow Fog Bob nose; his prominent, pointy chin; his thick mop of straight, brown hair; and those ample ears that stuck out a little too much.

Mok's breath caught with surprise before he returned the compliment, drinking in all that would keep her fresh in his mind while he tackled the challenging task at hand: her wild, curly mop of orange curls, skin that couldn't be more pale or delicate, those mesmerizing, one-of-a-kind kaleidoscopic eyes, and those overly generous yellow lips, which were right in front of him, waiting to be kissed.

"I love you too, Punkee. More than I know how to say." Mok leaned down and gently pushed his thin lips into the puffy lips that were hers. He embraced her tiny body, feeling the electricity that raced through his body vibrating within hers too. He wanted the moment to last forever.

But reality returned when a familiar voice broke the spell. Nick, who had been at the Bin since getting stung on his lip, approached, speaking through repeated yawns. "So, Mok, tell me where we are with the situation. What's the plan at this point?"

Mok released Kip from their embrace but kept an arm around her waist. "We're about to hit the sky on gum hoppers and do battle in the drill bugs' territory, Uncle Nick. We're going to cover the hubcaps with bait and sweep the skies until these nasty bugs are gone for good."

"Whoa, that's a tall order," said Nick, his eyebrows weaving into a frown. "But good for you. You're taking them head-on, and I'm proud of all of you. I sure wish I could help, but it looks like I'm headed for a deep sleep like RJ's. I can hardly keep my eyes open now."

"So sorry you got stung," said Mok sympathetically. "We really didn't mean to drag you into this mess."

"Of course you didn't. I'm the one who decided to come along, remember? But I believe this is a sign. You Vowellans are meant to work this one out on your own. So, I'll just snooze for a while, so you and the others can do what you need to do. I'll see you on the other side. Good luck." Nick patted Mok's free arm. His eyelids kept closing despite his standing pose.

Mok and Kip led Nick to a cot in RJ's room. He was asleep in no time.

With no further words, Mok reached for Kip's hand one more time before leaving her there to care for RJ and

Nick. They smiled at each other as their fingertips enjoyed one last touch.

Before Mok left the Fig Wig Bin, he stopped by Kip's room where Dr. Jon was tending to Jen, Nel, and Dok. He explained the newest battle plan to his father and told him that Dr. Pol would be accompanying them.

"Do you want to take a moment to go wish him luck before we leave, Pops? Papa would probably like to see you."

"I'm really busy here, son. Be very careful out there. I'll catch up with you and Father when you get back," stated Dr. Jon quite matter-of-factly. He was so engrossed in his duties that he hardly gave Mok a second glance.

Mok pinched his lips together, hopped to his father's side, and placed a hand on his back as Dr. Jon bent down to check Dok's pulse. "Okay, Pops, see you when we're done. Love you."

"You too, son," responded Dr. Jon without a second thought to the phrase's meaning.

Once Kip watched Mok descend the vertical steps of the Fig Wig Bin, she peeked in at Dr. Jon. Sadness washed over her body at the fact that the poor Fog Bob truly didn't know his son's love that he was allowing to slip through his fingers.

Mok returned to the anxious committee that awaited him at the operations base. With Brune cradling Dr. Jok and Krune carrying Pun, the group caravan went up the main tunnel toward the Rec Hall. Roz embraced a stack of schedules and various other papers while Jes pushed the wheelchair. Dr. Pol pulled his red wagon filled with gumhoppers, and the Rug Bums juggled stacks of freshly shined hubcaps while dragging the heavy containers of remaining bug bait. Dr. Jok and Pun jabbered along the way about how unfair it was that they weren't going to be able to participate. Gusee Rug Bum took up the rear, chuckling at the knowledge that her brother was once again well enough to be feisty. All carried within their chests the heaviness of the unknown outcome that loomed before them.

CHAPTER 23

For Love of Home

The determined Vowellan warriors, armed with practice hubcaps and led by Mok and Dr. Pol, headed outside toward the Council Porch. Lek, San, and a few available Fig Wigs stayed behind to bait up the battle hubcaps that would be used in rotation. Random confused drill bugs swirled around their heads and bodies, to force the Vowellans into retreating from the territory the bugs now claimed as their own.

Confident in their protective gear, the Vowellans went about the business of learning how to use the gum hoppers and the hubcaps. Dr. Pol shouted out basic training instructions above the irritating drone of the drill bugs' flapping wings. Most of the warriors had youth on their side, so getting the hang of jumping was easy. For Mok and the few Ham Bat warriors, getting used to wearing hubcaps on their elbows was a bit of a challenge, but once again, their youthfulness accelerated the learning process. The troops got used to flying by taking tall hops between the bait ball littered grassy area by the Council

Porch and the uncluttered lawn behind the Vowella Valley school, just as Pun and the Elders had done on their first flights. Gusee Rug Bum, who was older and more out of shape, practiced jumping twice as hard with Brune and Krune. They gradually became good at it, achieving acceptable heights. Whether they would be able to handle the flying part of the mission was more questionable. They kept working at it.

When Dr. Pol was satisfied that the troops were sufficiently trained, he pulled them into a huddle. Drill bugs continued to zoom by them as the ugly creatures tried to make sense of what the Vowellans were doing. "I think we're ready, everyone. Do you all feel comfortable in your gear?"

A collective "YEAH!" exploded from the small crowd, and the troops hurried toward the doors of the Rec Hall to retrieve their baited armor. While they carefully filed inside and closed the doors, the drill bugs individually hovered and watched them through the glass panels. The bugs were no longer the massive force they had once been.

Mok pulled Dr. Pol over to the side for a last minute discussion while the troops pulled the baited hubcaps onto their elbows. "Papa, are you sure you're ready to go up there with us? You're not as strong as the rest of us, even though you may think so."

"Ack, rubbish! The gum hoppers and the hubcaps do all the work. Nothing would make me prouder than to be up there with you and the others. What's all my work worth if I can't share in the good it does? I'll be fine," assured Dr. Pol. He grabbed Mok by his shoulders. "I'm so proud of you, grandson. You've become an excellent example of what not only a good Fog Bob but also a good Vowellan should aspire to be."

Mok swallowed the emotion that he felt in his body. "And I'm prouder of you and all you've done for Vowella."

They gazed into each other's deep blue eyes and cracked similar Fog Bob grins at each other.

Dr. Pol took the honorary place at the head of the pack with Mok and Dun side by side behind him in the Rec Hall. The other warriors fell into a loose V formation behind them while performing last minute adjustments on their hubcap armor. Lek and San stood at the tall glass northern doors, ready to open them when prompted. Dr. Pol raised his right arm high above his head. With his head held high and his chest inflated, he proclaimed, "This we do because we are strong. This we do because we are smart. This we do for all Vowellans. This we do for love of home!"

"WOO-HOO!" cheered old Dr. Jok and Pun Rug Bum from their chairs, their arms waving wildly. "Go get those buggers!"

Lek and San shoved the doors open, and the warriors charged forward. Having discovered that the giant ant hills behind the Rec Hall served as good launching pads, Dr. Pol, Mok, and Dun used them to bounce themselves into the sky with their gum hoppers. The others followed suit. The drafts easily embraced the warriors' hubcaps, and the Vowellans found themselves swooping through the air at speeds they would never have imagined were possible.

Mok and Dr. Pol headed southwest, to sweep the sky over and behind the Fog Bob Box, where the avocado orchard, Tok and Sil's tree house, and Brune's makeshift home stood in gloomy silence. Dun and Gusee glided south to sweep the air above the crumbled Rug Bum Hut, the maintenance yard, and the tennis court site. Tug and Gun swooped above the gum tree grove, the Fig Wig Bin, and the school grounds while the rest of the warriors wove back and forth over the Net Ken Den, the apple orchard, and the Ham Bat Pad.

The drill bugs were quick to realize that fresh bait was easily accessible to them, and they attacked the armor with vigor. Screwing their vicious stingers into the irresistible bait, they quickly loaded themselves onto the hubcaps. The Vowellans performed their duty in various directions, surfing the skies and slowly clearing the air of their nasty enemy. At one point, Mok wavered as the weight of the bugs began to pull him down, but he came upon a stronger draft that allowed him to do a little more work before descending. Similarly, Dun got caught up in a higher draft, which at first seemed to help him collect more bugs. But when the draft suddenly swooped him up past 900 feet, he blacked out for a few seconds, as Vowellans do when the oxygen level lessens. He fell into a nosedive until he returned to 500 feet, awoke with a start, and swooped back to his territory.

At Mok's signal, the warriors returned to the ground,

dragging hubcaps heavy with trapped drill bugs. Dumping their armor outside the Rec Hall doors, they hurried inside to equip themselves with freshly baited hubcaps. It was only then that they realized that Brune and Krune hadn't made it up to the drafts.

"I guess we're just too big and heavy." Brune's sadness made the words stick in his throat. Krune nodded, his droopy eyelids expressing his disappointment.

"Oh, Brune," comforted Mok. "I'm so sorry. I know you really wanted to help. But you know, you can still do a great deal from here on the ground. Those giant hubcaps can trap one heck of a lot of drill bugs, and there are still plenty of them snooping around at ground level. If you two run back and forth on Valley Road a few times, I'm sure you'll trap bunches of bugs. And you can certainly clean off the hubcaps for us and prep them with new bait."

"Yeah, I guess that's true, huh." Brune and Krune nodded at each other at the realization that they could still play an important role in the operation. After one last check on the status of their hubcaps, they hurried outside.

Mok peered through the southern glass doors toward the sky. He was pleased with the progress they had made. His keen eye suddenly noticed a slight line etched in the clearing sky that trailed to the south. It stretched well beyond the southern field. His eyes widened behind his spectacles.

"Look," he commanded attention from his troops. "Look at that trail up there. New bugs are heading toward us. The south seems to be where they're coming from.

We'd better get back out there."

Dr. Pol took a look and nodded. "So, we have a clue to the source. Now, we can use a little strategy to guide us."

"But Dr. Pol, we don't know what's at the other end," voiced Dun, whose brows wrinkled into a new knot.

"You're right, but at least we know that somewhere down there, there is an end. We just have to find it." Dr. Pol's logical wheels turned with vigor.

"Papa, why don't you stay here and manage the troops while a few of us head down there to scout it out?" suggested Mok, still leery of his grandfather's participation in the operation.

"Listen, Mok-Mok, while I appreciate your protectiveness, I want you to understand that this is what I've worked toward my entire life, to make a difference in our Vowellan lives. This is the culmination of that work for me. I developed the gum products and gum hoppers that have gotten us this far. And they're working, by gum. That is so rewarding to me. But now, I need to see this to its end. I want to see this evil enemy defeated, once and for all."

"I get it, Papa," Mok surrendered with a grin and a shake of his head. He hopped toward Pol and gave him an awkward embrace around protective gear and armor. "Let's go get these buggers."

"Yeah, I'm ready," echoed Auntee Gus, who had never felt so energized.

"Well, let's go then," encouraged Tug Rug Bum, just itching to get back up to the drafts.

"Wait," said Dr. Pol, with final concern for the Vowellan warriors. "Is your equipment working well for all of you?"

"Yeah!" the troops chanted.

"Then fall into formation, warriors," commanded Mok, checking to make sure his warriors were armed with fresh bait. "Papa Pol, do you still want the lead?"

"You bet!" Dr. Pol took his position at the head of the V, and the Vowellans once again rushed out of the Rec Hall and into the sky.

To the Vowellans' unfortunate surprise, the remaining drill bug army, quietly being replenished by the thin line from the south, had formed a V of its own while the Vowellans had chatted in the Rec Hall. By the time the home troops reached the drafts, the drill bugs wasted no time in charging toward them, full force. Accompanied by the aching drone of their madly flapping wings, the bugs caught the warriors by surprise, slamming into several of them, knocking them off-balance. Dun and Auntee Gus tumbled a couple of times before reclaiming their balance in the drafts. Bulky Tug and Gun had to use a butterfly swimming stroke with their hubcaps to work their way back up to that airspace. Mok, Nak, and some of the others were bumped sideways within the drafts.

But the most horrifying scene was that of the point of the drill bugs' V smashing straight into Dr. Pol, who, of course had headed the Vowellan V formation. His head gear was knocked out of position. As he descended through the airspace, the wire mesh of his face mask, no longer in a protective position, pressed against his right cheek and forehead. The crazed drill bugs attacked his face in force, their many stingers penetrating the wire mesh, lodging themselves into his exposed skin.

From the road in front of the Fog Bob Box, Brune and Krune witnessed the horror. Having already been racing back and forth on the ground beneath the warriors, they ran to position themselves beneath the tumbling form of Dr. Pol. Clenching each other's forearms, they were able to break his fall, awkwardly catching him in their giant arms. Pol's log-like body, usually so erect and proper, lay limp and crumpled in their embrace.

Brune gently placed Dr. Pol on the road as the rest of the Vowellans quickly descended from the sky and dumped their armor in a spot that was a safe distance from the scene. The angry drill bugs enthusiastically attacked the pile of baited armor, ignoring the Vowellans, who were now so much less important. Mok rushed to his grandfather's side, where he knelt and hunched to see for himself the damage the limp body had endured.

"Papa, Papa, wake up! Can you hear me? You must wake up. We're almost done, and we need you." Mok swatted away two of the ruthless invaders whose stingers were stuck in the mesh, removed Pol's headgear and cradled his limp head, so swollen with venomous stings, in his caring hands. "Papa, you're going to be all right. Just hang on."

Dr. Pol, barely a thread of a breath escaping his graying lips, forced his left eyelid open and gazed up at Mok's worried face. Before his eye closed again, he managed to whisper, "You're the one, Mok-Mok. I love you."

"What, Papa? I'm the what? What are you trying to say?" With pupils greatly dilated and his heart pounding wildly within his chest, Mok hugged his limp grandfather to his chest. He repeatedly whispered soothing words that Pol would never hear.

The moment dragged on in slow motion. The Vowellans stood frozen in shock at the scene. Brune, one knee on the ground next to Mok, placed his giant hand on his back as Mok rocked his grandfather to and fro.

"You know he's gone, Mok," said Brune tenderly. "I don't think he even understood what hit him."

Mok ceased his rocking and looked up at the gentle giant. "I know, Brune, I know."

Mok's voice quivered as he lifted Pol higher and hugged him hard. Struggling to keep some form of sense about him, he asked, "Will you help me get him inside?"

"Of course," Brune answered readily.

He gently lifted Pol into his burly arms, cradling him most carefully. He walked in steady strides toward the Rec Hall, where Dr. Jok, Roz, and the others who had witnessed the shocking event painfully awaited his arrival. The warriors filed into the Rec Hall in silence as Brune gently placed Dr. Pol in the comfortable chair that had been occupied by his father, Dr. Jok.

Dr. Jok knelt at Pol's side and rested his head on his son's arm. Roz and Mok knelt next to him in silence. Roz quietly noted the time on her wristwatch. The others lowered their heads in sadness and respect. No one needed to recount the event. Everyone had witnessed the tragedy at the same time.

Jes, with a further gesture of respect, covered his battered face with the fine, hand-embroidered lace doily that had been hanging over a nearby lounge chair. After several minutes of silence, old Dr. Jok stood, his chin held high, his body still weak from illness, to address the others.

"Let us pause to honor my son's finest moment. Because of his brilliant work, we WILL have our very lives back again. I don't know of a greater gift he could have given us. As is our Vowellan way, let us take a few silent moments to embrace our sadness. Then, we must tuck it away for his sake and move forward with our mission. Pol would want us to do that."

The mournful Vowellans and Huge Dudes lowered their heads and stood in silence around Dr. Jok. Each heart ached, and many a tear trickled down sagging cheeks. When old Dr. Jok raised his head, Jes escorted him to the nearby lounge chair and knelt to tend to him. Roz and Mok rose, embracing in deep sobs. Once their bodies calmed, Roz placed a gentle hand on each of Mok's wilted shoulders. He couldn't help but admire the strength his mother exuded. If anyone had ever been his strength, his rock, it was her.

"I know this is hard, son, but be assured that the pain will lessen with time. Papa would want you to remain strong and to carry on with true Vowellan spirit. He helped you get this far. Now, honor him by finishing the job. You're the leader everyone needs right now. I know you can do it, son."

Mok nodded and blinked away his remaining tears. "You're right, Moms. Papa's last words to me were, 'You're the one.' I don't know what that means, but I'm going to try my hardest to honor him in every way."

He turned to observe his silent warriors, who had quickly run outside to retrieve their armor, which they were now baiting for their final round of battle. "Tell them I'll be back, Moms. I need a few minutes to myself."

Roz gave his upper arms a few affectionate rubs, then backed away, giving her son space to move on.

Mok hopped through the south doors of the Rec Hall and surveyed the scene. A disgusting black heap composed of thousands of dead drill bugs lay ugly and still on the ground between the Ham Bat Pad and the badly littered crop fields. For the most part, the sky was blue, except for the thin line that continued to feed drill bugs into the valley from the southern horizon.

Tilting his head back to investigate the patch of sky from which his beloved grandfather had taken his final flight, Mok replayed the fateful scene in his mind, knowing that scene would forever haunt him. He suddenly felt an unfamiliar churning rising in his chest, something new and remarkably terrifying. Fury worked toward overtaking his body, though he rigorously tried to suppress it. Rewinding and replaying in his head Dr. Pol's fall only fed that mounting fury. When his mind couldn't handle seeing Pol land in the Huge Dudes' arms one more time, Mok pulled at the thick hairs above his ears and shook his head vigorously. With rage spitting from every pore of his young body, his fair skin now a deep shade of purple from his blood boiling within him, he screamed to the skies, "AAGH! HOW DARE YOU! HOW DARE YOU TAKE MY PAPA FROM ME! YOU WON'T WIN. YOU WILL NEVER WIN."

A phenomenal wave of air pressure blasted in all directions from where he stood. Buildings shook while the ground rumbled beneath him. Wind waves rippled through the sky, causing random clouds to disappear and the thin line of bugs to shatter. Drill bugs frantically sought out each other, hoping to regather their solidarity. Beneath ground, the tunnels shook as though caught in a severe earthquake. Kip, Dr. Jon, and the Vowellans still sick or caring for others had to grab on to something sturdy within the Fig Wig Bin, as did those above ground in the Rec Hall.

Mok felt a power emanate from his being like nothing he had ever imagined. His blue eyes widened behind his spectacles as he questioned whether all that force had actually come from his tall, log-like body. He turned toward the Rec Hall as the commotion of the stunned warriors exiting the building caught his attention.

Dun rushed toward him, his furry arms outstretched, his black eyes bugging as he babbled. "Dude, what the gum was that? The whole valley shook. Did you see that, boss?"

Mok stood stunned for a moment as the chaos within his body began to calm. His voice trembled, the force still needing more release. "Yes, Dun. I dare to say that I think it came from me."

"What? How could that be? What are you, some kind of wizard?" Dun stared at him with fresh eyes, as did the others.

"I don't know. I'm kind of freaked out right now." Mok's eyes darted from side to side, trying to understand what had just happened.

"Well, look! Those nasty critters are scrambling up there, and it looks like they're heading southward. We need to get them, boss. We can't let them get away where they could come back again." Dun paced in front of Mok while the troops nodded in agreement.

"Yeah, Mok, we need to get them where they live," offered Gusee, who was spitting mad at the latest developments.

Mok shook his head to get his brain back into leadership mode. He found himself repeating her words. "Where they live, where they live. You're right, Auntee Gus. That's exactly what we need to do."

The warriors nodded their agreement. Mok scanned the surroundings once more to determine their status. A new plan churned in his brain. "Tug and Gun, make sure those hubcaps are cleaned and ready for battle as soon as you can. Dun, round up as many backpacks as you can."

Mok's mind was suddenly formulating the new plan of attack at a furious pace. "Nak, you and Dap pack up water to take with us. Auntee Gus, get Sun, Lek, and San to help you round up whatever bait balls are left. Make more balls from the remaining bait mixture we have, wrap them, and pack them into the backpacks."

"Where are we going?" asked Brune in determined fashion. The sense of wrath he saw in Mok's face frightened him to a point where he felt it too. The gentleness within the giant was being pushed aside, being replaced by a determined soldier.

"We're going to get rid of these monsters once and for all," proclaimed Mok, his voice now strong and commanding. "We're going to find *their* town. We're going to destroy *their* home. These bugs are who they are. There's nothing we can do about that. But nothing and no one has the right to step in and keep us from simply being who we were meant to be and doing what we were meant to do. That's all that Papa Pol ever wanted. That's what all of us deserve."

"YEAH!" shouted the Vowellan troops. They efficiently disbursed to perform their assigned duties, reassembling in the Rec Hall in no time. San, Lek, Roz, and Jes carefully moved Dr. Pol into the quiet sitting room adjacent to the Ham Bat Café, where he would lie in peace until the war was over. The warriors strapped their backpacks and plenty of replacement armor onto their backs before sliding clean, freshly baited hubcaps over their elbows. With all in place, they once again fell into their V formation, this time with Mok front and center.

Chills rippled through Roz's body at the sight of the determination on her son's face. The thought of something happening to him too haunted her very being. She hopped to his side with all the strength she could muster. Once more placing a gentle hand on his arm, she simply asked, "Mok?"

"Don't worry, Moms. There's no way I'm not coming back to you. I love you too much."

Roz bit her lip, lowered her head, and nodded through giant tears. She backed away and joined Dr. Jok, who stood nodding proudly at his great-grandson.

"Are we ready, Vowellans?" Mok turned toward his troops with a face that meant nothing but business.

"Ready!" confirmed the troops.

"FOR PAPA POL! FOR LOVE OF HOME!" Mok proclaimed.

"FOR PAPA POL! FOR LOVE OF HOME!" shouted the proud Vowellans, along with a couple of equally proud Huge Dudes.

Mok and his small Vowellan army were out the door and into the sky with a few simple hops on their gumhoppers. Dun, Tug, Gun, Sun, Auntee Gus, several other Rug Bums and a few able Ham Bats followed Mok's lead. Incredibly, Brune and Krune even made it to the drafts, which suddenly held a force that had previously been missing. That force embraced their giant hubcaps. The Huge Dudes' strong desire to honor Dr. Pol and to help their new community of friends, who had so unselfishly made them part of their own, also took them there.

Upon discovery that their airspace was once again being invaded, the drill bugs split from their new line, fell into new formations and frantically circled the warriors, especially Mok, who fronted the pack. They stabbed their stingers at the warriors' protective gear from all angles, determined to penetrate the barriers surrounding each Vowellan. Their mission to defeat the troops overtook their attraction to the baited hubcaps. They swarmed Mok's head space, determined to defeat him as they had his grandfather.

Mok swatted at them as best he could while he struggled to maintain his balance in the drafts. Hard black bodies clanged against his wire mesh face mask while stingers ripe with venom tried to penetrate it far enough to reach his face. He pulled his head as far back in his headgear as he could, but there were only so many contortions he could accomplish while flying. He swooped high and low and side to side, trying to free himself of the swarm so focused on him. It did no good. Finally reaching a point of zero tolerance, Mok swooped through the airspace until he was able to resume his position at the front of the troops' V formation. Feeling a new wave of fury rise in his chest, he stared down the line of drill bugs still flowing toward Vowella and shouted," NO MORE!"

A wave of powerful wind blasted forward from his mouth toward the drill bugs, shattering their formation, scattering them in a thousand directions. The bugs tumbled through the air, numbed by the blast. The space around Mok's head cleared, and he watched in stunned silence. Behind him, the Vowellans flew unaffected by the wave. Once they caught sight of the flailing enemy, the troops sprang into action, swooping through the sky, sweeping as many stunned bugs into their sticky baited hubcaps as they could. Dun and Tug led smaller teams to the east and west while Auntee Gus and the Huge Dude brothers cleaned up the rear. The bug line beyond the airspace that had been affected by the blast made a U-turn and headed south.

Mok lowered his arms, allowing his body to descend to the ground. The troops followed suit. They quickly scraped the infested bait from their hubcaps and re-baited them with some of the bait balls they had packed in their backpacks.

Dun rushed to Mok. "Whoa, what kind of powers do you have, boss?"

Mok looked at Dun and the others with fierce eyes, his irises now a bright purple rather than their normal deep blue, his pupils hugely dilated. "We're about to find out."

He scanned the sky above Vowella. It was clear and crystal blue. But the sky on the southern horizon bore a trailing line of black. Mok then scanned his force of homemade warriors. The rapid movement of his eyes demonstrated how efficiently his mind was working. "Switch your backpacks around so you're wearing them in front, giving you easier access to the bait balls. Arm yourselves with triple hubcaps. Fly in pairs so you can assist each other if needed." He took a quick glance at the wristwatch on his left arm. "There's no time to waste. Let's go!"

Vowella's warriors hopped up to the drafts and headed south, systematically eliminating the thin trail of drill bugs that still dared to occupy the southern end of the valley. Auntee Gus, Brune, and Krune, now much less awkward in the sky, continued to take up the rear, capturing stray bugs that the other warriors had missed. As they flew over the southern field and RJ's airplane hangar, Mok alerted the troops to be conscious of the position of their face masks at all times and to monitor their altitudes. Every warrior's presence was crucial at this stage of their mission.

Just beyond the southern field, the landscape drastically changed. The twisted, tangled waterways of the dreaded southern swamp revealed their ugly presence. No Vowellan had ever traveled this far south. RJ had been the only one who had had any experience there, and that was a generation earlier, when he had first arrived in Heaven's Wait. The further south the troops flew, the thicker the air became with drill bugs. Mok shouted to the troops to brace for a rocky ride.

The troops were ready for the challenge. With newfound agility, they aggressively swept the sky, capturing hundreds upon hundreds of drill bugs. The clatter of the drill bugs' hard wings banging into each other was unbearable, especially to Nak. As individual teammates found their hubcaps sinking from the weight of the captured bugs, they allowed them to slide off their arms and down into the swamp. They slid clean hubcaps down from their shoulders to their elbows and slapped fresh bait onto them from their backpacks. The transfers were quick, and they lost little elevation in the process.

The warriors managed to achieve a clear enough view

of the swamp to observe the vast marshes and steaming waterways that lay below them. Mok's eyes widened with fresh determination when he spotted what he knew was the evil heart of the enemy.

Below them stood an ugly, black tulip-shaped plant, half the size of the dome-shaped Fig Wig Bin. A pulsing red glow radiated from its exterior, giving the enemy's home base the appearance of a devil's beating heart. A steady stream of drill bugs flowed from its center and fed the trail in the sky that the Vowellans were trying so hard to eliminate.

Mok studied the evil structure as he circled it from the air above. His logical Fog Bob brain computed its dimensions and composition. Its form included giant black petals, seemingly composed of a slimy, black rubbery material. Its center twitched with frantic drill bugs just itching to launch into the sky. This had been the source of all of the Vowellans' recent misery. This had been the reason he had lost his precious grandfather.

Mok pulled up to higher airspace, less dense with bugs, where he could communicate with his troops. He signaled them to again prepare their hubcaps and to report to various positions above and around the target. Nak and several Rug Bums flew in a wide circle around the warriors to keep as many drill bugs away from Mok as possible. Brune and Krune flew in a smaller circle between Mok and the other warriors to handle that airspace, while Gusee accompanied them to help them re-bait their armor. Dun flew next to Mok to feed him gumballs as needed while Tug and Gun closely flanked them.

"THIS ONE BELONGS TO ME!" Mok screamed above the racket.

The drill bugs were now enraged. They pounded on the troops' protective gear with their hard bodies. They zoomed around their face masks, trying to reach the vulnerable faces behind them with their stingers. As Mok and Dun descended toward the target, Tug and Gun zigzagged in front of them to try to clear a path for an attack. The trail of bugs streamed from the ugly black center, which made the view of it nearly impossible.

Mok and Dun circled back to higher airspace. Mok called Tug and Gun back to trade places with Brune. Brune flew in next to Mok as they circled.

"Brune," Mok shouted above the mind-boggling clatter. "We need to move the trail of drill bugs out of the way. I can't get a clear shot to the center as long as they're flying straight up at us. Could you somehow blow them out of the way like you did with the fog when we were in Jimmy's Jungle?"

"I don't know. Let me try. We'll see what happens."

Brune held his position next to Mok and blew downward toward the tulip. Bugs quickly scattered in all direction as his mighty breath reached the top of the tulip's petals. Now, even more bugs attacked each peripheral Vowellan warrior, making it even harder to sweep the sky and maintain flying position. Nak and Gusee were knocked sideways, barely able to spread their arms again to reenter the drafts.

Tug suggested that the Vowellans assemble themselves side by side so they could sweep the air in a circle around Mok, Dun, and Brune like the rotational blade in the coffee cooling machine at home. They pushed forward, capturing as many bugs as they could in their armor, but the armor was getting too heavy again, even for brutes like Tug and Gun.

Mok glanced at the mess in the sky, at his struggling companions, and at the ugly target below him. When his eye caught sight of Brune, the memory of him catching poor Dr. Pol flashed through his brain. His insides churned and boiled, and before he knew it, he announced for the last time, "FOR PAPA POL!"

The words blasted from his mouth in the form of a new and most powerful wind wave that rattled the very air in which they flew. Vowellans and bugs alike were tossed away from the Mok's position, only Dun and Brune exempt because of their close proximity to Mok. The airspace below him cleared and the ugly petals of the enemy's home flattened, exposing its pulsing center. Mok, Dun, and Brune dove straight toward that center. Brune blew as hard as he could to prevent new bugs from escaping the nucleus, clearing the way for Mok's attack. When they were within range, 50 feet from the tulip, Mok unzipped his backpack's bottom zipper, allowing bait balls to fall one after another into the tulip. The structure quickly weakened as the bait balls wounded its vulnerable petals. When Mok's supply was depleted, they swooped back up so Dun and Brune could hand more bait balls off to him as they circled. This was his battle, and he wanted to be the one to do the damage.

"Boss," hollered Dun as Mok was about to turn back

downward. "You need to sting that bugger right where it hurts. Just like we do when we whip rugs at you folks. Fire those gumballs right into its heart. You've already weakened it. Now, take it out for good."

Mok glanced at him with otherworldly purple eyes and dove one last time. The tulip was fully exposed and so was he. Dun and Brune followed closely behind. Mok fired the bait balls into the nucleus of the black tulip with a vengeance, finally suffocating what was left of the bug army that lived within its heart. The structure spit and sputtered, its center cracking open and heaving. They circled at low altitude and observed. With a final burst of life, it violently heaved, causing a giant black blob to emerge from the widened crack. Just as the Rug Bums had done to try to escape their sticky blobs of gum on a particular hot day in Vowella, this blob wiggled as though something lived inside. After quite a struggle, a giant screw-like stinger rose toward the sky, ripping through its encasement. A humongous drill bug emerged. It spread its armored wings and pulled its remaining body from the cracked center.

Mok and the others quickly retreated to higher airspace, but their fascination kept them near so they could watch. The remainder of the home team warriors, all battered but somehow able to recover from Mok's blast, joined them in their aerial surveillance of the drill bugs' damaged home base. Mok's mind churned as he realized that no more bait balls remained. What more could they do to at this point?

To everyone's surprise, the vile creature reached back

into the cracked center with its clawed foot and pulled out one of the tempting bait balls, which Mok had so generously gifted it. At first, it cradled the ball in its foot, examining it from every angle. With the curiosity of a cat, it poked at the ball with its giant stinger as though savoring its intoxicating limoncina scent. Then, it aggressively buried its evil stinger deep into the tempting bait. When it tried to extract the stinger, the gum stuck to it as well as the creature's claw, denying it the freedom it now desperately sought. It pulled and struggled, to no avail. One violent effort after another only weakened the creature. At last, limp and defeated, it collapsed to its side while remaining life oozed from its body. The pulsing red glow that had radiated from the ugly tulip when it had been vital slowly faded and disappeared. The only sound that could be heard was the faint buzzing of the few straggling drill bugs that hovered over the still, wretched body.

"Dude," Dun spoke in a quiet, astonished tone, the irritating clatter of the drill bugs' bodies no longer competing for Mok's ear. "You got the QUEEN! You got the stinking mother of them all."

Mok stared at the scene in wonder, the rage and adrenaline slowly draining from his body, which suddenly felt depleted and battered. His irises returned to their deep blue color.

"We did, didn't we! WE all did it. It's over. It's finally over." Mok mumbled the words, more to himself than the others.

Mok circled above the defeated enemy's home at a

casual pace, drinking in the sight that he never wanted to see again. The troops quietly fell in line behind him, leaving ranks only to capture final stray drill bugs into the few hubcaps, which here and there still held fresh bait available to their stingers.

Gusee Rug Bum swooped up to Mok's side, her hair loose and badly tangled from the drafts. "Mok, it's time we get back. We must hurry."

Mok glanced at his wristwatch and nodded. "Yes, we must."

With a swoop of his left arm, Mok signaled the troops that it was time to leave. Dun took it upon himself to radio back to Roz that all was done and that they were coming home. The quiet army followed Mok through the crisp blue sky northward toward Vowella. Mok wrestled his headgear from his head, allowing it to hang from his neckline.

Fresh wind beat against his face as the emotion of the day slowly crept into his being. Though he was aware that he ached inside, his brain, his skin, his entire being felt numb. The only thought that lingered somewhere at the outskirts of his mind was that of gratitude that Dr. Pol had gone so quickly. His grandfather had not suffered. As Mok became aware that his mind was slowly beginning to churn again, he realized that the Fog Bobs and the rest of the Vowellans were the ones who would now have to deal with their loss. And the time to honor him was quickly to be upon them.

Fortunately for the Vowellans, no one of Mok's generation had any experience with Vowellan death rituals. Past elders had left Heaven's Wait before they were born. Mok did know of the protocol, however. At the eighth hour after a Vowellan's passing, his body would leave for the heavens. Rituals were performed before that time to honor the beloved family member. Mok, as well as Gusee, who was old enough to have witnessed such rituals, knew they needed to make it back to town before the eighth hour. Mok shook his head in wonder as he realized all they had accomplished within that time frame.

As the airborne army approached familiar ground, they noticed that most of the horrible, bug-infested gumball litter had already been cleared from the valley floor. Dr. Jok, though emotional and sad, had had enough presence about him to direct San, Lek, and a few others who had stayed behind to remove the clutter and its bad memories from the valley as quickly as possible. They buried the ugly reminders of their ordeal in a grave that they had already dug in the southern field. The grave consisted of a group of tunnels that the Vowellans had prepared on a day of glorious fun and rewards, the day of the Game of Winnit. Lek waved up to Mok as he smoothed the dirt over one leg of the grave with a small rake. Mok faintly smiled down at lovely Vowella below, feeling at home in his heart and, though sad, at peace with the journey he had taken.

CHAPTER 24

From Now On

As soon as Mok and his troops had left town for the awful southern swamp and their final battle with the drill bugs, Dr. Jok, seeing the sky above Vowella turn a radiant blue and cleared of bugs, had begun to plan the immediate actions they could take to free the long-suffering folks of Vowella from their bondage. Then, when Roz had heard the news from Dun, Jok had sent Jes and her to the underground, first to free the bulk of the townsfolk and children from their sealed hibernation tunnel, and second to bring the news to the sick and their caregivers within the walls of the Fig Wig Bin. Those strong enough to help had removed the metal panels from the windows, doors, and skylights, allowing bright sunshine and fresh air to fill the dome with healing heat and light.

Roz had entered Kip's room, where RJ and Nick had been peacefully sleeping and Dr. Jon had been taking a quick snooze in a side chair. The sunlight had promptly roused RJ and Nick from their deep sleep, and their commotion had jarred Dr. Jon awake. With heads still foggy, all had eagerly searched Roz's face for information. Roz had hurried to RJ's side, touched his forehead with the back of her hand, and given him a hard hug as both joy and sadness spilled toward him.

"I'm so glad you're okay, RJ. And you too, Nick. Your sleep has now come to an end. Mok and the home team have defeated the drill bugs," she told them.

RJ's head dropped and shook with relief. He scratched at the scruffy beard that had grown on his face during his long nap. "I knew that boy could do it. I knew it."

"And how is Father?" inquired Jon, his voice as steady as it always was when he was looking for factual answers.

Roz looked at him as tears drizzled down her cheeks. "I'm afraid he's gone, Jon. He was the only casualty of the battle in the sky."

Jon shot her a cold stare. His jawline tensed as he clenched his teeth.

"Rozee, no!" RJ squeezed her hand, disbelief clearly etched in his expression. "Why was he up there? What was he thinking?"

Roz described the scene she had witnessed.

"He wanted to participate in the finest hour for his inventions," deciphered Jon in a logical manner, his face suddenly softening. He nodded with pride at his father's heroism. "He was a Fog Bob, through and through. I'm very proud of him."

"So am I," agreed Roz as she left RJ's side and patted the top of Jon's rigid hand. It softened as he pulled it away and placed it on top of hers.

"How long has it been?" asked RJ, who tried to shake the fog from his brain.

"A little over seven hours."

"Then we must hurry to get as many townsfolk as possible to his sendoff. Where will it be?"

"I believe G.G. wants to take him to Lake Marie," explained Roz. "There is much to do. Let's see how many of the folks here are well enough to make it there."

While Roz had been in conference with RJ, Nick, and Jon, Jes had spread the news through the Fig Wig Bin of the defeat of the drill bugs and of Dr. Pol's death. Most of the ill had progressed to the point where they could be escorted by their caregivers out the Fig Wig's front archway and into the fresh air outside. Only Bek Net Ken remained quite ill, so Jes hung back to care for him.

Once San was free of chores, he hurried to the Ham Bat tunnel to retrieve the recuperating flingbees. He carried them up to ground level, where they could readjust to the fresh air. Fahbee flew circles around the others in his excitement. Lucinda giggled at his antics and watched him with adoring eyes.

Kip took off up Valley Road as though she herself were an excited flingbee. She wove through the disoriented crowd of formerly hibernating folks that reunited and lingered on the road. She searched above many a head for her weary hero, not realizing that the troops had yet to return. Though she spotted several Fog Bob top hats in the crowd, none topped the protruding ears that distinguished Mok from the others. Just as she reached the crop fields on the south side of the Ham Bat Pad, the weary warriors appeared in the western sky. They circled the field once before lowering their beaten hubcaps and descending into the crop fields.

The crowd, many of whom had yet to learn of Dr. Pol's passing, hurried toward the troops to welcome them home and congratulate them on their victory. Mok stood by a row of battered broccoli, shedding his armor, then his two layers of protective suiting. Kip, having recognized him in his descent, squeezed her tiny body through a cluster of happy Ham Bats and raced to him, finally wrapping her delicate arms around his thighs.

The sight of her reduced Mok to a shaking heap on the ground. He hugged her tiny frame, sobbing into her shoulder. So many emotions had flowed through his body in such a short period that all he could do was let them go. She was the one, beside his mom, with whom he could share them. Kip rocked his body gently and ran her soothing fingers through his thick, damp mop of hair.

"I'm so sorry about Papa Pol, Munkee. You have to know how proud he was of all you did," she whispered in his ear, her words hoarse.

Mok backed up and looked into her turquoise eyes and then at his watch. Sudden realization smacked him in the face. "We have to hurry. The eighth hour is almost here. We need to find G.G."

Kip placed calming hands on his cheeks. "We'll find him. We'll be there in time."

They rose from the ground and hurried toward the Ham Bat's Rec Hall, where Mok had last seen his G.G. and his Papa Pol.

Peacefully at rest in his sleeping cot and carried high on the shoulders of Brune and Krune Huge Dude, Dr. Pol Fog Bob and the somber Vowellan community proceeded along the lazily winding trail to Lake Marie. Roz and Dr. Jon, escorting old Dr. Jok, who insisted he was strong enough to hop on his own, followed Dr. Pol. Mok and Tok, the remaining Fog Bob clan, the Ham Bat, Fig Wig, Net Ken, and Rug Bum clans, and the gracefully prancing wistas completed the procession. RJ and Nick, their curious and protective guardians, took up the rear. Each and every body was weary from its recent circumstance: illness, caregiving, hibernation, stress and worry, or active battle.

Once everyone was settled around the flat, lakeside rocks that served as their stage, Roz and Jon helped Dr. Jok hop onto the center rock to speak. Memories from a generation ago flooded RJ's mind of the time Jok had spoken similarly at the sendoff of his father, dear Cod Fog Bob. This time, Jok did his best to honor his son.

"My son spent his life doing what he loved. He researched; he experimented; he invented, all for the greater good of all Vowellans. He made the decision to be an active participant in this noble cause. I am so proud of all he did on our behalf, as all of you should be. Let's celebrate his contributions and remember him with respect and fondness. He will always be with us."

RJ and Roz spoke briefly, touching on various highlights of Dr. Pol's life. They draped him with the highest of praises and touched on his gentle side as well as his slyly comical side, which very few had been privileged to see. Mok and Dr. Jon, still too stunned to speak, listened and nodded at the accolades.

The wistas performed an elegant tribute dance for Dr. Pol, after which Kip took the stage to grace the mourners with her beautiful song, "One Moon." Though feeling shy and tentative since she had not spoken or sung since the drill bugs had forced her into silence, she raised her head. When her voice filled the air, her body once more responded to the magic of the moment, and her side fins flourished into a colorful fan behind her.

Didn't know that you were leaving,
Didn't know how life would change,
I can't touch your face with my hands,
I can't feel your warmth, how strange

One moon,
We're both looking at just one moon.
Even if you are a thousand miles away,
And you cannot come to stay,
Or you need another day,
I'll keep looking at that one moon,

Till you come back home, that one moon.
Cuz I know that where you are can't be too far,

Under sky, that's where you are,
Till you reach out from afar,
You'll be with me under one moon.

Somehow the lyrics, which Kip had originally written for her father, seemed so fitting in the moment. The song was especially soothing to the town's younger members, most of whom had no experience in dealing with loss. When the song ended, Mok hopped up to help her down from the rock stage. They embraced before resuming their places with their clans. The townsfolk ended their tribute by joining their voices to sing the Vowella Valley Anthem.

Many years past, in times before RJ's arrival in Vowella, the Vowellans' custom had been to call on the deity they had long worshipped, Halé. On Dr. Jok's cue, the Vowellans formed a large half-circle around Dr. Pol, who lay on his cot, covered with a fine white satin sheet, next to the lake's crystal blue waters. As the eighth hour struck on many a wristwatch, the Vowellans respectfully chanted, "Halé loves you, Halé loves you! Go to Halé, good Pol Fog Bob!"

Dr. Jok pulled back the silk drape that had been covering Jok's body. What had been his long, log-shaped body, with a tall, bespectacled head and round, floppy feet, was now a gently swirling cloud of rainbow colored mist. The cloud became less dense as it rose into the sky and hovered for a moment, fifty feet above ground. The older Vowellans applauded softly with their hands until the cloud gradually faded to nothing. The younger generation, as well as RJ and Nick, watched in awe at the miracle that unfolded before them.

The crystal-clear afternoon promised a brighter future as the townsfolk quietly strolled back from Lake Marie. The Vowellan clans made their way to their specific corners of the valley and spent time contemplating their future. For the Rug Bums, the future meant rebuilding their cozy Hut. They would camp out in tents in the gum tree grove in the meantime, and they would spend many an hour grumbling about the tents' confinement. For most of the others, it meant performing repairs to the structures and cleaning up the landscape within the valley. For all the residents of Vowella, the future meant a chance for fresh beginnings.

Mok and Roz escorted dear old Dr. Jok back to the Fog Bob Box. Lol, Dok, little Tok, and the other Fog Bobs followed closely behind. Several of the clan members noticed that Lol's long lost purple flowered pin was once again clipped to the back of her long, flowing brown hair. She had worn her handmade creation in tribute to her grandfather, who had so loved Fog Bob ingenuity and invention. She had received it back from Jen Net Ken in a surprise show of gratitude for the tender care she had given to Jen and Nel when they were so ill from drill bug stings.

The Huge Dude brothers retreated to their makeshift home below the tree house in the avocado orchard, where they told each other their war stories and shared their excitement over being able to fly.

Lek Net Ken, during the cleanup process at the Ham Bat Pad, discovered a couple of intact limoncinas. He quickly shoved them into his deep pockets and, with wary, spinning red eyes, returned to his room to hide them in his dresser drawer. He intended on sharing them with favorite schoolmates San, Kip, Mok, and even Dun in the near future.

San Ham Bat, busy in his bedroom fussing with Fahbee Flingbee over tiny Lucinda and the other recovering flingbees, received a sudden knock on his door. News arrived that his new little brother, Laz, had just arrived, and that his mom, Lan, was doing simply fine. San yelped with joy and hurried away, leaving Fahbee to tend to those of his kind. He flitted around the room in celebration before settling in next to Lucinda, who was resting on a cozy blanket atop San's frying pan bed.

"How are you, dear one?" asked Fahbee as he rubbed his wings against hers.

Lucinda's happy eyes flashed through her long lashes at him. "Much better, Señor Fahbee. Thank you so much for giving me and the others such good care. We are all eternally grateful."

"I was so worried about you," confessed Fahbee.

"No need now. I will soon be my old self," assured Lucinda. After hesitating, she shyly suggested, "Perhaps when I am, we could have a picnic in the jungle?"

Fahbee's tail curled into a tight swirl, and his crooked beak vibrated at the suggestion. "Of course, my dear. I cannot wait."

He snuggled next to her on the cozy blanket. She rested her delicate beak on his striped chest and drifted off to sleep.

Mok, having noticed that his father was nowhere to be seen within the Fog Bob Box, hopped out the front door to look for him. He didn't have to go far. Dr. Jon sat stoically on the outdoor stone bench that faced the Blue Zint Mountains. Mok slipped quietly onto the bench next to him and stared in the same direction. Nothing was said for a long period of time.

"I never took the time to tell him I loved him, you know," Dr. Jon finally confessed.

Mok nodded, still staring straight ahead. "I know, Pops."

"I've learned my lesson much too late, and now, there's no going back."

"Yes, there's no going back," repeated Mok as he slowly turned and placed his hand on his father's. "But, you know, Pops, it's not too late for the future. Tokee needs you. Moms needs you. We all need you. We've just been waiting for you to need us back."

"I do need you, son." Jon swallowed the lump in his throat. He placed his other hand atop Mok's. "I need all of you to help me get back on track. I wasted too much time thinking about myself and my own needs. And it cost me precious time with my own father. I'll never forgive myself for that. I admire you, son, for all you've learned on your own and for the great man you have already become."

"I didn't learn anything on my own, Pops. I watched, I listened, and I guess I paid attention more than anything."

"Well, you did it right, and I'm very proud of you." Dr. Jon looked directly into Mok's eyes.

Never in his lifetime had Mok heard those words spoken by his father. Warmth, instead of knots, suddenly filled his chest. "Thanks, Pops."

Dr. Jon stood and grinned softly. "Now, if you'll please excuse me, I think I need to have a conversation with a little toothpick of a brother of yours, who is probably in need of some comfort. Do you think I can find him at his favorite spot, the tree house?"

"I'd bet on it." Mok nodded and grinned.

The morning after the Vowellans freed their valley of the drill bugs, Mok emerged from the Fog Bob Box to find most of the townsfolk gathered on and around the Council Porch, while some sort of victory song played in the background. His Fog Bob curiosity made his floppy round feet hop over to see what was up. RJ, Nick, and the Council of Elders stood to applaud Mok as he approached. Soon, all the townsfolk were clapping wildly. Mok hopped onto the porch and scratched his head in puzzlement.

"What's going on, Mr. RJ? Why is everyone here?" Mok scanned the crowd of grateful faces.

"To honor you, of course." RJ beamed with pride. "You led your troops with bravery and smarts. You saved all of us here. We're so proud of you."

"But we all worked together as a team. It was all of us that made it work."

"No, dude, you were the one," Dun Rug Bum stepped forward to announce. He turned toward RJ and the Council. "You should have seen him, Mr. RJ. Three times, he got so worked up that it was like a bomb exploded from him. He blasted bugs left and right and almost knocked us out of the sky too. He's some kind of wizard or something. He's got powers, just like Frizzy Wig has when she sings."

"Is that what shook the underground during the battle?" asked Kip as she hurried onto the porch. "Munkee, is that true?"

"Yeah, I guess it is," confessed Mok with a shrug of his shoulders. "I don't know what it is. It's never happened before."

"Well, whatever it is, it worked at the right time." Dun marched up to RJ, where he flexed his muscles to display his strength. "Mr. RJ, do you think any more of us might have special powers, like the superheroes in the cartoons we watch on TV?"

RJ stood agape at the story he was hearing. With an astonished shake of his head, he looked at Mok and then at Kip with deep admiration and replied, "Why, I don't know, Dun. Who knows what you Vowellans are capable of if you reach the deep authentic place that I know lives within all of you."

"Well, I'm gonna be the next to reach it. You wait and see," announced Dun.

"No, it will be me," argued Auntee Gus.

"Afraid not, Gusee. It will be me," boasted Granny Zen.

"Okay, okay," interrupted RJ as Nick chuckled in the background. "That's enough. It looks like your classic quirks are kicking back in. That's a good thing. For now, let's honor your brave war hero, Mok Fog Bob, shall we? Let's hear three enthusiastic hoorays!"

Dr. Jok hopped forward to lead the cheer. While their new victory song rang through the town speakers, everyone robustly chanted and vigorously clapped. "Hooray! Hooray! Hooray, Mok Fog Bob!"

As the lunch hour approached, Mok found himself at a pause. He had spent most of the morning helping one clan or another clean and reorganize the many sections of the valley. After the emotions and the exhaustion of the previous day, the Vowellans had awakened perky and ready to restore their town to its previous charm. He had assisted the Ham Bats in tidying the crop fields. He and Lek had wrestled the Net Kens' rets into tubs to rid them of their sour smell after their long underground confinement. He had helped Kip, Niv and several Fog Bobs disassemble the makeshift hospital and return beds and supplies to their proper places while Wit, Fil and Zin had sanitized the dome, inside and out. Mok had worked with RJ and Nick to design a blueprint for the new Rug Bum Hut, and he had checked on Brune and Krune to make sure they were okay after their adventure in the sky.

Mok scanned the valley and grinned at the progress the Vowellans had made in such a short time. He then turned and headed up Zint Path toward the Cave of Hope. From the mountainside, he paused to view the treasured valley below him. Upon entering the cave, he caught sight of flickering light in the distance. Curious, he quietly hopped further inside.

Having been patiently waiting in the cave's main room, Kip stood and watched him move toward her. She had illuminated the room with the dozens of candles that were already tucked in their stone nooks. She had fluffed the rainbow sheers that hung from the ceiling and arranged many a colorful pillow around the cozy fire she had built.

Mok rushed to her and gently ran two fingers down the right side of her face. Finding several kinky orange tendrils flopping over her eyes, he slowly pushed them back from her forehead so he could drink in the beauty of her turquoise eyes. He didn't say a word. Nor did she. Understanding well what each had been through, they fell into a firm embrace and held it for what seemed like hours. Finally sinking onto the pillows, they looked deeply into each other's eyes and showered each other's faces with sweet kisses. A deep calm swept both of their bodies, and they knew they were truly back home again.

"I missed you, Munkee." Kip reached forward to run her gentle fingers through his thick hair.

"No, I missed you," he responded. A sudden devilish stare overtook his expression.

"But I missed you more," she proclaimed as she grabbed a small purple pillow and slapped his arm with it.

Mok's eyes widened as he grabbed a larger yellow

pillow and bopped her on the head with it. "That's impossible."

The pillow fight was then in full swing. They snatched pillows wherever they could find them and fired them toward each other. Giggles and yelps emerged from them.

Finally worn and satisfied, they plopped down next to each other by the fire on the cozy bed of pillows. They watched the light from the flames dance on the cave's ceiling. They held hands and chatted about a million things.

Kip rattled off facts to Mok regarding some of the silly Vowellan antics that had started to resurface while he had been so busy being responsible around town. "Believe it or not, Munkee, Granny Zen, Tes, and Jen had a big pow wow and finally decided to welcome Jes back into their clan. Do you know that little Fahbee Flingbee is now the heartthrob hero of the flingbee colony, since he shed his romantic hero facade and took such good care of tiny Lucinda and others who had fallen into exhaustion from being chased by drill bugs? Lucinda is totally in love with Fahbee now. And Brune, Dun, and even Lek have discovered their newfound celebrity as heroes, and they're loving every minute of it."

Mok chuckled at the thought of it.

"And Auntee Gus made sure to shove the fact that she had flown as a 'warrior' in the Vowellans' most important battle in Granny Zen's face. Granny congratulated her through gritted teeth before she headed back home for her manicure," Kip giggled. "Some things never change."

Kip sat up and started playing with the long, pointy fingers on Mok's right hand. "But seriously, Munkee. Thanks for saving us. We wouldn't be safe today if it weren't for you. I'm so very proud of you."

Mok sat up. "I'm proud of everyone, Punkee," he said humbly. "It took all of us to make this work. And we did make it work."

"Yes, we did." Kip rose to her feet and brushed down her simple, green cotton shift.

Mok hopped to his feet and wrapped her into his long, twiggy arms. "I love you, Kip Fig Wig. You are an especially important part of my life."

Kip looked boldly into his eyes, never again afraid to do so. "As you are to mine. I love you, too!"

Kip turned and skipped to the mouth of the cave. She hollered back at him, "Now, big Bob! Want to race to the bottom of the hill? I hear Uncle Jake and Auntie Bess are flying in soon to bring us doughboys and limoncina punch. We're meeting at the tennis court. Work resumes there tomorrow, you know."

She disappeared down the path. Mok let her take the lead as his grin widened. He knew it wouldn't be long, because of his long Fog Bob hops, before he caught up to her, the best friend he had ever had and now so much more.

It was late afternoon. Mok came upon an unexpected scene when he approached the Fog Bob Box. RJ, Dr. Jok and Dr. Jon occupied the stone bench and stared at the

Man-on-the-Mountain in the eastern sky. When they spotted Mok, RJ and Dr. Jon stood and moved onto Valley Road. Dr. Jon glanced past Mok's shoulder when the motion of Kip slipping through the front archway of the Fig Wig Bin caught his attention. His eyes shot to Mok, but he said nothing.

"Hey, everyone. What's going on?" Mok frowned. Before yesterday, he had never seen his father sit on the bench and look at the mountains.

"Hey, there, Mok. Glad you're here," said RJ fondly. "We were just talking about you."

Mok looked tentatively from face to face. "You were?"

Dr. Jok patted the empty seat next to him on the bench. "Here, Mok-Mok, come sit by me."

As Mok hurried to comply, Dr. Jok reached out and patted his leg.

Dr. Jon spoke first. "Son, it's been a while since I asked you what your goals are for the future. Have you given it any more thought?"

Mok shot his father a puzzled look. *Why is he asking this at this moment in time?* "To tell you the truth, Father, no, I haven't. Too much has happened, and it hasn't been my priority."

"That's okay, Mok-Mok," spoke Dr. Jok. "We're just wondering if you have some fresh goals now that you've had these experiences?"

Mok looked at his three elders and gave the question some thought. "Well, now that I know that much more exists beyond our little valley, I know that I need to explore whatever is out there. I think we Vowellans are barely aware of the bigger world that surrounds us. I think we deserve a chance to expand our awareness."

"I agree, Mok," said RJ as he beamed with pride. "When I first came here, I tried everything I knew to protect all of you from the outside world because you were all so innocent and naive to all that was beyond the valley. But you've all evolved so much over the years, and now I feel you Vowellans have proven that you're capable of taking on much more than I ever thought possible."

"And you, dear great grandson," added Dr. Jok, "have proven you're the one to lead as time goes on. But you're still very young. There is still so much you need to learn before any of us will feel good about setting you free to pursue your goals," added Dr. Jok.

"You're the natural choice to step into the key leadership position here in Vowella as time moves on," explained Dr. Jon. "We all see that. You have gifts that all of us envy. But we think you need help for the next couple of years, until you're 18, at which time you may certainly make your own decisions about your future and/or the future of the Vowellans. Will you allow us to mentor you during that time? Do you think you'll eventually like to take on this role?"

Such huge questions that demand such huge answers. Mok glanced at each of them, stunned at their confidence in his capabilities. "Of course, I'll allow you to mentor me. I want to learn all I can from each of you and the other Elders too. But I can't say I can answer the second question now. I think I need to wait until I turn 18, once

I've experienced so much more, to make that determination."

Mok's three elders nodded in unison. Dr. Jok spoke up. "Sounds fair enough. We're so proud of you, Mok. And we're so blessed to have you in our midst."

Mok's father and his G.G. excused themselves and quietly slipped into the Fog Box while Mok and RJ took their routine seats on the bench. It had been a while since they had convened there. They slouched so their heads rested against the front wall of the Fog Bob Box, allowing them to examine the Man-on-the-Mountain as they had done so many times before.

"I've learned so much, Mr. RJ. I wish you knew how much."

"I know you have. You were ripe for the lessons right from the start."

"Some things I should have known all along," confessed Mok with a shake of his head.

"Like what?" RJ casually placed his right ankle upon his left knee.

"Like the fact that there's always been so much meaning in who we are and what we do. Think about it, Mr. RJ. Truth has always been a factor in the Fig Wigs' lives. If they told a fib, their legs dipped. Lesson: always be truthful. When Kip got down to her truth in song, what do you know, her real colors emerged. The Rug Bums grumble beneath cooling suds and behind rigid armor. What if they could learn to calm themselves down without all of that? The Net Kens have many eyes, but how often do they really open them to all that they already have? Do the Ham Bats take advantage of their sensitive hearing to truly listen to the goofy language that prevents their genuine and caring nature from shining? And we Fog Bobs. We shouldn't let the fog be the only thing that determines when it's best for us put our work aside in favor of important relationships."

"I'll tell you what, buddy, you figured all of that out a lot quicker than I did," chuckled RJ. "I came here years ago thinking you Vowellans were all about the short vowel sounds my mother associated with you. I guess we don't see the right messages until we're ready for them to mean something to us, huh?"

"So what do you think about what happened to me?" asked Mok. "I mean, the very sky and ground shook. How was I able to do that?"

"I'm not sure, but just like Kip, I think you found the deep authentic place within you that gave you the power to overcome your greatest challenge. If only all of us were able to reach that place. It's a real gift."

"But Mr. RJ, does finding such a good place within yourself always have to bring out such darkness in others, like the drill bugs?"

"Absolutely not. I think the darkness only comes from those who are afraid to find their own truth, so they attack yours."

Mok turned to face RJ. With thoughtful eyes, he said, "Being authentic means taking on a big responsibility, doesn't it?."

"Being authentic?" asked the slow, deep voice of Brune Huge Dude. He suddenly hovered above them, tall and relaxed on the north side of the road. "I know about that."

"Brune, you do?" asked RJ, his voice filled with curiosity. "Tell us what you know about that."

"Why, that's the rule for finding never-ending happiness," Brune said matter-of-factly. "Being authentic. Everyone knows that."

"The rule for finding never-ending happiness," said Mok with an understanding nod.

"The rule for finding never-ending happiness," repeated RJ in agreement.

"NO WAY!" Mok and RJ shouted together as realization hit. "The Rule for Finding Never-Ending Happiness! RU-FO-FI-NE-HA!!"

"Mr. RJ," Mok said in an excited tone. "That's the phrase you said we Vowellans chanted on that eerie day when Auntee Dot disappeared, Mr. Fil, Mr. Zin and Ms. Jes came back, and when Brune came into our lives."

Brune jumped back, startled at their reaction. "Whoa! Did I say something wrong?"

"No, Brune, you said everything right." RJ laughed out loud.

"Okay, well, that's good." Brune gave a deep sigh of relief. "I've got to go now. Krune and I have a play date with Sil and Tok over at the tree house."

RJ and Mok chuckled. RJ looked up at the friendly giant and smiled. "You go, Brune. Have fun."

RJ turned back toward Mok. "I guess authenticity is always there, huh? It seems each of us just needs to find our own way of getting to it. Some need to disappear for a while to get to it. Others manage to get to it just living their normal lives. Everyone's different, huh?"

"It seems so." Mok had to agree.

RJ and Mok stood and gave the Man-on-the-Mountain one last glance before retreating to their respective homes. Before RJ rounded the corner to walk down the path to his place, where he would enjoy a cup of coffee in his vintage rocking chair, he hollered back to Mok one last time.

"So, Mok, what do you think about someday being the first mayor of Vowella? We don't have one of those here, you know."

Mok's eyebrows curled and his mouth puckered as he gave the question thought. He looked at his watch, then chuckled at RJ's boldness. "Sorry, Mr. RJ. According to my calculations, I have 669 days until my answer is due. Good night!"

ALSO BY BARBARA MCLAUGHLIN

TALES FROM VOWELLA BOOK ONE
HEAVEN'S WAIT!
RJ AND THE VOWELLANS

BARBARA MCLAUGHLIN

TALES FROM VOWELLA BOOK TWO

HEAVEN'S WAIT!
INNOCENTS AND CURIOSITIES

BARBARA MCLAUGHLIN

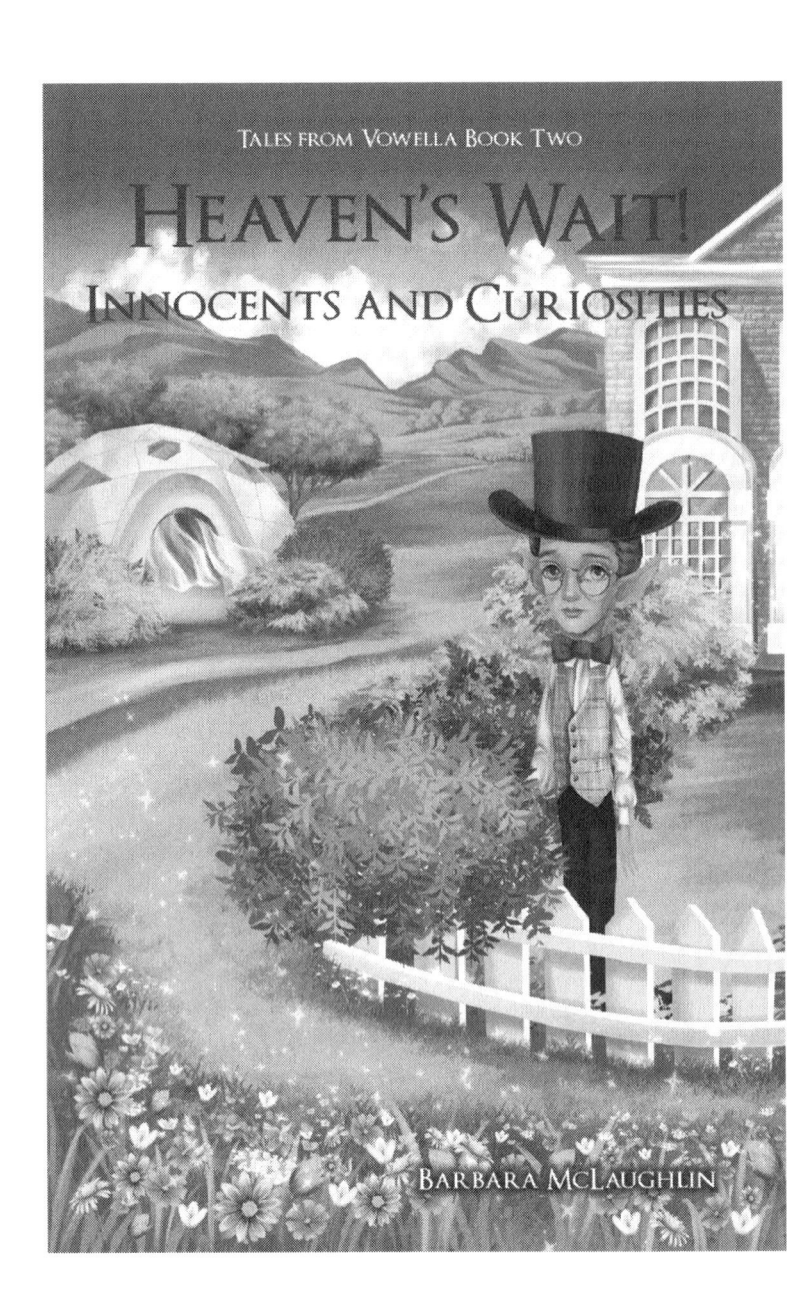

Tales from Vowella Book 3

Heaven's Wait!
Wonders and Truths

Barbara McLaughlin

FOLLOW BARBARA/HEAVEN'S WAIT ONLINE:

Heaven's Wait Official Website:
https://heavenswait.com

Heaven's Wait Facebook Page:
https://facebook.com/heavenswait

Heaven's Wait Instagram Page:
https://instagram.com/heavenswait

Heavens' Wait YouTube Channel:

https://youtube.com/@heavenswait

Barbara's Amazon Author Page:
https://amazon.com/author/bmclaughlin

THE AUTHOR AND HEAVEN'S WAIT

Barbara McLaughlin was born and raised in the San Francisco Bay Area, where she currently resides. She studied Early Childhood Education and worked in the field of education for several years before taking time out to raise her two sons. During that period, she not only helped her husband build their family-owned coffee roasting company; she self-published her first book, a remedial reading workbook filled with simple stories and quirky animated characters. When her dear father fell ill to a terminal illness, however, her creative spirit faded, and she abandoned the project.

Barbara directed her energies toward family and business for almost twenty years. All the while, her creative side continued to call to her. She eventually resurrected the animated characters that had been central to her remedial reading workbook and began to write a collection of life-lesson tales for her family. She didn't know her creative journey would lead her to fascinating places she never expected to explore or that she would become an accidental novelist during the process.

As the tales slowly morphed into a larger story, five main characters rose to the surface, as did the associated memory of her father's passing. Barbara found it fitting to create a character based on her father to bridge the gap between the world we know and the unlikely characters' new world, which became Heaven's Wait.

Since then, whenever she has found time away from family and work, Barbara has immersed herself in expanding the world of Heaven's Wait. Aside from work on her in-progress 7-part book series, she has further challenged her creativity by dabbling in illustration, musical composition, product development, and visions of a separate HW book series for young children. The flowering of her fantasy world has been her constant joy, and she finds her rewards in the knowledge that there are now believers in the magic of Heaven's Wait.

Learn more about Barbara McLaughlin and discover behind-the-scenes tidbits about the evolution of her Heaven's Wait world by visiting the Heaven's Wait website at:

https://heavenswait.com

Made in the USA
Columbia, SC
28 December 2022